BY JANET EVANOVICH

THE STEPHANIE PLUM NOVELS

One for the Money · *Two for the Dough* · *Three to Get Deadly*
Four to Score · *High Five* · *Hot Six* · *Seven Up* · *Hard Eight*
To the Nines · *Ten Big Ones* · *Eleven on Top* · *Twelve Sharp*
Lean Mean Thirteen · *Fearless Fourteen* · *Finger Lickin' Fifteen*
Sizzling Sixteen · *Smokin' Seventeen* · *Explosive Eighteen*
Notorious Nineteen · *Takedown Twenty* · *Top Secret Twenty-One*
Tricky Twenty-Two · *Turbo Twenty-Three*

THE KNIGHT AND MOON NOVELS

Curious Minds (with Phoef Sutton)
Dangerous Minds

THE FOX AND O'HARE NOVELS WITH LEE GOLDBERG

The Heist · *The Chase* · *The Job* · *The Scam* · *The Pursuit*

THE LIZZY AND DIESEL NOVELS

Wicked Appetite · *Wicked Business*
Wicked Charms (with Phoef Sutton)

THE BETWEEN THE NUMBERS STORIES

Visions of Sugar Plums · *Plum Lovin'* · *Plum Lucky* · *Plum Spooky*

THE ALEXANDRA BARNABY NOVELS

Metro Girl · *Motor Mouth* · *Troublemaker* (graphic novel)

NONFICTION

How I Write

DANGEROUS
MINDS

DANGEROUS MINDS

⊶⊷

A KNIGHT AND MOON NOVEL

JANET EVANOVICH

BANTAM BOOKS NEW YORK

Published in the United States by Bantam Books, an imprint of Random House, a division of Penguin Random House LLC, New York.

BANTAM BOOKS and the HOUSE colophon are registered trademarks of Penguin Random House LLC.

Hardback ISBN 978-0-553-39274-6
International edition ISBN 978-1-101-96606-8
Ebook ISBN 978-0-553-39275-3

Printed in the United States of America on acid-free paper

randomhousebooks.com

2 4 6 8 9 7 5 3 1

First Edition

DANGEROUS
MINDS

ONE

———⚇———

I T WAS A LITTLE AFTER ONE IN THE MORNING WHEN Riley Moon stopped struggling to make sense of the spreadsheet in front of her. She scraped her chair back from her desk, stood, and gave up a sigh. She was in a small room in a large mansion in Washington, D.C., and was surrounded by boxes, laundry hampers, and black garbage bags filled with official papers. She'd been hired to untangle the complicated financial affairs of the Knight family, who for generations had been brilliant at making money and pathetic at keeping records. Riley had been on the job for almost two months, and she'd reached the conclusion that it would be best for everyone if she just set fire to the office and destroyed every available document.

Her curly red hair was a rat's nest from a recently acquired habit of raking her fingers through it. Her brown eyes felt bloodshot. She thought a martini would fix everything, but she didn't have the energy to make one. She had two degrees from Harvard, a cute nose, a nice family back in Texas, and no social life. The closest she came to having a guy in her life was her boss, Emerson Knight, a man known far and wide as an "odd duck." True, he was rich, brilliant, and totally hot-looking, but that didn't alter the fact that he was quackers.

Emerson was the latest heir to the Knight fortune, and he had no interest in either making more money or keeping better records. He simply wanted to get his family's affairs in order so he could keep their many charitable trusts operating while he pursued a life of investigation.

Their backgrounds were worlds apart, Riley thought. Her father was the sheriff of a small, dusty county in north Texas. Her mother was a second grade teacher. Her modest childhood home had unfashionable, comfortable furniture, a small backyard that was fenced for the family dog, a kitchen table that seated seven, and a dining room table that could fit a tight ten but was only used for Thanksgiving dinner. Growing up she had to compete with her four brothers, so she knew how to shoot, throw a punch, hit a hardball, and cuss.

Riley glanced out her office's small window and considered her options. She could traipse downstairs, get into her black-and-white Mini Cooper, and drive home to her Georgetown apartment, or she could select one of the many guest bedrooms just down the hall and sleep here at the Knight mansion, Mysterioso Manor.

"The answer is obvious," Emerson said, standing in shadow on the far side of the room. "It would be more efficient for you to stay here."

"Crap on a cracker!" Riley said, whipping around, hand over her heart. "You just scared the heck out of me. How long have you been standing there?"

"That's an interesting question. On a quantum level, either always or never."

"And on the level we all live on except you?"

"About twenty seconds. I was checking the security monitors and I saw that your office light was still on."

"I can't reconcile money spent through your animal rights charitable trust with money received. You seem to have too much money, but I don't know where it came from."

"Is that a dilemma?"

"Yes!"

Only one of many, Riley thought, looking at her boss. Emerson had a peculiar intelligence that set him apart from other brilliant people she'd met. He was good at connecting the dots even when half the dots were missing. Unfortunately, he was also a charmingly annoying enigma with the right combination of charisma and resourcefulness to convince her of just about anything. And if that wasn't enough of a problem, he looked like a model for a romance novel cover. He was six feet two inches tall, with a lot of wavy black hair, smoldering dark eyes, and a hard-muscled, lean body. The dark hair and eyes were inherited from his Spanish mother. The muscle was the result of years of martial arts practice.

Riley agreed with Emerson that it would be more efficient for her to spend the night here. Problem was, the guest rooms were creepy. In fact, the whole mansion was creepy. It was a massive gray stone Gothic-Victorian architectural disaster with a wraparound porch, multiple chimneys, hidden passages, gargoyles, turrets, and lancet windows. It was filled with priceless bric-a-brac, elaborate woodwork, uncomfortable antique furniture, and heavy velvet drapes with gold tassels. Previous generations of eccentric Knights had lived in the mansion and filled it with their collected treasures, wives, and mistresses.

Riley was about to choose comfort over efficiency when Emerson's house security alarm screamed out, *"Intrusion, intrusion, intrusion."*

"What the heck?" Riley said, clapping her hands over her ears.

Emerson tapped a code into his smartphone. The noise stopped, and images from the house's security cameras appeared on the phone's screen.

"Follow me," Emerson said. "The game is afoot."

"Really?" Riley said. "Someone just broke into your house and you're quoting Sherlock Holmes?"

"It popped into my head. It seemed appropriate."

"Hiding in the closet and waiting for the police seems *more* appropriate."

"We would have a very long wait. The alarm system isn't connected to the police. I have my own top men who handle these sorts of problems."

"Who?"

"Vernon."

Vernon was Emerson's cousin from Virginia who'd taken up semi-permanent residence in a monster RV he kept parked behind the mansion. He was a big, good-natured guy who had a way with the ladies and preferred fishing to thinking.

"If there was any danger, Vernon would be here," Emerson said. "He has *unagi*."

"'*Unagi*'?"

"It's a state of total awareness. Only by achieving true *unagi* can you be prepared for any danger that might befall you."

Riley followed Emerson to the stairs, arming herself with a massive two-handed sword she'd appropriated from a suit of armor guarding a bedroom.

"First, Vernon doesn't have *unagi*," Riley said. "And second, there's no such thing as *unagi*. You heard about it on an episode of *Friends*."

"If there *is* an intruder I'll use my powers to cloud his mind so he won't see me," Emerson said.

"Awesome. Great plan. And what about me?"

"You have a big sword."

Riley mentally acknowledged that she did indeed have a big sword and that Emerson did have an uncanny talent for sneaking up on people.

They stopped on the second-floor landing and looked over the railing at a little man standing in the foyer below them. Bald head. Short. Asian ancestry. Orange monk's robe. Jesus sandals.

"Hello, Wayan," Emerson called down to the little man.

The man raised his eyes and smiled. He put his palms together, fingers up, and bowed his head slightly in greeting. Emerson repeated the palms-together greeting and went down the stairs to meet him.

"This is Wayan Bagus," Emerson said to Riley. "He's the Buddhist monk I studied with during my voyage of discovery."

"I thought your mentor was Thiru Kuthambai Siddhar."

"There are many paths to enlightenment," Emerson said. "The Siddhar was also a mentor." Emerson turned to the little monk. "How did you get here?"

"I walked," Wayan Bagus said.

"From Samoa?"

"I walked onto a boat. Then I walked onto a plane.

Then, when the plane landed in Virginia, I walked some more."

"How long did it take you?" Riley asked.

Wayan Bagus smiled politely. "Buddha tells the story of a granite mountain that reached many miles into the sky. Every hundred years it was wiped with a silk cloth held in the mouth of a bird until the mountain was worn away to nothing. So, not so long."

Riley suppressed a grimace and managed a tight smile. She didn't want to be rude, but, criminy, wasn't it bad enough she had to endure this philosophical baloney from Emerson?

"I suppose everything is relative," Riley said to Wayan Bagus. "Still, it had to have been a long, difficult trip. And how did you manage to get into the house once you found it?"

"The universe provided a way. Also, the door was unlocked." He turned to Emerson. "I need your help. The island I was using as a hermitage is missing. I think it was stolen."

"Define 'missing,'" Emerson said.

"Gone," Wayan Bagus said. "Vanished without a trace."

"Islands normally don't go missing," Emerson said.

"Nevertheless, it is missing just the same," Wayan Bagus said.

"Fascinating," Emerson said. "Where exactly did you see it last?"

"It was right where I'd left it. About two hundred miles north of Samoa."

"And what makes you suspect it's stolen and not just lost?"

"For the love of Mike, Emerson," Riley said. "You can't steal—or lose, for that matter—a whole island."

"That's exactly what makes it so intriguing," Emerson said.

"Last month some men appeared on my island and told me I had to leave," Wayan Bagus said. "When I objected they forcibly removed me and placed me on a different island. By the time I found my way back, my island was gone."

"What did these men look like?" Emerson asked. "Did you know any of them? Were they Samoans?"

"They were wearing khaki shorts and funny hats. Only one man spoke to me, and he spoke in English. Another man gave me an injection, and I woke up hours later in the cargo hold of a boat."

"Was there anything special about your island?" Emerson asked.

"I know of nothing that would be of extraordinary value. It was typical of the hundreds of uninhabited, unmapped islands around Samoa. It had a mountain and beaches and rain forests. It was a very nice place for a hermitage, except for the volcano."

"I'm quite fond of volcanoes," Emerson said.

"They are interesting," Wayan Bagus said, "but I find the energy can be disruptive to meditation."

When Wayan Bagus was comfortably settled in a third-floor guest room, Emerson and Riley made their way to the cavernous library, with its intricate parquet floor, hand-carved oak bookshelves, and a second-level balcony. Newspapers and magazines were neatly stacked on the floor, and half a dozen whiteboards were scattered about, covered with Emerson's cryptic notes. Some of the notes were devoted to the tangled estate left behind when Emerson's father had died under mysterious circumstances the previous year. Most were simply concerned with whatever sparked Emerson's imagination, ranging from quantum physics to tarantula crossings. A weather-beaten Coleman tent had been erected in front of the massive stone fireplace. Buddhist prayer flags hung from a line stretched between the tent and the fireplace mantel.

Emerson crossed the room, climbed a rolling ladder, and inched his way along, looking for a specific book in the science section.

"It's almost two in the morning, and the crazy little monk is asleep in bed," Riley said. "Why are we here in the library?"

"Wayan Bagus is many things," Emerson said. "Crazy isn't one of them. His mental and emotional acuity are exceptional. If he says his island is missing, then it is most certainly missing."

"And?"

"And we're going to help him find it."

" 'We'?"

"I'm changing your job description to 'amanuensis' so you can assist me in the search. You served as my amanuensis once before, and the results were excellent."

"We were almost killed!"

"The key word is 'almost.' We survived, and, you have to admit, it was exhilarating. This will give us an opportunity to once again marry our abilities."

"It wasn't exhilarating. It was terrifying. And I don't know about the marry thing."

"I'm using the term 'marry' in the broad sense of the word, as in 'join together.' I'm brilliant and intuitive, and you're practical and have a driver's license. We're the perfect team."

"Of course."

Emerson continued his search. "I thought I should clarify," he said over his shoulder, "because I recently read a book about body language and nonverbal cues, and I decided you find me irresistible."

"*What?* I don't think so. If anyone is irresistible here it's me."

Emerson paused, seeming to have found what he was looking for. "The two aren't mutually exclusive, but we need to maintain the sanctity of the amanuensis-client relationship despite our deepening physical attraction."

"Aha! So you *do* find me irresistible."

"Not at all. 'Irresistible' would indicate a lack of control, and I have control in spades."

Emerson reached for a book, his shirt rode up, and Riley sneaked a look at the bared skin and perfectly toned abs. She narrowed her eyes slightly and thought that she had pretty good control too. Otherwise her hands would be all over those abs.

"Look through this book for the section on Samoa," Emerson said, passing Riley a copy of *National Oceanographic and Atmospheric Administration Nautical Maps of the Pacific*. "I'll be right down."

By the time Emerson joined Riley at the desk, Riley had found the chapter. It was page after page of detailed maps, with information about water depths, latitudes and longitudes, natural and man-made hazards, currents, and anything else you would need to know if you wanted to navigate by boat through the Samoan island chain.

"As your amanuensis, I have to tell you this is insane. A bunch of men wearing khaki clothes stole an island? I mean, who's your prime suspect? UPS?"

Emerson flipped through the pages. "We would have to consider UPS. They're always *losing* things."

"What of yours have they lost?"

"Ice skates. A volleyball. A sculpture I'd created."

"And they never found any of it?"

"To be honest, Tom Hanks did personally deliver the sculpture to my house, but that was several years later."

Riley smacked her forehead. "You couldn't possibly be confusing your life with the movie *Cast Away,* could you? And if you are, Tom Hanks worked for FedEx, not UPS."

Emerson stopped flipping. "That explains a lot. I always thought it was weird that Tom Hanks would just randomly show up at my front door and give me a package."

"You're a very strange man."

"My Match.com profile says I have a quirky sense of humor."

"You have a Match.com profile?"

"Actually, no," Emerson said. "I just have a quirky sense of humor."

Riley stared at him for a couple beats thinking it was a good thing he had great abs because he wasn't going to get far with the quirky humor. She turned her attention to the book in front of Emerson. It was opened to a map of the Pacific Ocean, showing an area about two hundred miles north of Samoa.

"There must be at least a hundred islands," Riley said. "Any one of them could be your monk's island."

"And those are just the mapped islands. There are probably a hundred more that nobody's ever bothered to survey."

"It's like trying to find a needle in a haystack," Riley said.

"Then let's find the needle."

"You don't find the needle," Riley said. "It's a metaphor for an unsolvable problem."

"Ah, but the problem isn't unsolvable," Emerson said. "When Wayan Bagus told me he was going to spend a couple years living in solitude on a deserted island, I sent him an emergency satellite transponder. Fortunately he brought the transponder back with him, and he gave it to me before he went to bed."

Emerson pulled from his pocket a small orange device that looked a little like a walkie-talkie.

Riley turned the transponder to the ON position. This one had more bells and whistles than the ones she'd used hiking the Texas backcountry with her father and brothers, but it operated on the same basic principle: to send out a beacon signal with GPS coordinates so that first responders could locate you.

"What am I looking for?" she asked.

"The data history. We should be able to use it to track Wayan Bagus's movements over the past couple months."

Riley read off the first set of GPS coordinates, and Emerson plugged them into his laptop.

"That one is Rock Creek Park, Washington, D.C.," Emerson said. "Mysterioso Manor, to be more precise. They're in reverse chronological order. Skip backward until you find a period of time where he was in just one place for a while. We can assume anything else is him traveling to America."

Riley scrolled through the data. "He was at 8°24'34.2648" south and 115°11'20.1084" east for a couple weeks."

"That's a small island off the coast of Bali," Emerson said. "That's where he went after he was evicted from his stolen island. How about before that?"

"He was at 11°3'36.3544" south and 171°5'39.2232" west for six months."

"Bingo," Emerson said. "That's in the middle of the ocean, about two hundred miles from Samoa. He was either floating around in the Pacific for half a year or that's his deserted island hermitage."

Riley put the transponder on the desk and traced her finger down the map in the book to 171° west, looking to see if there were any islands in the approximate area. "Here! There's a little unnamed island, labeled with those exact coordinates."

"Odd," Emerson said. "This island had obviously been surveyed at the time of the book's publication ten years ago, but the image from Google Earth shows nothing but ocean at that location."

"Not surprising," Riley said. "Google Earth also shows an empty field where my parents live. Everybody knows it's just a compilation of various satellite images and still photographs. It's notoriously inaccurate when it comes to rural and unpopulated areas."

"Perhaps," Emerson said, accessing the National Oceanographic and Atmospheric Administration website.

"Let's check out the most current nautical maps. These were revised last year."

Riley looked over Emerson's shoulder as he found the set of online maps that corresponded to page 233 in the book.

"There's nothing at 11°3' south by 171°5' east," she said. "In fact, there's not even anything close to that location, except water. It doesn't make sense. The island was there five months ago. Wayan's emergency transponder proves that. And the NOAA mapped it more than ten years ago. So why isn't it on the most current NOAA maps?"

Emerson smiled. "There's only one explanation. Someone erased the island from the NOAA database."

"Why would someone do that?" Riley asked.

"For the same reason a murderer hides the body," Emerson answered. "To cover up a crime. Someone stole Wayan Bagus's island. Tomorrow we're going to hunt it down."

TWO

⎯⎯∞⎯⎯

RILEY WOKE UP AT EIGHT IN THE MORNING, stretched out on the giant sheepskin rug in the library. She was still wearing yesterday's clothes, and Emerson had obviously covered her with a comforter and put a pillow under her head sometime during the night. The NOAA book was lying next to her, still open to the last page Riley had read before falling asleep.

Her first thought was that it was sweet of Emerson to tuck her in. Her second thought was that there was something stuck to her forehead. She reached up and removed a Post-it note.

There are only two mistakes one can make along the road to truth: not going all the way and not starting. Having breakfast with Wayan.

Riley sat up and looked at the comforter Emerson had draped over her. It was covered with more Post-it notes. Emerson had been sticking notes on her while she slept as if she were a refrigerator. Most of the notes were work-related. A couple were personal reminders like "Find socks" and "Eat more vegetables."

"The man needs a keeper," Riley said to the empty room. Oh crap, she thought, that would be *me*. I'm his keeper.

Emerson's Aunt Myra was also his keeper. She was Vernon's mom and Emerson's father's sister. She was a no-frills, practical woman who'd stepped in when Emerson's father passed. She could usually be found in the kitchen, but this week she was in West Virginia tending to a sick relative.

Riley left the library and checked out the dining room and the kitchen. No Emerson. She helped herself to coffee and a piece of leftover pizza and set out for the conservatory. If Emerson wasn't in the library or the kitchen he was almost always in the conservatory, which was actually an immense greenhouse located a short distance behind the main house.

The garages and Vernon's RV were also behind the house. Riley was about to walk past the RV when its door crashed open and two young women in skimpy black maid's uniforms popped out, followed by Vernon. Vernon was buck naked except for a John Deere hat covering his privates. He was holding a feather duster in his free hand.

"Thanks for helping me clean up my RV," Vernon said. "Appreciate you ladies showing up on short notice. Hope you don't mind the job took so long."

The women giggled something that Riley couldn't hear, got into a Prius, and drove away.

Riley clapped a hand over her eyes. "For the love of Mike, Vernon. Put on some clothes."

Vernon looked down at himself. "I got all my nethers covered."

Riley peeked at him from between her fingers. "I'm looking for Emerson. I think he's having breakfast in the conservatory."

"I'm powerful hungry," Vernon said. "Wait up for me, and I'll go with you."

Two minutes later Vernon was dressed in jeans, cowboy boots, a tight-fitting white T-shirt, and he had the John Deere hat on his head.

"This here's my lucky hat," Vernon said, joining Riley.

"Apparently so. Did you hear the alarm last night?"

"Oh sure. But Emmie texted me not to come unless my *unagi* told me to. And I wasn't getting any *unagi* danger signals, which was a good thing being that I was busy with the maid service."

"They were here all night?"

Vernon grinned. "Turns out we had a lot to do, cleaning-wise."

"Good grief."

"It's not what you think," Vernon said. "Most people gotta pay for ladies in maid suits, but Jolene and Mary Beth and me went to high school together back in Harrisonburg. They live in D.C. now, and they come over on occasion to tidy up and enjoy my bachelor amenities."

Don't ask, Riley told herself. Best not to know too much about his amenities.

The grounds surrounding the main house and the conservatory were tended by a well-meaning but partially blind ninety-two-year-old gardener. The result was a riot of grasses and flowering plants run amok. Riley thought it suited the property perfectly because *everything* about Mysterioso Manor was amok. It was an extravagant display of wealth and bad taste set in a heavily wooded area of Rock Creek Park, in the northwest quadrant of Washington, D.C. It was horribly wonderful.

Riley led the way along the stone path to an elaborate iron and glass structure topped with a Victorian-era cupola. It was almost as large as the main house, and it contained a jungle of exotic tropical plants and fruit trees. It was, on one hand, a magical place. On the other hand, it was a living minefield. Spiders dropped from trees, birds shot through the air, assorted rodents and small animals scurried across walkways, and a larcenous colony of monkeys howled and screeched at visitors.

Benches were sprinkled throughout the conservatory, usually beside a small fountain or hummingbird feeder.

A larger sitting area had been placed in the middle of the greenhouse, under the cupola. A pretty wrought iron table with four chairs held court in the center. More fancy wrought iron chairs and benches were stationed along the perimeter.

Riley watched for mice and spiders as she made her way to the sitting area, and Vernon held on to his hat for fear a monkey would steal it.

"I don't know why Emmie likes this place so much," Vernon said. "Looks to me like a swamp. And I don't know why he puts up with the monkeys. They're all a pack of thieves. Especially that Mr. Manfrengensen. He's the worst. He takes anything not nailed down, and he don't even care if you yell at him."

"He listens to Emerson."

"I reckon. Emmie has a way with dumb animals."

Riley squelched a grimace. She hoped she didn't fall into that category.

Emerson and Wayan Bagus looked up from their breakfast when Riley and Vernon stepped into the clearing. Mr. Manfrengensen was on a nearby bench, eating a slice of dragon fruit.

Vernon pointed two fingers toward his own eyes and then one finger at the monkey. Mr. Manfrengensen kept eating.

"I'm watching you," Vernon said.

Nothing from Manfrengensen.

Vernon turned his attention to the food on the table. Lentils. Whole grain, seeded bread. Fruit from the greenhouse garden, and honey.

"Where's breakfast?" Vernon asked.

"This is my friend Wayan Bagus," Emerson said. "He's a Buddhist monk, so it's a vegetarian breakfast."

Wayan Bagus stood up and bowed to Vernon, who just kept staring incredulously at the lentils. "But where's the bacon?"

"Bacon's not a part of a vegetarian diet," Emerson said.

Vernon scratched his chest. "What about sausages and fried ham?"

"Those are all meats."

"Are you telling me he doesn't eat any of them? That's just all wrong. That's practically not even American."

"Wayan Bagus is Balinese," Emerson said.

"No shit?" Vernon said. "How cool is that!" He looked down at Wayan Bagus. "Well, Little Buddy, any friend of Emmie's is a friend of mine, even if you don't know how to eat breakfast."

Vernon grabbed the monk and gave him a big bear hug.

Emerson had his hand up, trying to get Vernon's attention. "Buddhist monks don't like to be touched," Emerson said.

"You're making that up," Vernon said to Emerson. "Everyone likes a hug." He lifted Wayan a couple inches off the ground and swung him side to side. "You're just a cute li'l ol' oompa loompa, aren't you?" he said to Wayan.

"Apologies," Wayan Bagus said in his quiet monk voice.

Next thing, Vernon was on his back, and Wayan Bagus was in his seat at the table carefully spreading a bit of honey on his bread.

Vernon pulled himself to his feet and grinned at the monk.

"I can see you like to wrassle," Vernon said to Wayan Bagus. "I'm a big wrassler myself. We're going to be good friends, Little Buddy."

Wayan Bagus nodded politely. Noncommittal. "All living things have Buddha nature," he said.

"I was thinking the same thing," Vernon said, reaching up to adjust his hat. "Hey, what the heck. Where's my hat?" He whipped his head around. No hat. No Manfrengensen.

"Sonofabitch! Damn monkey!" Vernon said. "That's my lucky hat. You'll have to excuse me from this here breakfast party while I kill that monkey."

Everyone watched Vernon stomp off and disappear into the vegetation.

"Right," Emerson said. "Now back to business. As soon as we're done with breakfast we'll head off to the Department of Commerce to meet with the NOAA administrator."

"Count me out," Riley said. "I slept in these clothes. I need to go home to freshen up."

"You can't go home," Emerson said. "You have to drive. You *always* drive."

Riley narrowed her eyes. "No."

"I'll let you pick out the car," Emerson said.

Riley blew out a sigh. Emerson knew how to tempt her. She'd grown up in a family that revered the flag, apple pie, and NASCAR. She'd spent weekends with her dad and her brothers restoring junker muscle cars. She'd driven in a couple local stock car races. Giving Riley access to the Knight garage was like giving a five-year-old the keys to a candy store. Emerson's father had amassed a mind-boggling collection of classic and luxury cars. Shelby Mustangs, Rolls-Royce Phantoms, Dodge Chargers, Pontiac Firebirds. The collection seemed endless to Riley.

Emerson had inherited the collection from his father, along with a menagerie of animals that ran loose on the Mysterioso Manor property, a bunch of charitable trusts, and a boatload of money. Emerson accepted the responsibility of maintaining the property and the trusts, and he found the money to be useful. At best, he was uninterested in the cars. He used them for transportation and the occasional bribe.

"I'll drive," Riley said, "but we'll have to stop at my apartment on the way to the Commerce Department."

"Deal," Emerson said.

. . .

Riley tapped the security code into the garage door opener, the doors rolled up, and she took stock of the cars that were lined up neatly in rows on the shiny white epoxy floor. Her personal choice would be something small and sporty, but she had to accommodate two more people, and Emerson was over six feet tall. There weren't any midsized cars in the collection so she went with the newest luxury car, the silver Mercedes-Maybach.

"Is the Maybach okay?" she asked Emerson.

"Good choice," Emerson said.

They got in and Riley drove the car out of the garage, past Vernon's RV, and followed the driveway to the front of the house.

"Have you spent much time with Wayan?" Riley asked.

"Seven years, off and on."

"What was that like?"

"It was like living with a combination of Yoda and Jiminy Cricket on a fifty-foot boat."

"He speaks excellent English, and he seems very worldly. Has he traveled a lot?"

"So far as I know, not at all. My understanding is that he's spent most of his life in a monastery in Bali, studying Buddhism and the martial arts. He seems worldly because he doesn't engage in unnecessary conversation. He keeps his own counsel."

"It was impressive the way he flipped Vernon onto his back. Does he have Jedi powers? Did he share them with you?"

"I was his student, but I doubt I'll ever achieve his level of power and control."

Wayan was waiting at the porch steps. He slipped into the Maybach's big back seat and shook his head.

"All this excess," he said. "It's not good. Not good at all. Down the path of *dukkha* it will lead you."

"*Dukkha* is suffering," Emerson explained to Riley. "It's caused by the three poisons, which are *raga* or greed, *moha* or delusions, and *dvesha* or ill will."

Wayan ran his hand over the ebony wood finish and plush leather seat. "Sitting on dead animals. Not good. Not good at all."

Riley turned to look at him. "What about the sandals you're wearing?"

Wayan looked down at his feet. "Faux leather. Very uncomfortable." His attention caught on the screen built into the back of Riley's seat. "What is this?" he asked.

"That's the entertainment center," Riley said.

She pushed a button and *The Little Mermaid* appeared on the TV screen. Sebastian was belting out "Under the Sea."

Wayan Bagus leaned forward. "It's a singing crab. Have you seen this, Emerson?"

"Yes," Emerson said. "He's excellent."

THREE

———∞∞∞———

T HIRTY MINUTES AND FOUR DISNEY SONGS
later, they reached Riley's apartment. She left
everyone in the car, ran into her building, and reappeared
in ten minutes wearing clean clothes, her hair still damp
from the shower.

She jumped back behind the wheel and drove them to
the Department of Commerce, circled a couple blocks,
and finally found a parking space close to the NOAA
administrator's office, near the White House. They entered
the building and paused in the lobby.

A short monk in a saffron robe, a tall eccentric rich
guy, and a woman with wet hair, Riley thought. They
looked like contestants from a bad reality show.

"Exactly how do you expect to get in to see the head of NOAA without an appointment?" Riley asked Emerson.

"I have a plan," Emerson said.

He pulled a pair of thick black-rimmed spectacles from his pocket and put them on Wayan.

"Showtime," Emerson said, opening the large glass door in front of them and making a sweeping gesture indicating they should all troop up to the desk beyond the door.

The receptionist glanced at them as they approached. She had a round face, short black hair shot with gray, deep red lipstick, and ears like Dumbo. She looked like she was counting the hours and minutes before qualifying for her government pension.

"His Holiness, the Dalai Lama, is here to see the administrator," Emerson said to the receptionist.

The receptionist stared down at Wayan, who really did look like the Dalai Lama in the glasses. "Are you really the Dalai Lama?" she asked.

Wayan Bagus nodded politely. "No."

She looked back at Emerson. "I'm feeling generous today. What else do you have?"

"I'm really, really rich?"

The woman leaned forward. "That's great. I really, really need a new Louis Vuitton handbag."

Emerson turned to Riley. "Do you have any money?"

"Are you kidding me?" Riley searched in her purse. "I

have seventeen dollars and fifty cents. Don't you have any money? You're the gazillionaire."

"I don't believe in carrying money," Emerson explained to the receptionist. "How about a million-dollar smile?"

"Only if I can use it to pay for a new handbag." The receptionist looked at Riley. "You're up."

What have I got to lose? Riley thought. I'm a nutcase by association.

"Dracula sent us to warn the administrator that Poseidon is about to release the Kraken," Riley said.

A tailored woman in her midforties opened the door behind the receptionist and smiled. "I'm Cheryl Rhoads. I'm the administrator. What's this I hear about the Kraken?"

"I'm Emerson Knight. This is Miss Moon, my amanuensis. And this is Wayan Bagus, who is a personal friend of the Dalai Lama," Emerson said.

"Lovely to meet you," Cheryl Rhoads said to Wayan. "Are you really a personal friend of the Dalai Lama?"

Wayan Bagus nodded politely. "No."

"Well, then, I'm a personal friend of the Dalai Lama," Emerson said, "not that it's important. We're investigating some unexplained discrepancies between your nautical maps in the Pacific Ocean."

"Discrepancies?"

Emerson pulled the NOAA book from his knapsack. He'd circled the monk's missing island in red pen. "I'm looking for an island that's not on your current online maps."

Cheryl came around to the receptionist's desk and accessed the NOAA maps. "You're right. It's not there. Weird. It could be that it was never there, that we made a mistake in the older maps and corrected it in the newer."

"Wayan was living at those exact coordinates five months ago," Emerson said. "That was after the most recent maps were published."

Cheryl shook her head. "An island doesn't just disappear from our database, unless somebody deletes it manually."

"That's why we're here," Emerson said. "We want to talk with the somebody."

Cheryl typed her password into the computer and logged in to her account. After a couple minutes, she looked up from the computer.

"Well, I'm sorry, but I can't really help you. It turns out that this island and all the islands around it are part of the National Park of American Samoa. All the national parks are mapped by the Department of the Interior. Everything else is the responsibility of NOAA, at least when it comes to bodies of water. It's been that way ever since the National Park Service was formed back in 1916. Interior is pretty territorial when it comes to the national parks."

"Excellent," Emerson said. "You wouldn't happen to know who we should talk to over there?"

Cheryl scribbled down a name and phone number on a piece of notepaper. "I'd recommend you speak with the Park Planning, Facilities, and Land Directorate. They're in charge of surveying all the national parks, including a lot of the waterways around American Samoa. If you want, I'll send an email so you can get to see somebody without bringing the 'Dalai Lama' along with you."

Emerson took the paper. "That would be helpful. Wayan Bagus isn't a very convincing Dalai Lama, and the National Park Service has had it in for Dracula for years."

The Office of Park Planning shuffled Emerson off to the liaison for the Pacific West Regional Office. The Pacific West Regional Office sent them to the Information Resources Directorate, and the Information Resources Directorate sent them back to Park Planning. Wayan Bagus had given up after the Pacific West Regional Office and was meditating in President's Park.

"Look, James," Emerson said to the paunchy middle-aged man sitting across the conference room table from him. "You're in charge of surveying the national parks. Aren't you the least bit curious how an island goes missing? An island that has been deleted from your survey, despite the fact that this emergency beacon clearly shows someone was living there?"

James shrugged. "Doesn't seem especially significant to me."

"And you don't think it's odd that my friend was forcibly removed from that same island, and when he came back it had disappeared?" Emerson asked.

James shifted in his seat and glanced at the security camera in the corner of the room. "Not really. These things happen all the time."

Emerson paused for a moment. He leaned across the table and looked the bureaucrat in the eye. "Actually, they don't." He turned away and stared directly into the camera. "In fact, under normal circumstances, this *never* happens."

"I'm not sure I'm the right one to help you," James said.

Emerson continued to stare into the camera. "That's the first honest thing anybody has said to me today. I won't take up any more of your time."

James stood to leave, but Emerson remained sitting.

"Um. Are we done?" James asked.

"*You're* done. However, I am not."

James turned the knob and opened the conference room door a couple inches. "You're not coming?"

"No, I'd prefer not to."

James opened the door fully and walked out into the hallway. He turned around to look at Emerson and Riley, still sitting at the conference table. "So, you're really not coming?"

Emerson smiled politely. "Thank you. I'd prefer to stay here."

"Okeydokey," James said. "Can I get you anything? Coffee? Water?"

"No. We're good," Emerson said.

James stood in the doorway for a beat, unsure what to

do next. He glanced at the security camera one last time, shrugged, and walked away down the hall.

Riley and Emerson sat in silence for what seemed like an eternity to Riley.

"So what are we going to do now?" she finally asked.

"Nothing."

"Nothing! We can't just do nothing!"

"Why not?" Emerson asked.

"Why not? Because this isn't the couch in your living room. It's a moldy old conference room in some government office building."

Emerson slouched lower in the chair, getting more comfortable. "*Wu wei.*"

"Wu what?"

"It's the Zen art of doing nothing. If we can do nothing in just the right way, the universe will provide the answers to all our questions."

"How do we know if we're doing it in the right way?"

"Spring comes effortlessly, the grass grows by itself," Emerson said.

Riley gave him her most withering squint. "If you answer me with one more vague and basically meaningless piece of philosophical crap I'm going to kick you in the knee."

Emerson opened his mouth to say something, thought better of it, and made the sign that he was zipping his lips shut.

Fifteen minutes later two men entered the conference room. The first was tall with a Mediterranean complexion and a lean and hungry look.

"Emerson Knight and Riley Moon? My name is Eugene Spiro. I'm chief scientist for the National Park Service."

"The Park Service has a chief scientist?" Riley asked.

"It's a relatively new position. I report to the director on the scientific assets of national parks and federal lands. I'm responsible for protecting park resources, ranging from dinosaur fossils to giant redwood trees."

Emerson stood. "Then you'd be concerned to know that an entire island under your protection is missing."

Spiro smiled. "I suppose an entire island would qualify as a park resource. Except that it's impossible for an entire island to disappear. Do you know the principle of Occam's razor? Given two explanations, the simpler one is usually correct."

"I agree," Emerson said. "Except that Occam's razor assumes there are two explanations. I can think of only one."

"And that is?"

"It's been stolen."

Spiro shook his head. "Even if such a thing were possible, and it's not, then by whom? For what purpose? The entire area is an uninhabited marine sanctuary. It's worthless except to a bunch of green turtles, humpback whales, and seabirds."

The second man was at parade rest a couple feet behind Eugene. He was very fit. Closely shaved head and a three-day-old beard. Tattoo of two crossed sabers with a number one above them on his right hand. Both men appeared to be in their early forties. Both were wearing gray suits and white dress shirts. Top button open. No tie.

Riley thought neither looked like a scientist. She thought the man with the tattoo looked like a hired assassin, and Eugene looked like his pimp.

"We ran a background check on you just now," the man with the tattoo said to Emerson. "Bottom line is, you're a well-known troublemaker."

"That's nice of you to say," Emerson said. "But I'm not sure how well-known I am. Maybe in certain circles I've achieved some degree of prominence, but I wouldn't really describe myself as famous. Really, I just put my pants on one leg at a time, like every other troublemaker."

"Is that supposed to be clever?" the man said.

Eugene stepped to one side and turned slightly. "This is my associate, Tim Mann, but everyone around here calls him Tin Man. He's in charge of protecting park resources for the Pacific West Region."

"Tin Man," Riley said. "That's a clever play on your name."

"And like the Tin Man in *The Wizard of Oz*, I could be kind of human if I only had a heart."

"Well, that's certainly not extra creepy," Riley said.

Emerson nodded. "I agree. There are so many other less creepy explanations you could choose. Like, I'm a grown man who collects tin soldiers in my spare time. Or, hello, would you like to see my tin thimbles, which happen to belong to me, a man?"

"Criminy, Emerson. That's even worse," Riley said. "Who asks someone he's just met if she'd like to see his thimbles? That's serial killer creepy."

Emerson looked from person to person around the room. "Can we all just agree that Tin Man is creepy, but not, you know, serial killer creepy?"

No one offered any objection.

"Bottom line is, all those islands are protected marine sanctuaries, and unless your friend had a research permit from the NPS, he shouldn't have been there in the first place," Eugene said. "Notwithstanding that he broke about ten different federal laws and disturbed a fragile marine ecosystem, we'll look into it and correct the maps during the next update."

"So you don't mind if we continue to look into it as well?" Emerson asked.

Tin Man locked eyes with Emerson. "Suppose I told you we *do* mind?"

"I would continue to look into it anyway," Emerson said.

. . .

Eugene and Tin Man walked through the double doors leading to the private office of the director of the National Park Service. The director, Bart Young, was standing in front of a large window, watching Emerson and Riley leave the building.

"Boys," Bart Young said, "the National Park Service was formed in 1916, and since that time there have been eighteen directors. And every one of those directors has been responsible for protecting probably this country's biggest national secret. I am not going to go down in history as the director who failed to keep that secret."

"I did a fast read through the dossiers on Knight and Moon," Tin Man said. "Is this their complete history?"

"You were given the short version," Bart Young said. "They were already in the system. It was easy to pull them up. Not long ago they created an international incident. Knight wanted to see his gold holdings, and things got out of hand."

"We wouldn't want things to get out of hand this time," Tin Man said. "I would be happy to sanction them for you."

The director looked over at Tin Man. "This is why I personally recruited you from Special Forces to lead the Rough Riders. Bloodlust. It's a gift, really. Has there ever been anybody you haven't wanted to kill?"

Tin Man smiled.

"Using this psycho and his army of thugs at this point

is like using a cannon to kill a mosquito," Spiro said. "Knight and Moon don't know anything. They're just stumbling around trying to pacify the monk. I think we should wait to see what they do next."

"I'm inclined to agree," Bart said. "A dead billionaire could draw some unwanted attention, and we don't need that kind of scrutiny right now. How are you doing with your special project?"

"On time. More or less."

Bart stared at him. "More or less isn't acceptable."

"Understood," Spiro said. "We'll be ready on time."

"Follow Knight and Moon," the director said to Tin Man. "Get wiretaps on their phones and monitor their Internet access."

"And if they make trouble?" Tin Man asked.

"Then you do what you do best. You kill them."

FOUR

⸻⸘⸺

RILEY AND EMERSON COLLECTED WAYAN BAGUS in President's Park. He rose when he saw them, bowed slightly, and followed them to the car. No questions asked.

Riley thought the monk's heartbeat was probably around ten beats per minute. Her heartbeat was up there at hummingbird level. She was getting sucked into another whackadoodle conspiracy theory obsession that was going to step on all the wrong toes. Last time Emerson went off on a tangent like this, it was a disaster. Okay, so it ended well, but getting to the end was a freaking horror.

The ride back to Mysterioso Manor was quiet, Riley and Emerson thinking their own thoughts, Wayan Bagus watching *Beauty and the Beast* on his little screen. Riley parked the Maybach in the garage and told Emerson and Wayan Bagus she would see them in the morning. She walked across the circular driveway to her Mini Cooper, and Emerson walked with her.

"Now that you're once again my amanuensis and we're involved in another investigation, I feel it would be best if you moved into Mysterioso Manor," Emerson said.

"For how long?"

"I was thinking permanently."

Riley stopped breathing for a beat, not sure what he was suggesting.

"Permanently is a long time," she said.

"Not as long as until the end of time or forever. That would indicate the potential for infinity."

"Where would I stay?"

"It's a mansion. There are plenty of guest rooms. Anywhere you want. Although I was hoping you would spend tonight with me in the library."

"The library," Riley said. "That's where you sleep."

"Yes. I sleep in the tent. I find it more restful than the cluttered, elaborate bedrooms."

Holy crikey, Riley thought. He wanted her to spend the night with him. In the library. She supposed that was flattering, and she did find him attractive, but she wasn't sure she was ready. How would it affect their work relationship? And he was just so darn odd.

41

"This is so sudden," Riley said.

"I suppose it is. I was hoping we could jump right into it, but I guess it would be okay if you wanted to go home and pack a few personal things to bring back here."

"I don't know if I'm ready to *jump* right into it. I mean, I like you. And there is a certain physical attraction . . ."

"Yes," Emerson said. "I realize there's a potential for distraction, but I'm sure we can work our way through that for the sake of the investigation."

"The investigation."

"Yes, and not just any investigation either. This one is worthy. A missing island. *Sweet!*" Emerson was practically vibrating with excitement. "We can do some research on the National Park Service tonight. Get a head start on tomorrow."

"So you want me to drive all the way home, pack up a few personal things, drive all the way back here, and stay up all night doing your scut work?"

Emerson smiled. "Precisely."

"And you want me to move in," Riley said, making exaggerated quote marks with her fingers, " 'permanently,' so I can be at your beck and call twenty-four hours a day?"

Emerson smiled again and looked relieved. "Exactly. So glad you understand."

"For the love of Mike, Emerson. In the entire history of ideas, that one has to be one of the worst."

Riley slid behind the wheel, cranked the engine over,

and rolled away, talking to herself all the way down the driveway.

"Idiot, idiot, idiot," she said, rolling her eyes, wrinkling her nose. "What was I thinking? What is *he* thinking?"

She took the back way home along Beach Drive, following Rock Creek and weaving around the National Zoo. While she waited for the traffic light at Massachusetts Avenue, she got a text from Emerson.

> I do not contend with the world, rather it is the world
> that contends with me.

Taken at face value she thought this sounded a tad egocentric. Since it came from Emerson she suspected it had a loftier meaning. And because she didn't have sufficient energy to suss out the meaning, she texted back that she would see him tomorrow morning at nine.

A black Cadillac Escalade pulled up behind her and followed her through the light and onto Rock Creek and Potomac Parkway. Several miles later she turned onto M Street and then again onto Wisconsin Avenue. The Escalade was still there. She pulled to the curb by the Apple Store, and the Escalade sped past before she could get a glimpse at the car's interior.

She texted Emerson.

> Think I was being followed by an Escalade. It's gone
> now. What do you think?

Moments later she got his response.

Terrible. Only gets 15 mpg. Also, be careful. #unagi.

A half mile later Riley parked in the alley behind her apartment. She was renting half of the third floor of a redbrick townhouse in a great location on a tree-lined street. It was long on charm and short on plumbing. The heating system clanked, and the hot water was slow in arriving, but the crown molding was stunning. It was a one-bedroom, one-bath, and it was furnished in comfortable contemporary pieces, mostly from Crate and Barrel.

Riley walked into the dark apartment and flipped on the light switch. It was good to be home. Her apartment felt calm and sane. It reflected her tastes and her hope for a bright, successful future. It screamed "young professional." It also whispered "small town Texas girl." There were pictures of her parents, grandparents, her brothers, and the family dogs. Scuffed-up, square-toed shitkicker cowboy boots were in the closet beside four-inch stiletto-heeled Christian Louboutins.

She poured herself a glass of wine, pulled some mac and cheese from the freezer, heated it up, and added some Texas Pete hot sauce. She ate at the little table she'd placed in a corner of the kitchen, and she wondered about Emerson. What was he eating? Probably nuts and berries with Wayan Bagus. Or a vegetarian breakfast bar.

She forked into the mac and cheese and toyed with the idea of returning to Mysterioso Manor. As much as she hated to admit it, there was a decent possibility that an island had vanished. Been blown up, possibly, and sunk into the sea. What else could have happened to it? And there was also a decent possibility that the government was involved and trying to cover its tracks. They'd met too much resistance today. It felt off.

She had a second glass of wine and decided to stay in her apartment. She'd get a good night's sleep and get an early start in the morning.

Shortly after two A.M. Riley was dragged out of sleep by a car alarm. She padded barefoot to the kitchen window and looked out at the dark alley. There were three cars parked there beside hers. The alarm was coming from one of the cars. She fumbled through the purse she'd left on the kitchen counter, found her keys, and pressed the panic button. The alarm stopped wailing. She squinted at the parked cars. Everything seemed okay. No extraneous cars lurking in the shadows. No one skulking around. She ate half a tub of mint chocolate chip ice cream and went back to bed.

At seven the next morning, Riley finished the tub of ice cream and washed it down with two cups of coffee. By eight she was showered and dressed and had her coffee mug rinsed and in the dish drain. She had a small overnight bag packed with a few essentials in case she decided to spend the night at Mysterioso Manor. Wouldn't hurt to have this in her car, she thought. She grabbed a sweatshirt, headed downstairs, and walked out the back door to the alley. She pulled up short when she reached her car. A hatchet was sticking out of the Mini Cooper, the blade embedded in the hood.

Her first reaction was to run through her extensive vocabulary of cuss words. Her second reaction was to look around, because if the jerk who vandalized her car was still there she was going to punch him in the face. The face-punching phase was cut short when it occurred to Riley that the vandal might be a psychopathic maniac. At closer inspection she saw that there was writing on the hatchet handle. *Curiosity killed the cat.*

She took a picture of the car and the hatchet with her smartphone and tried to pull the hatchet out of the hood. It wouldn't budge, so she got into the car and headed for Mysterioso Manor. She was halfway there when Emerson called.

"Are you on your way?" he asked. "I've been working all night and have something very interesting to show you."

"I'm on the road. I have something interesting to show you too."

FIVE

⸺◦◦◦◦⸺

Vᴇʀɴᴏɴ ᴀɴᴅ Eᴍᴇʀsᴏɴ ᴍᴇᴛ Rɪʟᴇʏ ᴀs sʜᴇ pulled into the circular drive. Both men stood hands on hips, looking at the hatchet. Riley got out of her car and joined them.

"That's not going to do you any good at trade-in time," Vernon said.

Emerson glanced at Riley. "I believe it's safe to assume this isn't your work."

"Someone set my car alarm off at two o'clock this morning. When I stepped out of my apartment to come here, I discovered the hatchet. The message on the hatchet handle is *Curiosity killed the cat.*"

"Ominous," Vernon said. "Being that you don't have a cat."

"I like my Mini," Riley said. "And now it has a big gash in it."

"Looks like they sliced a hose," Vernon said. "You're leaking vital fluids. You're lucky you made it this far."

Riley looked at the liquid trickling out from under her car. "I'm really mad at *someone*," she said.

"If you connect the dots between the message on the handle and yesterday's confrontation at the Park Service office, you might deduct that a hatchet serves as Tin Man's calling card," Emerson said.

"Like in *The Wizard of Oz*," Vernon said. "The Tin Man always had a hatchet! You know what I'd like to see? One of them flying monkeys from that movie. Boy, they were really something. I loved those monkeys. The Wicked Witch had a whole army of them."

"I'm going to need a raise if I have to deal with a psycho with a hatchet," Riley said.

"How about a million-dollar smile?"

Riley accepted the smile and followed Emerson into the house. She thought it was an interesting idea that someone named Tin Man would be running around impaling cars with his hatchet. Sort of funny, right? Unless it was *her* car. Still, that didn't mean it was true. Hard to believe she had made herself enough of a nuisance to warrant Tin Man defacing her car in the middle of the night. Surely he had better things to do.

"How's Wayan Bagus doing?" Riley asked.

"He's experiencing a period of adjustment. He exploded a bean burrito in the microwave this morning. Aunt Myra won't be happy when she returns."

"I thought you had a cleaning service."

"They quit. Vernon left the door open two days ago, and one of the zebras strolled in and left a package in the kitchen."

"When your father created his own personal zoo I don't imagine he envisioned a zebra in the kitchen."

"My father had a large staff of professionals. I'm working with a skeleton crew of mostly geriatric leftovers."

"From what I see of your finances I think you could well afford to keep the large staff of professionals."

"They were annoying. Leaf blowers, power washers, prima donna animal groomers and landscape artists. People underfoot in the house and on the grounds all day long. I prefer to let the animals roam and the weeds take over, and be at one with nature."

"What about the package in the kitchen?"

"I gave it to the gardener. I believe he needed it for the tomato plants."

Riley made a mental note not to eat the tomatoes. "You said you found something interesting."

Emerson led Riley into the library. He pulled an extra chair up to the table he was using as a desk, and they both sat down. The massive book on the table was titled *Plumes: A Journey to the Center of the Earth.* A bunch of newspaper articles had been stacked up alongside the book.

Emerson opened the book to a world map showing red, green, and yellow dots of differing sizes at various geological locations. Samoa had a big red dot, and there was a circle drawn around it with black marker.

"I suppose this means something?" Riley said, tapping the circle.

"It does, but I want you to see for yourself. Read through the first stack of newspaper articles."

There were fifty-two different stories, spanning the last couple years. Riley read through some of the headlines. *USA Today:* "Hikers Disappear Without a Trace in Yellowstone." *Hawaii Tribune-Herald:* "Murder in Volcanoes National Park." *The Oregonian:* "Brothers Drown in Crater Lake." *The New York Times:* "Australian Tourist Boat Vanishes in Galapagos—20 Presumed Dead."

"Last month there was a news story about a couple hikers who fell into one of the hot springs at Yellowstone and were boiled alive," Emerson said. "The acidic water completely dissolved them within a day."

"Horrible."

"I agree. And it might be the perfect crime. Turns out there are stories every year about visitors dying or going missing in our national parks."

"Another conspiracy theory for Vernon's blog?"

Vernon's main claim to fame was a blog called

Mysterioso, where he published Emerson's many theories, crackpot or otherwise.

Emerson smiled. "You studied statistics at Harvard as part of your MBA, right?" He opened his laptop and downloaded a list of deaths at every national park, by year, since the early 1900s. "What do you make of this?"

It was almost one o'clock by the time Riley finished charting the national parks deaths. "Do you know anything about regression analysis?" she asked Emerson.

"It tries to see if data gathered from something fits into a mathematical model."

"Right." Riley held up the paper with her calculations. "In this case I used the data you gave me on deaths at national parks and tried to fit it into an actuarial model used by insurance companies to predict accidental deaths. If you look at the total number of deaths in national parks over the past ten or so years, there's nothing statistically significant."

"And when you look at individual parks?" Emerson said.

"At a handful of them, there are statistical anomalies. Too many accidents resulting in fatalities when compared to other parks. Statistically speaking, there's less than a three percent chance it's mere coincidence. Of course, there could be other variables, ones I don't know about, affecting the results."

"Exactly," Emerson said. "There could be other variables. I'm interested in those other variables."

"Don't you want to know which parks?"

"I already know which parks."

Emerson returned to *Plumes: A Journey,* still open to the world map, and he used the marker to circle the rest of the red and yellow dots in the United States. "Yellowstone, Hawaii Volcanoes National Park, Oregon Crater Lake, and, of course, the National Park of American Samoa."

"That's right! How did you know?"

"Wayan Bagus's stolen island. It has beaches and rain forests. But most important, it has a volcano. I found it odd that certain national parks were death magnets and thought there might be a connection."

"What's the connection?"

"Hawaii Volcanoes National Park is the site of Mauna Loa and Kilauea, two active volcanoes. Crater Lake National Park in Oregon is the deepest lake in the United States and the ninth deepest in the world. It's the caldera of an ancient vast volcano that forms Three Sisters Wilderness. And Yellowstone is one of the most geothermally active areas in the world and the site of an inactive super-volcano."

"Volcanoes are dangerous," Riley said. "Boiling hot springs are dangerous. Couldn't that explain it?"

"It might. Except that these aren't just any volcanoes.

Plumes: A Journey identifies all the sites as suspected mantle plumes."

"What's a mantle plume?"

"The vast majority of volcanoes are formed from shifting tectonic plates, and the magma comes from fairly close to the surface of the earth. Rarely, they're fueled by magma directly from the earth's core. Volcanoes fueled directly from the earth's core are called mantle plumes."

"So we have statistically unlikely accidents occurring at national parks that just happen to have been created on the sites of mantle plumes."

Emerson smiled. "Seems rather unlikely that they're accidents, don't you think?"

"Then what?"

"Murder. Somebody is murdering people at these national parks, but the really interesting question is why."

He was connecting the dots again, Riley thought. And he was doing it with at least half the dots missing, so what were the chances he was reaching the right conclusions? She thought the chances weren't good. It was a big stretch to connect a bunch of murders to mantle plumes. Not that this surprised her. Emerson was a conclusion jumper. It was the way his mind worked. It was a game for him. And sometimes he actually jumped to a significant conclusion. Other times, the idea would run its course and get discarded.

"This is *really, really* good," Emerson said, beaming out

happiness. Radiating excitement. "We now have a missing island *and* a murder mystery!"

Riley didn't want to ruin his fun, but she thought this was right up there with Tom Hanks delivering a sculpture to Emerson's house.

SIX

⸻◦◦◦⸻

EMERSON HAD HIS KNAPSACK HUNG FROM HIS shoulder and his hand wrapped around Riley's wrist. He was tugging her forward, out of the library, out of the house, and toward the garage, making sure she kept up with his long strides.

"I had a Tesla delivered an hour ago," Emerson said. "It's fuel-efficient, and only the steering wheel is made of leather. The seats are genuine cloth. This car is almost entirely karma-friendly."

She was all in favor of friendly karma, Riley thought, catching sight of the shiny new Tesla. Maybe some of the good stuff would drift over onto her Mini Cooper. God knows the Mini needed some help. It was parked next to the Tesla, and Vernon was standing on the hood, trying to remove the hatchet and not having any luck. Wayan Bagus was watching.

"I can't get this dang thing out," Vernon said. "It got wedged between something in there. Offhand I'd say Tin Man got a mean streak."

"We aren't sure Tin Man did this," Riley said. "It could have just been a random maniac."

Emerson handed the Tesla key fob to Riley, and an iPad to Wayan.

"What is this?" Wayan asked.

"It's an iPad," Emerson said. "I loaded Angry Birds onto it for you." He motioned to the car. "Everyone in. The game is afoot."

Riley looked over at Emerson. "You said that two nights ago."

"I like saying it," Emerson said. "It's one of my favorite things to say. The game is afoot. The game is afoot."

Wayan Bagus and Vernon got into the back seat, and Vernon leaned forward.

"Where are we going?"

"George Mason University," Emerson said. "I have some questions to ask the vulcanologist."

Vernon grinned. "Well, shoot, Emerson, it's about time. Course, them scientists living in their ivory towers don't know anything but theories. I've got what you call practical experience."

Riley put the car into gear and drove down the driveway. "Vernon, do you know what a vulcanologist studies?"

"I sure do." He ear-muffed Wayan Bagus. "It's all about lady parts."

"A vulcanologist studies volcanoes," Emerson said. "You're thinking of a *vulva*-ologist. And also, there's no such thing."

"Well, shoot. That's disappointing." Vernon removed his hands from Wayan Bagus's ears and turned to his cellphone. "Emmie, I got another one of them emails threatening to sue us for defamatory comments in the blog."

"Who's threatening to sue us this time?"

"Government lawyers. They didn't like the entry I posted last night." He grinned. "It was awesome. I called it 'Death Parks: Fact or Fiction?' They say I'm causing irreparable damage to the reputation of the national parks and inciting panic."

"I'm surprised you haven't heard from Tin Man," Riley said. "Shocking that he didn't sneak into your RV and whack your laptop with his hatchet."

Emerson looked over at her. "I suspect you made your statement in jest, and while it was a humorous thing to say, there is an underlying element of *perhaps*."

"Perhaps what?" Riley asked.

"Vernon's blog goes out at midnight. Two hours later someone inserted a hatchet into the hood of your car. *Perhaps* it was Tin Man. Think about it."

"Okay, I might consider the possibility of a connection, but why me?" Riley said. "I didn't write the stupid blog."

"*Perhaps* he decided you were a good target," Emerson said. "You separated yourself from the pack."

"Yeah, and it would have been a bitch to stick a hatchet in the Maybach," Vernon said. "That thing's built like a tank."

"I need to report the hatcheting to the police," Riley said. "My insurance company is going to want a police report."

"Waste of time," Emerson said. "I'll trade this car for your Mini. I can use the Mini for a lawn ornament. I like the addition of the hatchet."

"I have destroyed the greedy pigs' defenses," Wayan Bagus said. "I have secured the survival of the angry birds."

"That's good, Little Buddy," Vernon said. "Let's see what you do when I bump you up a level."

"Child's play," Wayan Bagus said. "I am the master of this game."

Thirty minutes later Riley pulled into the Exploratory Hall parking lot at George Mason. A large, modern-looking brick building with a wetlands area behind it and a greenhouse on the roof, Exploratory Hall housed the Department of Atmospheric, Oceanic, and Earth Sciences.

Wayan set his iPad aside and unbuckled his seatbelt. "Am I to be the Dalai Lama today?" he asked.

"It's not in my game plan," Emerson said, leading everyone across the parking lot and into the building.

Vernon looked around. "I always knew some day I'd get to college . . . and here I am."

"It's vastly overrated," Emerson said, stopping at the elevator, tapping the UP button. "It's far better to be born rich."

"Contentment is the greatest wealth," Wayan Bagus said. "It is better to be born contented."

"Do we know where we're going?" Riley asked.

"I want to talk to Professor Marion White," Emerson said. "She's on the third floor, and she's currently having office hours."

Marion White was at her desk when Emerson knocked on her open door. She was in her midthirties with dark brown hair pulled back and tied at the nape of her neck. A sliver of red tank top peeked out from under the deep V-neck of her white lab coat. The tank top showed a couple inches of cleavage.

"Do you have a moment to talk?" Emerson asked. "I have some questions about mantle plumes."

"I'll be happy to answer your questions," Marion said, and she gestured toward some chairs surrounding her desk.

Her office was small and filled with books, papers, and various lava rocks. Scaled-down models of volcanoes covered a folding table set against one of the walls. Charts and maps and whiteboards covered most of the wall space.

Riley, Wayan Bagus, Vernon, and Emerson carefully walked around the stacks of books and took a seat.

"There are only seventeen known mantle plumes in the whole world," Marion said. "It's really one of the more interesting fields of study in geophysics."

Emerson pulled *Plumes: A Journey* out of his knapsack. "I've read through this book. But it doesn't completely explain the differences between volcanoes formed from mantle plumes and volcanoes formed by plate tectonics."

"For one thing, volcanoes formed from mantle plumes are generally much larger. As you probably know, mantle plumes originate at the center of the earth. They begin as a relatively narrow pipe at the core and expand into a giant mushroom head by the time they approach the earth's surface. Most of them are massive, up to two thousand kilometers in diameter. One of the biggest and most famous mantle plumes is responsible for creating the entire Hawaiian Islands chain."

"Woo-wee," Vernon said. "That's mighty interesting. I sure would like to take you to dinner tonight and talk some more about eruptions and such."

The little monk slapped Vernon on the back of the head.

"You got to pardon my grandfather," Vernon said. "He's old, and I'm the only one who's willing to take care of him on account of his disposition."

Marion looked at Vernon and then at Wayan Bagus. "Your grandfather is an Asian monk?"

"Oh, well, he's adopted," Vernon explained, putting his hand on the monk's shoulder.

Wayan Bagus batted Vernon's hand away.

"Maybe that's what happened to my missing island," Wayan Bagus said to Emerson. "Maybe it collapsed and sunk into the ocean."

"You're here about a missing island?" Marion asked. "It's unlikely. Most mantle plumes form what are called shield volcanoes. They generally create landmasses, not destroy them."

"Generally?" Riley asked.

Marion pointed to a map on her office wall of Pangaea, the ancient supercontinent that existed before separating into today's seven continents. "Some people theorize that a mantle plume could cause a massive tectonic uplift, powerful enough to break apart a continent."

Vernon opened his mouth to say something about powerful uplifts, looked over at Wayan Bagus, and decided it wasn't worth getting slapped again.

"Is there anything of value in a volcano formed by a mantle plume?" Emerson asked. "Something somebody would want to steal?"

"Not really. Mostly just basalt and silica rock and sulfuric acid gasses. The lava does contain higher than normal amounts of rare earth elements, like osmium."

"What's osmium?" Riley asked.

"It's similar to platinum, and it's the densest naturally occurring element in existence. It's worth about four hundred dollars per ounce but would likely cost more to extract than you could sell it for."

Vernon picked up one of the model volcanoes and examined it. "I made one of these in seventh grade for the science fair."

"That one's a scale model of Krakatau," Marion said. She turned to Emerson. "Mantle plumes also extrude some primordial isotopes from the earth's core. They're very rare but not valuable to anybody except an astrophysicist."

"Why not?" Riley asked.

"It's mostly just things like rare forms of helium. But primordial elements are materials that existed before the earth was formed. Sort of cosmic leftovers from the big bang. No one has really ever seen the earth's core, so it's kind of a clue to the forces of creation."

Emerson thanked Marion for her time, and everyone trooped out of her office and out of the building.

"Now what?" Vernon asked.

"Now we go back to Washington," Emerson said.

SEVEN

—⊗⊗⊗—

E MERSON EMPTIED THE CONTENTS OF HIS
knapsack onto the table at the Organic Kitchen, a
local health food restaurant halfway between George
Mason University and Washington, D.C. There were two
books about volcanoes, including *Plumes: A Journey*, three
manila folders labeled "Yellowstone," "Crater Lake," and
"Hawaii Volcanoes National Park," a yellow notepad, and a
replica of Dumbledore's magic wand from the Wizarding
World of Harry Potter.

Riley set her Succulent Summer Smoothie aside, picked
up the magic wand, and waved it at Emerson. "Does this
work?"

"It reminds me that magic is all around us," Emerson
said. "All you have to do is believe."

"Believe in what?"

"It doesn't matter. Santa Claus. The power to cloud someone's mind. Love."

"I guess I'd like to believe in those things too," Riley said.

Emerson looked across the table at Wayan Bagus, who was sipping on a cucumber and kale smoothie and watching *Revenge of the Nerds* on his iPad. "Wayan once told me that the moment you doubt whether you can fly, you cease to be able to do it forever."

"No second chances?"

"Take Peter Pan, for instance."

Riley raised a single eyebrow.

"He had some good times on that island," Emerson said. "Fighting pirates. Rescuing Indian princesses. Spending time with the mermaids. Good times. Good times."

"All because he believed?"

"Exactly."

"Maybe he just had an overactive imagination and was delusional."

"Nevertheless, he could fly. Peter Pan, Tinker Bell, Rudolph. All excellent flyers."

She couldn't dispute it. They were all excellent flyers. And there was something oddly compelling about a man who, in a time of cynics and doubters, embraced the value of believing.

"What's the next step?" Riley asked Emerson.

"Flying-wise?"

"Mantle-plume-wise."

Emerson passed one of the manila folders over to her. "This is the file on a newlywed couple who disappeared without a trace in Yellowstone one month ago. They were staying at the Old Faithful Inn and went out to do some backcountry hiking. Search and Rescue looked for them for weeks. The bodies were never found. The Park Service speculates they fell into a hot spring and were boiled alive. Officially, it's a closed case."

"But you don't think it was an accident."

"They were experienced hikers," Emerson said. "Worked as mountain guides in Colorado during the summer and backcountry ski instructors during the winter. No, I don't think it was an accident."

"What's in the Crater Lake file?"

Emerson opened the folder. "Zachary, Taylor, and Adam Brolowski. Brothers. Have a popular YouTube channel where they stream themselves doing all manner of extreme sports. Call themselves the Bro Brothers."

"And they're missing too?"

"Dead. At least, Taylor and Adam. Taylor was killed during a deep dive into Crater Lake two weeks ago. Adam was killed in a car crash one week later. Zak told his parents he was going hiking in Three Sisters Wilderness three or four days ago and hasn't been heard from since."

"And you think they were murdered?" Riley asked.

"Three brothers die or go missing within weeks of each other in separate incidents. And, it all happens in one of our death parks."

"You said yourself they were into extreme sports. It could be just coincidence."

"I don't believe in coincidence," Emerson said. "I do believe in conspiracies."

Wayan Bagus looked up from the iPad, having heard something that interested him more than the Nerds getting revenge on the Jocks.

"How we explain coincidences depends on how we see the world. Is everything connected or do things merely co-occur? It's all in how you think."

"Well, what do you think?" Riley asked.

Wayan Bagus went back to watching the movie. "I am one with the universe. So are the Nerds. And so are the Jocks. The Nerds will never know the Jocks' world and the Jocks will never know the Nerds'. And yet, we are all connected by the Tao, Nerds and Jocks alike."

"In-ter-est-ing," Riley said, and she turned back to Emerson. "What about Hawaii Volcanoes National Park?"

Emerson tapped the folder labeled "Hawaii." "I think this one is the key. Half a dozen missing persons or deaths in the past three years. The local police just found a mutilated body near one of the volcano's vents, Puu Oo, on the east side of Kilauea. He was chopped to pieces."

"And you think Yellowstone, Crater Lake, and Hawaii Volcanoes National Park are all connected to the missing island?"

Emerson put the files back into his knapsack. "It is a statistical impossibility for all of this to be random. It might be explained by many things, but my favorite explanation is that these are not accidents, but murders. More importantly, I believe these murders are being committed by one person or group of people for some purpose we do not yet know. The same person or persons who stole Wayan Bagus's island."

Riley was willing to entertain the possibility that at least some, if not all, of the murders were the work of one person. Emerson lost her on the island connection.

"Our next stop on the day's agenda is the United States Park Police," Emerson said. "Everyone drink up."

Riley, Vernon, Wayan Bagus, and Emerson stood outside the massive gray stone fortress with DEPARTMENT OF THE INTERIOR chiseled above the entrance. They walked through the middle of five doors and made their way to the U.S. Park Police Office.

On their way, Vernon read from a tourist brochure he'd picked up from the information kiosk. "The U.S. Park Police was founded in 1791 by George Washington and is one of the oldest uniformed federal law enforcement agencies in the United States. The U.S. Park Police shares law enforcement jurisdiction in all lands administered by the National Park Service with a force of National Park Service Rangers. The Park Police is a unit of the National Park Service, which is a bureau of the Department of the Interior."

Riley paused at the large glass door leading to the Park Police offices. "We're going to look like a bunch of crazies announcing to the police that we've uncovered some conspiracy to murder tourists at national parks."

Emerson pushed the door open and motioned everyone through. "I wouldn't worry," he said. "Three things cannot be long hidden. The sun, the moon, and the truth. And if we were to add a fourth thing it would be missing islands." He approached the police sergeant manning the front desk. "We're here to report a murder."

Wayan Bagus nodded. "Also a stolen island."

"And, I'd like to talk with someone here about the government's war on coal," Vernon added. "America!"

Five minutes later they were escorted out of the building by two uniformed police officers.

"In retrospect, I suppose it probably wasn't the best idea for a monk, a blogger, a known conspiracy theorist, and his amanuensis to march into a police station," Emerson said.

Riley was taking deep, calming breaths. Thank goodness she didn't see any reporters hanging out because if this got into the papers she would be a complete laughingstock in the legal community. She would be working for this nutcase forever, because no one else would ever hire her.

"You think?" she said to Emerson.

"On the positive side, we made our concerns known."

Riley stared at him incredulously. "They threatened to get a restraining order against all of us!"

Emerson shook his head and smiled. "I'm rich. You have to do a lot more than that to get a restraining order when you're rich. Wayan Bagus is just a harmless little monk, and Vernon gets a restraining order at least once a week."

Vernon waved his hand dismissively and blew a raspberry. "Restraining order, shmestraining order."

"So, there you have it," Emerson said. "Nothing to worry about."

Riley stuck her thumb at herself. "What about me?"

"Oh, you're definitely getting a restraining order," Emerson said.

"Seek not to contend. Where there is no contention there is neither victory nor defeat," Wayan Bagus offered.

"All this not contending is making me hungry," Vernon said. "Being as this is Little Buddy's first time in our nation's capital, let's show him the sights. Little Buddy, you ever touch a genuine moon rock?"

Emerson turned to Riley. "Every time Vernon visits Washington, D.C., he makes a pilgrimage to the National

Air and Space Museum to get an ice cream sandwich at the cafeteria, touch a moon rock, and take a nap at the planetarium."

"Yup," Vernon said. "Planetarium naps are just about the best kind of naps there are."

They walked along the National Mall, past the Washington Monument to the National Air and Space Museum. As soon as they were inside, Vernon made his way to the cafeteria, and Emerson, Riley, and Wayan Bagus headed for the second-floor exhibit halls.

It was late in the day, and the museum was emptying out. Some school groups and clumps of tourists were still wandering around, but the earlier crowds had disappeared.

Riley was drawn to the special World War II Aviation traveling exhibit. Emerson and Wayan Bagus's interests took them elsewhere.

This was nice, Riley thought, browsing through a collection of photographs and documents. She lived in Washington, D.C., but she didn't take advantage of the culture. She didn't visit the museums. She worked during the week, and on weekends she did laundry and food shopping.

She walked to the railing to look at the large prop bomber. The plane was suspended from the ceiling and hung just below the second-level balcony. She was looking down at the plane, imagining what it must have been like to be part of the war effort, when she was grabbed from behind, lifted off her feet, and pitched forward. Her knees hit the top of the railing, someone cursed behind her, and shoved her over the edge. She went into a free fall with arms flailing and eyes wide open, looking at the cement floor thirty feet below. There were no thoughts in her head. Just raw terror.

The plane was directly beneath her. She hit it square on the fuselage, couldn't get a grip, and tumbled down onto a wing. Her momentum carried her off the edge of the wing, but she was able to grab on to one of the large propellers.

She dangled precariously, holding tight to the propeller. She felt the blade slowly rotate from horizontal to near vertical, and her grip started to slip. She looked down at the floor, felt panic sweep over her, and shouted for Emerson.

She looked from the floor to the balcony and saw Emerson launch himself over the guardrail and drop onto the wing. He stabilized for a moment and then grabbed her wrist from above and held tight.

"If you want to avoid situations like this in the future, we're really going to have to work on your *unagi*," Emerson said.

"S-s-sure," Riley said. "Whatever. Just don't drop m-m-me."

Emerson pulled her onto the wing and held her tight against him.

"Don't move," he said. "We aren't entirely secure."

Riley had no intention of moving. Her heart was

pounding, and she could barely breathe. She had her eyes squinched closed and her fingers curled into Emerson's shirt. She thought she might have wet her pants a little. She hoped he couldn't tell.

"My *unagi* tells me you'd like to be kissed," Emerson said.

Riley opened her eyes and looked at him while he kissed her softly on the lips.

"How was that?" he asked.

"It was nice. You're a good kisser."

"I enjoyed it," he said. "We should do it more."

"And it helped to take my mind off our problem."

"What problem is that?"

"The plane," Riley said. "We could slip off and die."

"That would be unpleasant," Emerson said.

People were scrambling below them. Museum guards, Park Police, curious tourists. Sirens from first responders could be heard in the distance. EMT trucks, fire trucks, police cars.

"This is a nightmare," Riley said.

"Perhaps, but a brush with death is always interesting. And the kiss added a certain something."

Riley didn't want to be ungrateful, because, after all, Emerson had risked his life for hers, but criminy, explaining their kiss in terms of "a certain something" was just about the most unromantic thing she'd ever heard.

"A certain something?" she asked Emerson.

"Je ne sais quoi," Emerson said.

Okay, Riley thought, it sounded better in French, but it wasn't going to get him another kiss anytime soon.

There was a loud *SPLAT*, and someone shrieked in another part of the hall. A school group was rushed out of the area, running underneath Riley and Emerson.

"What's going on?" Riley yelled down.

"Someone fell," a guard said. "Not as lucky as you, I'm afraid."

Riley locked eyes with Emerson. "Where's Wayan Bagus?"

"I don't know," Emerson said. "He went off on his own. I believe he was interested in the planet exhibit."

First responders arrived. Half ran to the area by the front entrance, and half stopped under the prop plane and looked up at Riley and Emerson.

"Hang on," a museum employee called from the floor. "We're going to lower the plane."

Riley heard gears turning overhead. The cables holding the plane jerked, and the plane slowly inched down. Riley strained to see what was happening on the first floor. A lot of people were clustered around something lying on the ground. It was difficult to see from her vantage point, but she supposed it was a body. Not Wayan Bagus at least. No orange robe. And not Vernon. No white T-shirt.

Hands reached out to her, easing her off the wing. She set foot on terra firma and stood on shaky legs. She took a couple deep breaths. Emerson climbed down next without assistance.

A paramedic offered aid, but Riley dismissed him. She had a skinned knee and some leftover fright, but no other damage had been done. A museum PR person and a guard had questions. The information Riley could provide was brief. She was pushed from behind. She heard a man swear. She didn't see him.

Emerson didn't see the man either. He'd been in an adjoining room that had been set up to resemble the quarterdeck of an aircraft carrier. He'd run to the railing when he heard Riley call his name.

Riley and Emerson shared a moment of relief as they spotted Wayan Bagus standing quietly off to one side next to a uniformed police officer.

A few feet away from Wayan Bagus an overweight middle-aged man wearing a shirt he'd obviously just purchased from a gift shop was talking with a homicide detective.

"Never saw anything like it," he said. "That big goon, who's splattered all over the floor, bum-rushed the little monk in the orange dress and, *poof*, the little monk just sort of disappeared for a second." He gestured a second time at the dead body. "His momentum kind of carried him right over the balcony on the second floor."

Riley looked at Emerson. "Nobody can disappear."

Emerson shrugged. "Taoists believe the greatest one to walk the earth is nobody."

"So you're saying he can disappear because he's nobody?"

"I'm saying *if* he was nobody he could disappear."

Riley shook her head. "That almost makes sense."

The detective finished with the tourist, walked over to Riley, and handed her his business card. "I've already talked with museum security, and I'm guessing you're Riley Moon. You were attacked first. Are you okay?"

Riley looked at her skinned knee. "Just a couple bumps and bruises. Who was he?"

"We were hoping you'd know. He didn't have an ID. Hopefully we'll be able to identify him once CSI has had a chance to examine the body. Is there anybody who would want to kill you? Any enemies?"

"So you're thinking this man who tried to attack the monk is the same man who pushed me off the balcony?"

"We don't know at this point, but it's possible."

"I suppose I might have some enemies," Riley said, "but the Buddhist monk standing over there hasn't any. Or, rather, he hadn't any until today."

The detective looked over at Wayan Bagus. "So you all know each other."

"His name is Wayan Bagus. He's from Bali. He's my employer's houseguest," Riley said.

The plainclothes cop turned his attention to Emerson. "And Ms. Moon's relationship to you is?"

"She's my amanuensis."

"Your what? Never mind. What you two do behind closed doors is none of my business." The detective

75

motioned to the police officer standing with Wayan Bagus. "I want to talk with the monk now."

Wayan Bagus approached them and bowed slightly.

"So," the detective said. "Is there anything you can tell me?"

"Anything?" Wayan Bagus asked.

"Yes, anything."

"Lord Buddha teaches that even death is not to be feared by one who has lived wisely."

The detective had a pained look on his face. "I meant about the dead guy."

Wayan Bagus nodded. "He fell."

"Some of the witnesses said you disappeared just before he was about to push you over the balcony."

"Nobody can disappear, though, can they?" Wayan Bagus said.

EIGHT

⊛

R ILEY AND EMERSON SAT SIDE BY SIDE ON A
bench outside the planetarium while they waited
for Vernon. Wayan Bagus had gone off in search of a quiet
place where he could meditate and pray for the dead man.
It was near closing time, and the museum was almost
empty.

"I'm exhausted," Riley said. "I expended a lot of
adrenaline, and I'm toast."

"I have to admit, I'm also a little toasted," Emerson said,
"but I can't stop thinking about the attacks just now."

"Hard to believe they were random. I think we were
targeted."

"I agree," Emerson said. "And I think this is the result

of us asking questions about the stolen island and the unexplained disappearances and deaths at the national parks."

"I'm having a problem with that. The cause doesn't justify the effect. Look at us. We're ridiculous. A monk, an eccentric billionaire, a big goofy guy, and me. We barge into a couple offices, ask totally off-the-wall questions, and get shuffled out onto the street."

"You're assuming that the questions are off-the-wall. Maybe the questions are spot-on."

"Even if the questions are spot-on. Someone tried to kill Wayan and me. That's not an appropriate reaction to a spot-on question. That's not normal."

Emerson nodded. "True, but what if there's something happening out there that is so huge and beyond normal that it justifies murder at the slightest provocation?"

"You have my attention. Keep going."

"I believe that the incidents we've been looking at, from our missing hikers in Yellowstone to our missing island in Samoa, are all the result of something occurring at exactly the same location. The earth's core. Imagine lines from the earth's core to each of the death parks, plus Wayan's island."

"And?"

"That's the connection."

"That's all you've got?"

"It's not sufficient?" Emerson asked.

"It's *nothing*," Riley said. "You've got nothing but an idea. It's not even an idea that makes any sense. I can draw lines from the center of the earth to anything. Anybody can. Even Vernon."

Emerson thought for a beat. "There are a few blanks to get filled in. Albert Einstein famously said if at first an idea is not absurd, there's no hope for it."

"You got me there," Riley said.

"So we're all on board," Emerson said.

"No."

"Partially on board?"

"Maybe."

"Good enough," Emerson said. "We're going to Yellowstone to find the missing newlyweds."

"The ones that were boiled alive?"

"That's speculation."

"Have you ever been to Yellowstone?"

"No, but I read Frommer's Yellowstone National Park travel guide. It's more than two million acres of boiling hot sulfuric springs, bubbling mud pots, vast lakes of brilliant blue, red, and yellow, huge geysers, and massive canyons and waterfalls. The entire Yellowstone National Park is an active volcano rumbling beneath the visitors' feet. It has the potential for a magnitude eight eruption."

"And if one of these magnitude eight eruptions happened now?"

"It's an extinction-level event. The amount of ash

expelled into the atmosphere would trigger massive climate change and could be the end of the human race. Most scientists predict that Yellowstone will erupt again in about sixty thousand years."

"Wow, only sixty thousand years."

"It's a ticking time bomb," Emerson said. "In 2013, scientists discovered a humongous blob of magma stored beneath Yellowstone. If that blob was released, it could fill the Grand Canyon eleven times over, but no one is predicting that will occur anytime remotely soon. Yellowstone is extremely stable, for an active volcano."

The planetarium was starting to empty. Vernon was one of the last to leave.

"That was a real good show," Vernon said to Emerson and Riley. "I hardly slept at all." He looked down at Riley's bloody knee. "What the heck happened to you?"

"A maniac threw me off the balcony."

"No kidding. Are you all right?"

"Yes. Fortunately I fell onto a plane that was hanging from the ceiling."

Even as she said it she realized the whole thing sounded ridiculous. It was almost as if she'd dreamed it.

"Did they catch the guy?" Vernon asked.

"Yes and no. He sort of flew over the second-floor railing, smashed onto the ground floor, and died," Riley said. "At least we think it was the same guy."

"What did this guy look like?" Vernon asked.

Wayan Bagus joined them. "I took a picture with my iPad. It was accidental but the quality is actually quite good. I was taking a picture of a plane when the unfortunate man came up behind me. After he fell I leaned over the balcony to see him, and my iPad snapped another picture."

Wayan Bagus brought the picture up on his iPad and showed it to Vernon.

"Oh man," Vernon said. "That's awful. His head exploded. There's brains all over the place. And I think I see guts squishing out of him. Did he poop himself? I bet he pooped himself. Dead guys always do that. 'Specially if you crush them. I mean I don't know firsthand, but it seems reasonable, right? This is making me sick. I might hurl. I feel faint. I gotta sit down." He did some deep breathing. "Okay, I feel better now. Anyone want an ice cream sandwich? If I hurry I might get to the snack bar before it closes."

"We'll meet you outside the front entrance," Emerson said.

Vernon ran off to get ice cream, and Emerson studied the photo on the iPad.

"Interesting," Emerson said. "Very interesting." He enlarged a part of the picture to show Riley. "You have to see this."

"I don't want to look if there are brains or guts," Riley said. "I haven't totally got it together. My heart is still skipping beats, and my stomach is queasy. It was awful to get thrown off the balcony. Seeing a dead guy with an exploded head isn't going to help my stomach."

"I want you to look at a close-up of his hand," Emerson said.

Riley looked at Wayan's iPad.

"He has the same tattoo as Tin Man," she said. "Two crossed sabers and a number one above them."

"It's a symbol for the 1st Volunteer Cavalry Division in the United States Army."

"So, they're both military?"

"Not unless they're both 120 years old. This insignia hasn't been used by the army in about a century. It's the insignia of the Rough Riders," Emerson said.

"As in Teddy Roosevelt?"

Emerson smiled. "Precisely. The same Teddy Roosevelt who led the Rough Riders in the Spanish-American War. The same Teddy Roosevelt who, as president, signed the Antiquities Act of 1906, allowing the president, with the stroke of a pen, to seize control of any lands he deems of natural, cultural, or scientific importance. It's been used hundreds of times since 1906 to create national parks and federal monuments. Millions of acres have been put under permanent conservation. That's why Teddy Roosevelt is often seen as the father of the national parks system."

"It's a pretty cool emblem," Riley said. "I could see why someone might want it as a tattoo. Not me, of course, but someone."

"It might be more than that. The Rough Riders were officially disbanded in 1898, but maybe Teddy Roosevelt had some use for them other than fighting Spaniards. Something important. Something he wanted kept secret."

"Oh boy," Riley said. "Now you're going to drag poor Teddy Roosevelt into this."

"Yes," Emerson said. "I think it might have all started with Teddy. Although at this point in time there's no way to know for sure if it was the man himself or someone close to him."

"And you think Tin Man and the dead guy are both members of some underground Rough Rider society?"

"That's my theory."

"Seems like a stretch," Riley said. "One hundred twenty years is a long time to keep a secret."

Emerson did a full-on smile. "It must be a real doozy!"

Riley spent the night at Mysterioso Manor. She didn't want to be alone with her thoughts, and Emerson's house felt safer than her apartment. She woke up slowly, assessing her injuries from the day before. Her knee had scabbed over, and she was generally achy. All minor issues. Her life's direction was more serious. Her life's direction was panic-attack material.

She got out of bed and saw two suitcases in the middle of the floor. Medium size. Black. New. The nice kind that rolled around on four wheels. One had an orange tag that said "Yellowstone" and the other had a red tag that said "Hawaii." She looked down at herself and realized there was a Post-it note stuck to her pajama top.

Flight for Jackson Hole, Wyoming, leaves Dulles at noon.

"Crap on a cracker," Riley said. And she padded off to the bathroom.

A half hour later she was showered and dressed in new undies, new bootcut jeans, a new plaid flannel shirt, and new Ariat cowboy boots that she had found in the Yellowstone suitcase.

Emerson, Wayan Bagus, and Vernon were already halfway through breakfast when Riley walked into the kitchen. Vernon's and Emerson's packed bags and three backpacks were sitting by the table. Wayan Bagus was trying to fit an assortment of supplies from Emerson's guest room into his little duffel. L'Occitane shower gels, bath salts, and Charmin Ultra Soft toilet paper.

It was clear it wouldn't all fit.

"The root of suffering is material attachment," Emerson said.

Vernon was eating a big stack of waffles smothered in butter and maple syrup, with orange juice, bacon, and sausages on the side.

"Well, I've got to differ with you there, Emerson. I kind of like all my attachments."

Riley sat down next to Emerson. "Do you think it's weird that you're a multimillionaire with lots of stuff who believes that material possessions are the root of all suffering?"

Emerson shrugged. "What choice do I have but to be myself? Everyone else was already taken."

"Is that more Buddhist wisdom?" Riley asked him.

"It came from a fortune cookie I had last week. I thought it might be appropriate. My life is complicated and even contradictory at times, but it's my life and I'm comfortable in it. Also, my lucky numbers are seven, fourteen, two, and nine."

Riley took a piece of bacon off Vernon's plate. "Since we're on the subject of being yourself, could you be a little less yourself from time to time, primarily from when I fall asleep to when I wake up? I mean, who sneaks into someone's bedroom in the middle of the night, sticks a note on them, and leaves suitcases filled with clothes? And I'm not even going to ask how you know my bra size."

"I must confess I had little to do with the clothes selection," Emerson said. "I employed a professional shopper."

Vernon looked up. "Personally, I don't believe in sexualizing women's bodies by making them wear bras and such," he said, his mouth full of waffles. "Free the nipple! Make America great again!"

"You needed the clothes for Yellowstone," Emerson said. "It was in the interest of expediency."

Riley threw her hands into the air. "For the love of Mike, I never agreed to go to Yellowstone. In fact, you never even asked if I wanted to go to Yellowstone."

"Because you wouldn't have agreed if I asked."

"Of course not. We'll probably be killed or worse."

"Will you go to Yellowstone with me?" Emerson asked.

Riley stole another piece of bacon. "I suppose I have to. My suitcase is already packed."

She also didn't want to remain in Washington, D.C., alone, trusting in her own *unagi*. Plus she had to secretly admit she was loving the new cowboy boots.

Wayan Bagus was still working on his duffel. He discarded the shower gels and bath salts, settling on packing the toilet paper.

"The devils at Procter and Gamble have seduced me with their Western cushiony comfort and two-ply construction," Wayan Bagus said.

"Welcome to my world, Little Buddy," Vernon said, pushing back from his empty plate. "I don't know about anybody else, but I'm ready to take off."

"Excellent," Emerson said. "We just have one quick stop before we go to the airport. We're going to the morgue."

NINE

⊗⊗⊗

THE WASHINGTON, D.C., OFFICE OF THE CHIEF
Medical Examiner was just off Route 395 and, as it
happened, half a mile from the Smithsonian National Air
and Space Museum. It was in an uninspired high-rise that
looked a little like a cross between a big, practical office
building and a classy parking garage.

"This is creepy," Riley said, pulling into a parking lot.
"I don't want to look at this dead guy. I don't even want
to go into this building."

"I'm not going in either," Vernon said. "Me and Little
Buddy are watching *Cinderella,* and she's about to get
Bibbidi-Bobbidi-Booed. It's my favorite part."

"Vernon tells me Walt Disney can change mice into

prancing white stallions," Wayan Bagus said. "I am anxious to see this."

Riley parked the car and grimly followed Emerson down the sidewalk and into the building.

"We aren't going to look at the deceased," Emerson said. "At least not in person. That would require political assistance that I could certainly get but don't desire at this point. I've arranged to get a copy of the dead man's file and some forensic photographs. I'm hoping they've managed to identify our mystery attacker. I'm willing to bet he worked for the Department of the Interior. And I would like to get a better photo of his tattoo."

"I guess I'm okay with that," Riley said, looking around. "This lobby reminds me of a hospital."

"Most lobbies feel like hospitals," Emerson said. "In this case, the feeling is accurate, because this facility functions very close to a hospital. An autopsy is a surgical procedure performed on a lifeless body."

A slim Asian man in khakis and a white dress shirt approached Emerson.

"This is Milton," Emerson said to Riley. "We first met in Sri Lanka several years ago."

"Emerson did me a very great favor at that time," Milton said. "I am happy to help my friend with this small thing." Milton handed a large yellow envelope to Emerson. "No one has claimed the body as a friend or family. His fingerprints were not in the system, and initial testing showed traces of heroin and meth. Most likely this is a homeless person."

"Do we have photographs?"

"Yes. There are six photographs plus a copy of the report. Four photographs of his hands, front and back to the elbow, as you requested."

Emerson removed the photographs from the envelope and paged through them.

"This isn't the man who fell off the museum balcony," Emerson said. "That man had a very distinctive tattoo on his hand. My friend took a photo of it at the crime scene. Your John Doe doesn't have a tattoo."

"That's troubling," Milton said. "This was the only body we accepted yesterday. And I took these photos myself."

"There's really only one explanation," Emerson said. "Someone stole the body and left this one in its place."

"That would be very difficult," Milton said. "The entire building is monitored by security cameras and guards. The body storage room is always locked. No one could have done that without being seen."

"Then the body was switched between when he was picked up at Air and Space and when he arrived here. Do you know who delivered the body?"

Milton pulled the report out of the envelope and read down.

"The Park Police performed that service."

"Is that normal procedure?" Emerson asked.

"There are several ways a body can be transported," Milton said. "Most commonly it is by the coroner, but at times it will be delivered by the Park Police or a city ambulance." He handed the report back to Emerson. "This is a very serious matter. Why would someone do this?"

"To conceal the attacker's identity," Emerson said.

Emerson thanked Milton, they did a complicated man-to-man handshake, and Milton walked away toward the bank of elevators.

"Will he get into trouble for this?" Riley asked.

"Unlikely. I simply circumvented procedure. The photos and the report are made available upon request."

"I assume Milton works here."

"He's a forensic photographer."

Emerson and Riley left the building and walked in silence to the Tesla. Riley got behind the wheel, and Emerson took the passenger seat next to her. Riley looked over at Emerson.

"Honestly? Really?" she said.

"What?" Emerson said.

"You're gloating."

"Not at all. Gloating implies a smug satisfaction in one's success."

"And you're telling me you're not feeling just a little smug."

"I'd only be smug if I had an exaggerated self-opinion."

"Heaven forbid."

"Do you still doubt the existence of a secret society of Rough Riders?" Emerson asked her.

"I might have a little less doubt, but I'm not convinced. And at any rate I'm not ready to pin it on Teddy Roosevelt."

"I like Teddy," Vernon said. "He carried a big stick, if you know what I mean."

Wayan Bagus smacked Vernon on the back of the head.

"Everybody knows that," Vernon said. "Common knowledge."

"The idea that there might be a society of Rough Riders is unsettling," Riley said. "One psycho axe murderer is bad enough, but a whole army of them is truly disturbing."

"It is written that the army, which the world with all its false gods cannot overcome, can be smashed with discernment."

"Okay, then, Little Buddy. Let's go to Yellowstone and discern the hell out of them," Vernon said.

One of the many "attachments" that Emerson inherited from his late father was a Gulfstream G550 jet. It was configured to carry as many as fourteen passengers, two pilots, and a flight attendant up to 6,750 miles nonstop.

Riley appreciated it for the two Rolls-Royce engines and its engineering. Vernon appreciated it because it was stocked with a bottomless supply of Oreos, M&M's and little bottles of rum. Wayan Bagus, for his part, looked like he was still deciding whether he appreciated it or not. It was, after all, a $50 million attachment, but the seats were extremely comfortable, and each had its own personal television. Not to mention the restroom had soft two-ply toilet tissue and tiny bottles of minty mouthwash.

Four hours into the flight, Vernon and Wayan Bagus were asleep. Riley and Emerson were wide awake.

"What's your plan?" Riley asked Emerson.

"I reserved rooms for us at the Old Faithful Inn. It's right in the center of the park and where the newlyweds were last seen. So I think it's a good base of operations for us."

Riley ate a strawberry off the catered fruit platter. "Search parties looked for them for two weeks, but the park is a thirty-five-hundred-square-mile wilderness. Nobody found anything."

"They didn't know where to look."

"And you do?"

Emerson nodded. "If our theory is correct and the disappearances have something to do with the locations of mantle plumes, then our search area is limited to the blob of lava bubbling underneath Yellowstone."

"That blob is enormous," Riley said.

"Fifteen hundred square miles."

"Criminy, Emerson, that's the size of Rhode Island. It would take a hundred years. Maybe five hundred years."

"As I could only reserve the hotel rooms for five days, I'll just have to be extra discerning," Emerson said. "Between my ability to discern, Vernon's *unagi,* and Wayan Bagus's special talents, it should be a piece of cake."

Riley didn't think it was going to be a piece of cake. She thought the investigation was going to be difficult and dangerous. Even if the homicidal lunatics didn't show up at Yellowstone, there were the bears. She wasn't a fan of bears. She could grab a snake with her bare hand and squash a spider with her shoe, but she didn't like bears.

"What's my role?" she asked Emerson.

"You're the glue that holds our disparate personalities and talents together. You're our Professor X."

"The bald guy in Marvel comics? The founder of the X-Men?"

"Exactly! Only instead of being a bald dude, you have a lot of pretty red hair and you're a girl."

Riley stared at Emerson, trying to decide whether he was complimenting her, coming on to her, or just being, for lack of a better word, Emerson. She settled on just being Emerson.

"Thank you for thinking my hair is pretty," Riley said.

"No problem," Emerson said.

"So, what are Wayan Bagus's special talents? Can he really disappear?" she asked.

Emerson gave a noncommittal shrug. "Some Taoists

believe that it's possible to develop certain supernatural powers, or *siddhi*."

"Like being able to disappear."

"Something like that," Emerson said. "One of the *siddhi* is supposed to be the ability to move the body wherever thought goes."

"Are there any others?"

"There are five primary *siddhi*. They include clairvoyance, being able to tolerate extremes of heat and cold, and being able to read minds. There's also a bunch of secondary ones. Things like being undisturbed by hunger or thirst, being able to hear or see things far away, being able to assume any form desired, and being able to make yourself very big or very small."

"Your Aunt Myra calls it all a lot of hogwash and magic tricks," Riley said.

"It's difficult to dispute Aunt Myra. On the other hand, there are things that defy explanation."

The plane landed and taxied down the Jackson Hole Airport runway. Emerson gathered his papers up and dumped them into his knapsack.

"If you had told somebody in the year 1800 that there were invisible things called germs and that they were responsible for the common cold, he would have thought that you were crazy and believed in magic," Emerson said. "Today, everybody simply accepts it as fact, despite that they've never seen or knowingly touched a germ."

"Assuming it's possible, how would you go about learning to read minds or make yourself small?"

Emerson went to wake Vernon and Wayan Bagus. "Concentration."

"Doesn't sound too hard."

"There's a catch. You have to learn to concentrate for a sustained period of time. It's much harder than it sounds. Try to focus your mind on one thing."

"Like what?"

"Something simple to start." He picked up one of the strawberries from the platter. "Like this piece of fruit." He held it up in front of Riley. "Try to think about only this strawberry and nothing else."

Riley concentrated on the strawberry. "Have I disappeared yet?"

Emerson smiled. "Most people can't concentrate for more than a couple seconds before their mind starts to wander to all sorts of things. The other fruit on the platter. The person standing in front of you. What you ate for lunch. If you were able to focus on that strawberry and only on that strawberry for even just one full minute, Wayan Bagus would tell you that you might be able to learn one of the *siddhi*."

"If that's true, why isn't the world full of clairvoyants?"

"It can take decades, even a lifetime, to train your mind this way. Most people will never be able to do it. Once in a rare while, you might be able to do it for a short time and get a glimpse of that world. Haven't you ever had a moment of déjà vu or a premonition of something?"

Riley focused on the strawberry. After a few seconds, her mind drifted to the missing newlyweds. Emerson had a way of making the impossible sound reasonable. "Maybe," she said.

TEN

⊶⊷

A RENTED FORD EXPLORER WAS WAITING ON THE tarmac of the Jackson Hole Airport. Riley left the plane and walked to the SUV. She looked at the snow-capped Teton mountains in the distance, and took a deep breath of the fresh, crisp air. The town of Jackson was the sole vestige of civilization in the area. It was about seven miles south of the airport and completely surrounded by the Gros Ventre Wilderness. To the north was Grand Teton National Park and beyond that Yellowstone.

They piled into the car and drove out of the airport, turning left on U.S. Highway 26. After a couple miles, Riley exited the main highway onto the more scenic Teton Park Road. They passed crystal clear Jenny Lake and a couple miles later, fifteen-mile-long Jackson Lake came into view. They drove in silence along the lake, appreciating the natural beauty of the wilderness, the occasional elk at the side of the road, and even a grizzly bear rummaging through the marsh.

"This really is the middle of nowhere," Riley said.

Emerson was reading through the Yellowstone guidebook. "Yellowstone is home to sixty-seven different mammals, including bears, wolves, bison, cougars, wolverines, bighorn sheep, beavers, and coyotes."

"I sure would like to see a beaver or two on this here vacation," Vernon said, ducking before Wayan Bagus could slap the back of his head.

The scenery became increasingly dramatic, and after a little over an hour of driving they passed through Yellowstone's South Entrance. Conifers covered rugged hillsides. Streams meandered through high country meadows. Smoking pools of geothermally heated water dotted the landscape, and huge hairy bison grazed along the side of the road and posed for photos, slowing traffic through the park to a near standstill.

At Yellowstone Lake, Riley turned left onto the Grand Loop Road. A little later, a huge rustic-looking log hotel with a steeply pitched shingled roof and gables came into view. Riley pulled up to the front entrance, and a valet parked the car.

Vernon looked up at the building and whistled. "That's one big log cabin."

"The biggest in the world," Emerson said. "Even more impressive considering that it was built back in 1903."

Riley, Vernon, and Wayan Bagus walked through the front doors and explored the lobby while Emerson got their room keys from the front desk. Like the exterior, the inside of the hotel was luxuriously rustic, constructed from logs and four stories tall with balconies encircling each level. A massive stone fireplace with a beautiful ironwork clock and hearths on all four sides dominated the space.

There was a steady exodus of people from the lobby. It had been almost an hour since the last eruption of Old Faithful and crowds were beginning to form outside to watch six thousand gallons of boiling water shoot up to 180 feet in the air.

"I have to admit this would be pretty awesome, if it wasn't for the fact that there's a secret society of crazy park rangers after us," Riley said to Emerson when he returned.

"So you have finally come around," Emerson said. "You acknowledge the Rough Riders."

"I acknowledge something. I'm not sure what it is."

He handed her a room key. "I rather think the possible presence of the Rough Riders adds to the experience. The difference between adventure and adversity is attitude."

"It's hard to have a good attitude about someone trying to throw you off a balcony," Riley said.

It was five P.M., and a tour group was forming, led by a pretty twenty-something-year-old park ranger wearing a gray two-pocket shirt, green shorts with a belt, and a broad-brimmed khaki campaign hat. About a dozen hotel guests were standing in a circle around her, waiting for the last tour of the day to begin.

Wayan Bagus pointed at the park ranger. "Emerson," he whispered. "That's the same uniform the men who forced me off my island were wearing, except the shirt and pants are a different color."

"One more indication that we're on the right trail," Emerson said.

Riley tagged after the tour guide, and Emerson, Vernon, and Wayan Bagus tagged after Riley.

"Hello, everyone, my name is Beth," the guide said, "and this is the south section of the Upper Geyser Basin tour. The tour starts here with Old Faithful. Old Faithful is one of many geysers in this part of the park. It isn't actually the biggest or even the most regular, but it is the biggest most regular geyser in Yellowstone."

A chuckle went up from the crowd, and Emerson shifted his body weight from side to side. Small talk was Emerson's kryptonite, and he was already losing patience with the tour.

Beth spent a couple minutes regurgitating facts about Old Faithful before moving on to its history. "Back in the nineteenth century, before the National Park Service was created, the United States Cavalry was in charge of

Yellowstone and used Old Faithful as a makeshift laundry. They'd put their soiled uniforms in the geyser, and they'd be ejected clean and warm. But don't any of you get any bright ideas! The inn's housekeeping department does a much better job!"

There was another chuckle from the crowd and an audible groan from Emerson.

After a couple more minutes of stock jokes about Old Faithful, the tour moved on to its next stop, a conical mound with an opening in its top.

"This geyser is named the Beehive Geyser. Can anyone here tell me why it's named Beehive?"

No one from the crowd said anything. Emerson looked like he was about to jump out of his skin. Vernon was grinning from ear to ear.

"Anyone? Anyone?" Beth said. "I'll give you a hint. It's not because it's filled with honey."

Vernon raised his hand. "I reckon it's because it looks like a house of bees."

Beth smiled at Vernon. "Correct." She looked over the crowd. "Does anyone have any questions so far?"

Emerson perked up. "I do have a question. Where is the top-secret government research facility?"

"Pardon?" Beth said.

"I'm only interested in the one located over the giant pool of lava capable of destroying the earth," Emerson said.

The crowd was silent. An older couple took a step away from Emerson.

"You know. The one where you keep the kidnapped visitors who"—Emerson made air quotes with his fingers—"'know too much.'"

Riley nudged Emerson and whispered into his ear. "For the love of Mike, Emerson. Asking crazy questions during a public tour is rude, not to mention insane. How do you know if you can trust this guide? She could be one of your Rough Riders. She could text Tin Man that we're here."

Emerson nodded at Riley and gave her a thumbs-up. "Right. Understood. I'll find out." He turned back to the tour guide. "One follow-up question. Do you have any unusual tattoos?"

Riley smacked her forehead. The rest of the crowd was staring at the park ranger, waiting for her response.

"Um. No secret government labs, but at any given time, there are a wide variety of scientific studies being conducted at Yellowstone," Beth said. "The Yellowstone Center for Resources is responsible for coordinating all the research programs. It's with all the other administrative buildings at Mammoth Hot Springs in the northwestern corner of the park."

"Do you really kidnap people who know too much?" a twelve-year-old boy in the crowd asked.

"Yellowstone has its own court and jail and police force, also located in Mammoth," Beth said. "But they only detain people for actual crimes, and that doesn't include knowing too much."

Beth walked away down the path, and the group followed her to the next attraction on the Upper Geyser Basin tour.

"What the heck was that all about?" Riley asked Emerson. "Haven't we gotten thrown out of enough places? What happened to *wu wei*? Remember, the Zen art of doing nothing but enjoying the scenery and letting the universe solve the world's problems all by itself?"

"We're looking for a couple missing hikers in an area the size of Rhode Island, so I'm burning down the haystack. We make a big enough spectacle, and I suspect that it's only a matter of time before Tin Man or one of his associates decides to take us to the same place those missing hikers ended up."

"The bottom of a boiling acid-filled lake?"

Emerson shrugged. "It's not an exact science. Sometimes you need to follow your gut and know when to *wu wei* and when to make a little trouble."

ELEVEN

———∞∞∞———

RILEY WOKE UP TO A BRILLIANT BLUE-SKY DAY. The inn was charming, and her room was beautiful with a full-on view of Old Faithful. She stood at her window and stared out at the geyser. Hard to believe it hadn't been conceived and constructed by a Disney Imagineer. Also hard to believe she was there to investigate the disappearance of an island.

She'd had a restless night, waking and reviewing everything that had happened in the past couple days. In her heart she wanted to discount Emerson's ideas about mantle plumes and murders and secret societies. Her head told her to pay attention. They poked the bear and the bear attacked. And as long as they kept poking the bear it wasn't going to go away. Sooner or later the bear was going to find them at Yellowstone.

She wasn't ready to buy into the mantle plume theory connecting the island with the park deaths, but she knew with certainty that something bad had happened . . . and maybe was still happening. She knew this not because there was irrefutable evidence of a crime. She knew this because the people in question had overreacted and overplayed their hand.

She thought about her dad back in Texas. He never closed his eyes to things that were wrong. Even when he wasn't acting as sheriff, he refused to look the other way when someone was behaving badly or breaking the law. She knew she couldn't either. Like it or not, she was going to help Emerson find out why the bear didn't like getting poked.

She left the window and went to the dining room to meet Emerson for breakfast. She found him already at a table, studying a map of the park.

"Have you eaten?" she asked him.

"Breakfast buffet. I recommend it. Fast and healthy if you make the right choices."

Riley looked over at the buffet. It looked amazing, and she was sure she would make all the *wrong* choices. Bacon, eggs, pancakes, sausage, Danish pastries.

She signaled the waitress. "Coffee, fresh fruit, and two eggs scrambled." She turned to Emerson. "So what's the plan for today?"

"You and I are going to park headquarters in Mammoth Hot Springs. I want to talk with the Center for Resources and find out more about the mantle plume underneath the park. Then I want to talk to Visitor Protection and get a sense of where Search and Rescue looked for the missing hikers."

Vernon waved from the entrance to the dining room and joined them.

"Did you see that buffet?" Vernon said. "I'm gonna eat everything there. Maybe not the smoked salmon and fish eggs, but everything else."

Beth, the tour guide, walked into the room. Vernon waved at her, and she made her way to the table.

"We spent some time together last night, if you know what I mean," Vernon said. "And I invited her to breakfast. I hope that's okay. It's her day off, and she said she'd show me and Little Buddy the sights."

Beth was out of uniform, but still in tour guide mode. She greeted everyone with a smile and asked if Riley and Emerson were enjoying their breakfast. And were their accommodations satisfactory?

Riley and Emerson assured her they were indeed satisfactory.

"And what are your plans for the day?" Beth asked.

"Riley and I are going to Mammoth," Emerson said. "I'd like to talk to someone about the newlyweds that disappeared."

"That was a terrible tragedy," Beth said. "They were a really nice couple."

Emerson sat a little straighter in his chair. "Did you know them?"

"Not really. They'd hike the backcountry for a week, then show up at the inn and stay for a couple nights, then go off on another weeklong adventure. They were ski instructors, so they weren't working. They planned to spend the entire summer at Yellowstone as a kind of honeymoon. I spoke to them from time to time."

"Do you know where they went last, just before they were reported missing?" Emerson asked.

"No, but I think they always told the hotel concierge where they were headed before they'd leave for the backcountry. You know, for safety's sake or just in case family wanted to reach them. It was the concierge who alerted the Park Police when the man and woman didn't return to the inn on time."

Beth pointed at a man kneeling beside a table on the other side of the dining room, drawing on a map with a red pen. "The concierge is actually right over there, helping that family, probably with driving directions. I'll tell him to stop by after he's done."

"Isn't she the best?" Vernon said. "She knows everything about everything. And you want directions you don't have to ask that concierge, because Beth can give directions."

Beth rolled her eyes and gave Vernon a punch in the arm. They went off to the breakfast bar, and Beth stopped on the way to talk to the concierge.

Riley was halfway through her eggs when the concierge walked across the room to talk with them.

"I hear you guys need some directions to Mammoth Hot Springs," the man said.

"Actually we're looking for information on the newlywed couple who went missing a month ago," Emerson said. "We heard that you were the one who reported them missing."

The concierge hesitated. "Are you friends of theirs? I was kind of told not to talk to anyone except the Park Police about it since it's still officially an open investigation."

"It's still an open investigation? I thought Search and Rescue stopped looking for them a week or two ago," Riley said.

The concierge nodded his head. "True. I guess it's not a state secret. They wanted to spend a month hiking some of the most off-the-beaten-path backcountry areas in the park. They were interested in the Pitchstone Plateau, the Lamar Valley, and the Gallatin Range. They disappeared in Lamar Valley, hiking from the Northeast Entrance down to Fishing Bridge at Yellowstone Lake."

"Is the Lamar Valley dangerous?" Riley asked.

"The entire park is dangerous, but Lamar Valley is especially wild. Lots of predators, like grizzlies and wolves.

There are some hazardous thermal features as you get closer to Yellowstone Lake. Unless you're experienced, I wouldn't recommend hiking there without a guide. And even with a guide you would need to apply for a backcountry permit from one of the ranger stations or visitor centers. Plus, some areas of the park are restricted access. It's mostly for visitors' safety so that the rangers know where to look if they get lost."

Emerson nodded. "Did the lost hikers have a permit? And what kinds of areas are restricted?"

"There are lots of different areas," the concierge said. "Most of them are bear management areas with high densities of dangerous grizzlies. Others have ecologically sensitive hot springs and mud pots. There are also some that are used as dumping grounds for bison and other animal carcasses. And yes, I believe they had a permit."

"Where would we obtain backcountry permits?" Emerson asked.

"If you're going to Mammoth Hot Springs, you can get them at the Mammoth Visitor Center." He shook Emerson's and Riley's hands. "I need to move on. Hope you folks have a good day."

The concierge's words ran through Riley's head. *Have a good day.* She supposed there were all kinds of good days.

Some would undoubtedly be better than others. This good day she wasn't so sure about.

She was at the wheel of the rental car, chauffeuring Emerson to Mammoth. He had spent the morning reviewing maps and geology articles, but they were finally on the road. The ninety-mile drive around Yellowstone Lake and past the Grand Canyon of the Yellowstone was breathtaking.

The hot springs themselves were an otherworldly outcropping of terraced crystallized calcium tinted in unnatural shades of red, orange, and green. Geothermally heated water flowed from the top of the terrace down to Boiling River.

Fort Yellowstone came into view just past the Hot Springs. Constructed in 1891 by the U.S. Army, it originally contained sixty structures, some made of wood and some of sandstone, that included barracks, a jail, a chapel, and a hospital. Today, thirty-five buildings survived, mostly used as administrative offices and personal residences for park staff.

Riley parked near a one-story wooden building with a red roof. The sign out front read YELLOWSTONE CENTER FOR RESOURCES.

"What's the plan?" she asked Emerson.

"I want to talk with somebody from the Physical Resources and Climate Science Branch. They're responsible for monitoring the Yellowstone Caldera."

The inside of the small building housing the Physical Resources and Climate Science Branch was set up very simply as a central reception room with three cluttered offices off to the sides. No one was in the reception area.

"Hello," Emerson called out. "Is anyone here?"

A ponytailed college-aged guy dressed in jeans, hiking boots, and a flannel shirt poked his head out of one of the offices. "Can I help you?"

"I'm Emerson Knight, and this is Riley Moon. We were hoping to talk with one of the scientists about the volcanic activity underneath the park."

"Sorry, there's usually just a skeleton crew manning the offices. Everyone spends most of their time out in the field. I'm Dan. I started working here last month, so I'm sort of low man on the totem pole."

"Perhaps you can answer some of our questions," Emerson said.

"I can try. I'm a grad student working on my PhD in geology, so I know the basics of the area."

Emerson pulled a map of Yellowstone from his knapsack. "There's a giant blob of magma buried underneath the park. Do you know the boundaries?"

Dan took the map and spread it out on the table. "It's roughly the same as the Yellowstone Caldera." He got out a red pen and started drawing a rough circle on the map. "The caldera extends pretty much from the western boundary of the park to the eastern side of Lake

Yellowstone. Shoshone Lake is on the south side, and on the north, it's the Grand Canyon of the Yellowstone. The Gallatin wilderness sits to the northeast of the caldera. Old Faithful is more or less in the center of the circle."

Emerson frowned at the map. The area delineated in red was a huge circle with a diameter of at least forty miles. "We still need to narrow this down by quite a lot. Is there anything of value in the area?"

Dan looked surprised. "Of monetary value? No. However, from a scientific perspective, it's unique. Really one of a kind."

"Are there any research programs or studies being conducted on the caldera right now?" Emerson asked.

"Tons of them. It's technically an active super-volcano, so the NPS monitors it very closely for any changes."

"How about in the Lamar Valley?" Riley asked.

"Most of the more exciting research is in the Lamar Valley. The lava reservoir is shallow there. Ten to fifteen miles beneath the surface of the earth. So it's easier to study. The shallowest spot is at Sour Creek Dome. The reservoir is probably less than a mile deep at that point."

Emerson and Riley looked more closely at the map at the area around Sour Creek Dome. It was in a remote area of the park midway between the canyon and Fishing Bridge, with no nearby roads.

Riley looked at Emerson. "That's smack in the middle of the path joining the North Entrance to Yellowstone

Lake, where the newlyweds had told the concierge they wanted to hike."

Emerson nodded. "It looks like it would be at least a day or two hike through the wilderness to reach Sour Creek Dome."

"Yeah. It's pretty rough terrain," Dan said. "But you can't go there. It's a restricted bear management area. In fact, it's one of the most active spots for grizzlies in the park."

"Are they dangerous?" Riley asked.

Dan laughed. "Only if you consider a highly territorial, ten-foot-tall, eight-hundred-pound monster with four-inch claws and a bad attitude to be dangerous."

Riley and Emerson thanked Dan for his help, left the Center for Resources, and walked to the Albright Visitor Center. In 1909, the large two-story gray stone building had served as bachelors' quarters for the U.S. Army cavalry officers. It had been renovated over the years and now contained a bookstore, wildlife and historical park exhibits, and various offices.

Riley followed Emerson to the Mammoth Backcountry Office on the first floor.

"We're interested in doing some hiking in the Lamar Valley," Emerson told the ranger at the desk. "We were told we could obtain a backcountry permit here."

The ranger slid an application form across the desk and handed Emerson a pen. "Absolutely. I just need to get some information first. How many people are in your party and where do you want to hike?"

"There are four of us, and we would like to hike from the North Entrance to Fishing Bridge."

"Whoopsie," the ranger said. "I can't issue you a permit for that. You would have to cross through bear country and some dangerous thermal areas. There are a lot of great, safer hikes in the park."

"We're investigating the disappearance of Emma and Joshua Bulfinch, the newlyweds who went missing last month," Emerson said. "We think they may have disappeared in that area."

The ranger shook his head. "Like most of the rangers, I was involved in the search. They didn't go missing in Lamar Valley. They were in the Gallatin wilderness on the other side of the park."

"Interesting," Emerson said. "We believe they intended to hike through Sour Creek Dome to Yellowstone Lake."

The ranger went to his computer. "All the permits are scanned and entered into our database." He typed "Joshua Bulfinch" into the search engine and turned the computer screen to Emerson and Riley. "You see. They applied to hike in Gallatin. There's even a notation in the file that they checked in with the ranger station in that area before they began their hike."

"So no one searched for them near Sour Creek Dome?" Riley asked.

"No. The search focused on where they were last reported seen."

"Who reported that they saw them in Gallatin?"

"The ranger's name isn't noted on the permit. You'd probably have to ask the deputy chief ranger in charge of field operations. He's responsible for all the law enforcement and search missions in the park."

"Is he available now?" Emerson said.

"I'll go see. Can I tell him who's asking?"

"Emerson Knight."

The ranger disappeared through a door that read AUTHORIZED PERSONNEL ONLY.

"Do you think it's a little weird that they didn't bother to search Lamar Valley when the hotel concierge reported that was where they wanted to hike?" Riley asked once they were alone.

"Not at all," Emerson said. "It's perfectly logical that they would search fifty miles away, clear on the other side of the park. They didn't want the newlyweds found, probably because the people responsible for searching for them are the same people responsible for their disappearance."

TWELVE

⟨⟨⟨

Two stocky men dressed in green pants, gray shirts, and campaign hats walked through the AUTHORIZED PERSONNEL ONLY door and approached Emerson and Riley.

Riley glanced at their hands and saw that both men had the crossed sabers tattoo. She was sure Emerson saw it as well.

"I'm Bob Smith," one of the men said. "My partner is Jim Jones. If you'll come with us we'll take you to the deputy chief."

Bob had a large ragged scar that ran from the corner of his mouth to his left ear. Riley thought he was the better looking of the two.

Bob led the way down a narrow corridor and motioned Riley and Emerson into an office at the very end. A tall man with a gaunt face and a sinewy body was standing in front of a desk. He was wearing a park ranger uniform and he had the requisite tattoo. The nameplate on the desk identified him as Francis Scully, deputy chief ranger. Tin Man was standing next to him.

"What a pleasant surprise," Emerson said to Tin Man. "Did you bring your hatchet?"

The tall man stepped forward and smiled at Emerson and Riley. Friendly. "I need to ask you some questions. Would that be okay?"

Emerson smiled back. "Oscar Wilde said it's never the question that's indiscreet, only the answers."

Scully dropped the smile. "Just so. Let's just say that we're all going to be able to part as friends so long as there aren't any indiscreet answers."

"And if there are?" Emerson asked.

Scully gestured to Tin Man. "Then I leave the room, and he asks the questions."

Riley raised her hand. "Um. Yeah. I'm kind of against this plan. Discretion's not really his thing."

Emerson nodded in agreement. "That's true. This is a lot of pressure. Could I possibly be allowed just one indiscreet answer?"

Scully shook his head. "I'm afraid not. It's a matter of national security. I'm sure you understand. Why are you so interested in finding Joshua and Emma Bulfinch?"

"I'm not," Emerson said. "At this point, I'm presuming they're dead."

Scully smiled. "A very good response."

Emerson gave Riley the thumbs-up and mouthed "Nailed it" before turning back to Scully. "I'm much more interested in why you purposefully misdirected the search to the Gallatin wilderness, all the way on the other side of the park from where they disappeared."

Riley smacked her forehead.

"The only plausible answer is that you did not want a search party poking around Sour Creek Dome," Emerson said.

"It's a bear management area," Scully said. "It's filled with grizzlies."

"It's also the area where the volcano bubbling underneath the park is most active."

"Another reason why it's a restricted area."

"How convenient," Emerson said.

Tin Man leaned forward. "Still peddling your crazy conspiracy theory that people are being murdered at national parks?"

"Not all national parks," Emerson said. "Just the ones built over mantle plume volcanoes, like Yellowstone."

"One final question," Scully said. "If you're no longer interested in the missing hikers, what do you want?"

"I want to know who or what you're hiding at Sour Creek Dome."

"That is a horribly indiscreet answer," Scully said. "I'm afraid I'm going to have to turn the whole matter over to my associate. Final requests?"

"I'd like an explanation," Emerson said.

Scully went silent for a beat before nodding agreement. "It's a secret that the U.S. government has gone to great lengths to protect. The National Park Service was created over a century ago. The public mission was conservation of America's most beautiful, unique lands, but that was a smoke screen."

"For what?" Riley asked.

"To hide a secret within millions of acres of wilderness, protected in perpetuity from development or private ownership. Originally, back in the nineteenth century, the U.S. Army was put in charge of Yellowstone, but it was only a temporary solution. A military installation the size of a small country would have aroused too much attention. So, the idea of hiding it in plain sight under the guise of a national park was formed."

Riley looked at Emerson. "A needle hidden in a million-acre haystack."

"An apt analogy," Scully said. "In 1903, President Theodore Roosevelt secretly authorized the creation of an elite network of rangers responsible for protecting the 'needle,' at any cost."

"Rough Riders," Emerson said.

Scully again nodded in agreement. "The army has its Green Berets. The navy has its SEALs. I suppose you could say the National Park Service has its Rough Riders."

Riley cut her eyes to Emerson. "You're gloating again, aren't you?"

"Big time," Emerson said.

Riley turned her attention back to Scully. "Why haven't I ever heard about these Rough Riders?"

"Their very existence is highly classified. There are whispers, of course, but even 99.9 percent of the people working for the Park Service have no idea who we are or what we do. Tin Man will take it from here. I think we can all take comfort in the fact that your deaths are going to be for the greater good."

Scully left the office, and Tin Man pulled a hatchet from a holster under his jacket. "Does this answer your question?" he asked Emerson.

"You probably buy them in bulk and get them at wholesale," Emerson said. "Personally, I think the whole Tin Man hatchet routine is a little clichéd."

"It serves my purpose," Tin Man said.

Bob and Jim stepped into the office.

Tin Man gestured at Emerson and Riley with his hatchet. "Truss them up and let's move them out."

THIRTEEN

※

R ILEY STRAINED TO ADJUST HER SITTING
position so that the zip ties binding her wrists
together would be just a little less uncomfortable. They had
been sitting in a small cell in the back of the Yellowstone
jail for almost four hours.

"Well this is a fine mess you've gotten us into," Riley
said to Emerson.

"It's not over until it's over," Emerson said.

The door to the cell opened, and Vernon and Wayan
Bagus were shoved in, hands tied behind their backs. The
door closed and locked behind them.

Vernon grinned. "Well, I sure am happy to see you two.
Although I can't say I'm impressed with the facilities here.

They got all the basics but none of the amenities you'd find in one of your higher class jails."

Wayan Bagus reached into his robe and pulled out an assortment of bath soaps, shower gels, and little bottles of Listerine he'd borrowed from the Old Faithful Inn.

"I would be happy to share these with you," Wayan Bagus said to Vernon. "Except for the Listerine, these complimentary products make your hands smell like flowers."

Riley looked at Wayan Bagus. The zip ties that had been binding his wrists were lying on the floor.

"How did you get out of those?" she asked.

Wayan Bagus shrugged. "A wise man, recognizing that the world is an illusion, does not act as if it is real, and so he escapes suffering."

The door to the cell opened again, and Bob walked in. "Everyone out. We're going for a ride."

Jim was in the hall with his service weapon drawn. Lights in the hall were dim. The building was silent. As far as Riley could see they were the only detainees.

Outside the jail, it was dark except for an idling Chevy Tahoe's headlights. Emerson, Riley, Vernon, and Wayan Bagus were herded into the SUV. Bob and Tin Man were in the front, separated from the back by a police partition cage.

Emerson leaned forward. "Where are we going?"

"Not far," Tin Man said. "We're tending to your bucket

list. You wanted to see some of the park's restricted areas."

Fifteen minutes later, Bob pulled off the main highway onto a smaller one-lane dirt access road. Tin Man got out and unlocked a gate, marked by a sign that read NO TRESPASSING.

Past the gate, the road was heavily rutted and the Tahoe crept along for a couple more miles before coming to a stop. Tin Man and Bob got out of the SUV and opened the rear door.

"Out," Tin Man said, holding a flashlight so everyone could see the step down onto the dirt road.

"I see you traded in your semiautomatic for that big-bore bolt-action rifle," Vernon said to Bob. "I do some hunting myself, and I know that there's one heck of a gun."

"What do you hunt?" Bob asked.

"Squirrel mostly," Vernon said. "You might not think that's got a high difficulty rating, but they're devious devils."

"I mostly hunt bear," Bob said. He looked over at Tin Man. "He hunts people."

Tin Man flicked the flashlight beam into the tall grass at the side of the road. Several sets of eyes reflected the light before the animals backed off and retreated into the darkness.

"Enough talk," Tin Man said. "We let this drag on and it's going to eat into my recreational time."

Tin Man moved off the dirt road, onto a rough path

that led through the brush. "Follow me and watch where you're walking. I don't want anyone to break a leg ahead of time. And don't even think about wandering off the path, because Bob will shoot you if you so much as stray five inches."

Riley, Emerson, and Vernon walked single file into the brush, stumbling over branches, struggling to keep themselves upright in spite of their bound hands. Wayan Bagus was having an easier time. No one had noticed he had escaped the zip ties. He kept his hands hidden in the folds of his orange robe.

Vernon was directly behind Tin Man. Wayan Bagus was behind Vernon. Riley was between Wayan Bagus and Emerson. The temperature was in the low forties, but Riley was sweating with the exertion of the forced walk at the high altitude and the fear of what lay ahead. She tripped and went down to one knee. The march stopped while she pulled herself up. She stood tall and they continued walking.

"Wait for it," Emerson said softly behind her.

She knew he was encouraging her not to lose faith. He was reminding her to stay vigilant for an opportunity to turn things around.

The air was increasingly foul with the smell of sulfur and rot. The moon peeked from behind a cloud. Not enough moonlight to show whatever was beyond the path, but clearly something had died and was decomposing in the inky blackness of the night.

"You got some day-old roadkill out here," Vernon said.

Tin Man shone his flashlight off to the side of the path, panning the beam across the field. Not far from where they were walking were piles of dead and rotting buffalo, mule deer, and elk. They littered the landscape of rolling scrub grass.

Tin Man inhaled deeply. "The smell of death. Nothing like it."

Riley was taking shallow breaths. Her stomach rolled with nausea, and sweat dripped off the tip of her nose. "What is this place?" she asked.

"A dumping ground for dead animals," Bob said.

"It's not a 'dumping' ground," Tin Man said. "This is sacred ground. Here there's no rank, there's no rich or poor, black or white, Christian or Muslim. Here you don't even have a name. Here you're either a killer, a scavenger, or fresh meat."

"Which are we?" Emerson asked.

"You'll find out soon enough."

Riley looked out at the acres of bones and carrion. She couldn't see them without the aid of the flashlight, but she could feel the weight of the dead animals. "You don't bury them?"

"Bury them? These animals were all killed by natural causes. Ideally, they'd be left where they died for scavengers to eat, but it's too dangerous to do that where tourists sightsee, so we relocate them here for the coyotes, wolves, and bears."

They walked for several more minutes before Tin Man

told them to stop. The moon was emerging from behind the cloud, so Riley could see they were standing at the end of the path and on the edge of an excavation. She guessed it had to be at least twelve feet deep. A big yellow backhoe was parked a short distance away. A couple freshly dead, half-ripped-apart buffalo were at the bottom of the pit. A pair of backpacks lay beside them, along with some barely identifiable human remains.

"Is that Joshua and Emma Bulfinch?" Emerson asked.

Tin Man ignored Emerson's question and motioned toward the pit. "Get in."

Emerson looked into the hole. "I don't feel that would be in our best interest. You're certain to kill us once we're down there."

"You have it all wrong," Tin Man said. "I don't intend to kill you. My associate is just going to shoot each of you in the leg. Then, we'll leave you here to discover for yourselves whether you're predator or prey."

Vernon lowered his center of gravity and started to sway back and forth.

"What's he doing?" Bob asked.

Vernon did an awkward-looking somersault, struggled back to his feet, and continued to sway.

"I'm about to go all capybara on your ass," Vernon said.

"Isn't a capybara a rodent?" Bob asked Tin Man.

Tin Man smiled. "I think he means 'capoeira,' the Brazilian martial art based on dance and acrobatics."

Everyone was mesmerized by Vernon.

"Has he really been studying capoeira?" Riley asked Emerson.

"He had a Groupon at a local dance studio for a free introductory Zumba class last month," Emerson said, "but the instructor was sick, so they stuck him in the capoeira class instead."

Riley caught a flash of orange in her peripheral vision and turned in time to see Wayan Bagus spin and perfectly execute a flying kick to Bob's gut. Bob doubled over on a whoosh of expelled air and dropped his rifle. He staggered back and tumbled into the pit. Wayan Bagus grabbed the rifle, and threw it into the brush.

"Nice move," Tin Man said, "but it was a big mistake to get rid of the rifle."

"It was of no use to me," Wayan Bagus said. "I could not let you use it to injure my friends, and I could not use it to injure you. I would prefer not to contend."

Tin Man pulled a pair of hatchets from a concealed holster. "And I *intend* to contend," he said. "The rifle wouldn't have been much use to me either. These are my weapons of choice."

Tin Man threw the first hatchet at Emerson, missing him by less than an inch. He brandished the second and moved past Riley and Emerson, toward Wayan Bagus.

Vernon roared, doing his best imitation of a pissed-off bull moose. "Capybara your ass," Vernon yelled, charging

Tin Man and head-butting him from behind, knocking him into the pit beside Bob and the buffalo.

"Thank you," Wayan Bagus said to Vernon. "It was thoughtful of you to come to my aid."

Riley peered over the edge of the pit. Tin Man was slowly getting to his feet. Bob was standing but looked dazed and uncomprehending.

"I have to admit, I was a little worried there for a while," Riley said.

"No need for that when you got Little Buddy and me tag-teaming," Vernon said. "Isn't that right, Little Buddy?"

"What is 'tag-team'?" Wayan Bagus asked.

"Tag-team's what they do in the WWE. That's World Wrassling Entertainment. Don't tell me you don't follow the WWE. Where've you been all your life?"

"In a monastery and then on an island . . . until someone stole it," Wayan Bagus said.

"I'm thinking it's lucky for you someone stole that island," Vernon said. "Otherwise you might have lived your whole life without the WWE and two-ply toilet paper."

"I do like the two-ply toilet paper," Wayan Bagus said, retrieving the hatchet Tin Man had thrown at Emerson.

Wayan Bagus used the hatchet to free Riley, Vernon, and Emerson from the zip ties, and everyone moved to the edge of the pit. Tin Man was clawing at the rocks and dirt, trying to climb out, not having any luck at it.

Emerson leaned over the edge. "We have to be going

now. We're going to borrow your Tahoe. You two can stay here and work on your survival skills."

It was difficult to see Tin Man's face in the dark shadows at the bottom of the pit, but Riley could hear him swear. She saw the flash of a hatchet blade, and her breath caught in her throat as, without warning, Tin Man buried the blade deep into Bob's chest. Bob fell back and lay motionless, the hatchet still in him.

Riley clapped a hand over her mouth to keep from retching. The smell, the dead animals, the brutality at the bottom of the pit was overwhelming. The only thing stopping a flood of tears was the fact that she was completely dehydrated.

"Remember this," Tin Man shouted, pointing at Emerson. "I worked with this man for the past seven years, and I liked him. He's dead because of you. I want you to take a good look so you know exactly what I'm going to do to you the next time we meet."

"We'll see," Emerson said. "Now I have a hatchet too."

Riley thought it was a good thing the flashlight was at the bottom of the pit with poor dead Bob, because without it the rifle was hopelessly lost in the brush. She knew for certain if she had the rifle she'd shoot Tin Man, and it would put a big black mark on her karma.

Emerson led the way out, and everyone found it easier to follow the path with their hands free and the moon shining down on them.

There were occasional rustlings in the brush, and Riley

caught the sound of what she suspected was an animal gnawing on a bone, but she kept her head down and forged ahead. Relief washed over her when she saw the brush give way to the road and the parked SUV.

The Tahoe was unlocked, and the keys were in the ignition. Not much chance of auto theft in grizzly backcountry.

Riley looked in the glove compartment and under the front seats.

"What are you looking for?" Emerson asked.

"A gun," Riley said. "I'm contemplating shooting Tin Man."

"That would not be a good thing," Wayan Bagus said.

"He's a killer," Riley said. "And he's going to continue to kill. He needs to be stopped."

"I'm with Riley," Vernon said, "but it doesn't matter, because there doesn't appear to be another gun."

Riley looked at the hatchet Emerson was carrying.

"No way," Emerson said. "It's too risky."

He was right, she decided. Her daddy had taught her how to use a gun. She had no experience with a hatchet.

FOURTEEN

⸺∞⸺

I T WAS CLOSE TO MIDNIGHT WHEN RILEY PARKED the Tahoe behind the Old Faithful Inn. It had been decided that they would all go to their rooms, ransack their minibars, and meet back in the parking lot in no more than ten minutes.

Riley and Emerson were the first to return to the SUV.

"I'm not comfortable with this," Riley said, chugging a bottle of water and tucking into a granola bar. "This is the first place anyone would think to look for us."

"If Tin Man succeeds at getting out of the pit, it will take him at least another hour before he can make his way back to park headquarters in Mammoth."

"You don't know that for certain," Riley said. "He could know a shortcut. He could already have a search party out looking for us."

"Unlikely," Emerson said.

"Why are you and Vernon and Wayan Bagus so calm about all this? It's like I'm the only one who worries about anything."

"Vernon isn't smart enough to worry. Wayan Bagus is at peace with the universe. And I'm pure bravado. I've found that I can bluff my way through almost anything and talk myself into believing it."

"Wow."

"You hadn't figured that out?"

"No," Riley said.

"Well, then, I'm sorry I told you. I suppose I've ruined my image as a hero."

Riley smiled at him. "You have your moments. You saved my life in the museum."

"I did," Emerson said. "I was excellent."

"As long as I'm the designated worrier, let's think about this stolen Tahoe. We can't ride all over creation in it."

"We aren't riding all over creation. We're going to hike to Sour Creek Dome. Vernon is bringing the backpacks."

"I understand your need to get to the bottom of this, but hiking to Sour Creek Dome is a dumb idea. There's a psycho axe murderer and his small army after us. Even if we can get past them, there's a bunch of hungry bears and wolves ready to eat us in Lamar Valley. Wouldn't it be better to get out of Yellowstone and go to the police?"

"Which police?" Emerson asked. "The park rangers who turned us over to Tin Man? Or the Bozeman, Montana, police, who are eighty miles away, have worked with the U.S. Park Police for years, and, in the near future, will most likely be informed that four dangerous fugitives killed a park ranger and stole his car?"

"How about the FBI?"

"Whatever we've stumbled upon is at the highest level of national security. Best case scenario is they'll lock us up and throw away the key."

Riley pawed through the stolen minibar stash and came up with a couple tiny bottles of whiskey. She gave one to Emerson, and she unscrewed the cap on hers.

"Here's to good times on Sour Creek Dome," she said.

"Good times," Emerson said.

They clinked bottles and chugged the whiskey.

Riley felt the liquor burn her throat and warm a path to her stomach and beyond.

"I feel inspired," Emerson said.

He grabbed Riley by her flannel shirt, pulled her close, and kissed her. There was some tongue involved this time, and when he released her they both licked their lips.

"You taste like whiskey," Emerson said. "I could use more."

"Whiskey?"

"Yes. That too."

"I don't think I have any more whiskey."

"Well, then," he said. And he leaned in for another kiss.

"I hate to be a party pooper," Riley said, "but I keep going back to the part about us getting locked up and the authorities throwing the key away."

"It's very simple," Emerson said. "We need to uncover the secret being hidden at Sour Creek Dome and expose it to the world. Without a secret to protect, Tin Man and the Rough Riders' usefulness to the U.S. government will come to an end. I suspect they'll become more of a liability than an asset."

"What if it truly is a matter of national security?" Riley said. "What if we'd be endangering people if we went public?"

Emerson nodded. "I thought of that, too. I'm certain that back in 1903, it was part of a noble plan to protect the American people from something really terrible, but I'm equally certain that the plan has been corrupted over the years."

Vernon rapped on the driver's side window. He was carrying two large North Face backpacks. Wayan Bagus was standing next to him, holding a third pack and his little duffel.

"We might have a problem," Vernon said. "The Park

Police just showed up. I saw them in the lobby talking to the front desk, so we skedaddled out the back door."

Vernon pitched the backpacks into the back of the SUV and climbed in after them with Wayan Bagus. Riley put the Tahoe in gear and drove out of the lot. She breathed a sigh of relief as she pulled onto the Grand Loop Road, and the inn receded into the night.

Fifteen minutes later, Riley arrived at the intersection of the Grand Loop Road and Yellowstone Lake. To the right was the South Entrance. To the north, Canyon Village.

"We're literally at a crossroads," Emerson said. "We can go north to Sour Creek Dome, or south out of the park and back to our plane waiting for us in Jackson Hole."

"I'm not even sure we're going to be able to get out of here at this point," Riley said. "There are only four entrances to the park, and they could have roadblocks set up for us at each."

Emerson nodded. "There's risk in either choice, but I've never lived my life making decisions based on risk. Innocent people are being killed. I have to see this through, but everyone else here needs to decide for themselves whether they're in or out."

"Mostly, I'm sort of the kind of guy who prefers to be in," Vernon said from the other side of the police partition.

"It is fortunate that you know so very little," Wayan

Bagus said to Vernon. "A man who does not know fear cannot die, because death has no place to enter."

Vernon grinned. "Well, I appreciate that, Little Buddy."

"The universe put me in the middle of this mystery, and I believe it is my Tao to follow it to its conclusion," Wayan Bagus said. "I'm in."

Riley didn't see where there was much of a choice. Even if she went home to Texas and led the life of a recluse, she suspected she would be hunted down and eliminated. These people were serious about guarding their secret, and she was in the uncomfortable position of knowing too much and not knowing enough. And, most important, her daddy wouldn't be happy with her if she didn't see this through.

"I'm in," Riley said.

"Well, this sure is a nice moment," Vernon said. "In the movies, they'd hug it out."

Wayan Bagus looked at Vernon. "Like in *Frozen* when Elsa and Anna hug at the end because of true love?"

"No. Yuck. What the heck are you talking about? That's girlie hugging stuff," Vernon said. "There's only two kinds of movie hugs that aren't totally lame. The first is a *Rocky III* hug. You know, when Apollo and Rocky hug because Rocky finally gets his confidence back and they know he's gonna kick Mr. T's ass."

"I know nothing of these people," Wayan Bagus said, "but I understand the concept."

"I'm almost afraid to ask about the second kind of hug," Riley said.

"A *Godfather* hug," Vernon said. "You know the kind of hug somebody totally boss, like Al Pacino, gives someone really annoying, like Fredo, just before he kills them."

"I will reflect seriously on the matter," Wayan Bagus said.

Riley thought it was unclear which type of hug Wayan Bagus was considering giving Vernon.

While all the hugging talk was going on Emerson had reached over and placed his hand on Riley's. She thought it might have been just a gesture of camaraderie, but it felt warm and intimate. Whatever it meant, Riley liked it. She left her hand under his for a few seconds, then withdrew it and turned the steering wheel. The Tahoe veered left toward Canyon Village.

"I guess we should find somewhere to hide for the night," Riley said.

"There's a campground near Fishing Bridge at the northern part of the lake," Emerson said. "We'll hide the SUV there and start off into the backcountry at first light."

It was dawn when Riley got out of the Tahoe and stretched, glad to exchange the stale air and cramped sleeping arrangements for the fresh smell of conifer trees. They were at the bottom of a gulch and about a mile from the campground. Emerson and Vernon were laboring to camouflage the car with branches and leaves.

"Do you think they'll find the Tahoe?" Riley asked Emerson.

"Undoubtedly. However, I don't care *if* they find it. I only care *when*. We need to find what we're looking for before Tin Man discovers the Tahoe and knows for certain that we're still in the park."

"Okay, then. How long do you think that will take?"

"It's going to take two days to hike to Sour Creek Dome and two days to hike back out. At any rate, we have enough food to last a week and no more."

"If there's something big going on at Sour Creek Dome, wouldn't there be a road leading to it?"

"Most likely, but it's not on any map, and we could waste a lot of time trying to find it. With any luck we'll be able to take it out."

The three backpacks and Wayan Bagus's duffel were propped up against a nearby tree. Emerson strapped one on and handed another to Riley. He pointed at an unassuming hill in the distance. "That's Sour Creek Dome. It's about ten miles as the crow flies from here."

"And you think it's a two-day hike?" Riley asked.

Emerson removed a map of Yellowstone from his pocket. "I don't really know. There's no established trail so it'll be slow going."

Riley looked at the map. "Why is the entire area delineated in a green bubble?"

"It's the area of the park with the highest density of grizzlies. That's one of the hazards."

Riley cut her eyes to Emerson. "*One* of the hazards?"

"There may be one or two others."

Vernon and Wayan Bagus joined them. Vernon had already strapped on his pack and changed into a camouflage hunter's jacket and tan pants. Wayan Bagus, still dressed in his orange robe and sandals, had the duffel slung over his shoulder.

Vernon looked the little monk up and down and shook his head. "Are you the Lorax?"

Wayan Bagus looked confused. "Who is the Lorax?"

"He's a little orange man who 'speaks for the trees.' At least that's according to Dr. Seuss."

"I speak only for myself," Wayan Bagus said.

"That's what I thought," Vernon said. "So if you're not the Lorax, you have no business wearing his clothes on a two-day hike through this here upcountry forest. You're going to freeze your ass off."

Wayan Bagus was his usual pleasantly calm self. "These clothes should suffice. I am just a simple monk, but I will overcome the cold."

Vernon looked at Emerson. "What the heck is he talking about?"

"Some Buddhist monks are able to withstand extreme temperatures," Emerson said. "It sounds crazy, but it's been documented that they can raise their skin temperature by as much as seventeen degrees and lower their bodies' metabolic rate by up to sixty-four percent."

Vernon looked back at Wayan Bagus. "Is that true? How do you do that?" he asked.

"Simple concentration. You must focus your mind on nothing else but the image of a flame running down your spine."

"Huh, I reckon there just might be something to it," Vernon said. "I focus my mind on an image of boobs, and it raises my wiener by as much as ninety percent. Works every time. Do you think it's the same thing?"

Riley stared openmouthed at Vernon. Emerson smiled. Wayan Bagus looked skeptical.

"Only problem is I'm not loving the idea of a flame going down my back, so I'll just stick with my wool socks and fleece pants," Vernon said. He pulled a .45-caliber revolver from a holster inside his hunting jacket. "Besides which, there's no good place to keep this in a monk robe."

Wayan Bagus wagged his finger at Vernon. "Guns. Very bad for our karma."

Vernon put the gun back in the holster. "Little Buddy, this here's my lucky gun. The only bad karma this gun has is for any woodland critter we happen to come across at dinnertime."

Wayan Bagus shook his head. "The Sage teaches us first

learn how to live and then learn how not to kill. No good. Very bad."

"Right. On that note, off we go," Emerson said, walking in the direction of Sour Creek Dome. Riley followed him into the woods. Vernon and Wayan Bagus lagged a little ways behind, still bickering about guns and karma.

FIFTEEN

F OUR HOURS, SEVEN HILLS, AND FIVE MILES of breathtaking terrain later, Riley was drenched with sweat. The thirty-pound pack, which had seemed manageable at the beginning, weighed heavily on her back, and her legs ached with every step. She was ready for a break, but wasn't about to be the one to suggest it first.

Emerson paused on top of a ridge and set his pack down. "What do you say we stop for lunch?"

Riley looked out over the valley floor below. Sour Creek Dome was on the other side and looked not much closer than it did four hours ago. She turned back to look in the direction they'd traveled. No sign of civilization. No sounds from the highway. Except for the occasional bear print the size of a dinner plate, there was absolutely no evidence that any creature had ever been in the area in the last thousand years.

Riley put her pack down next to Emerson's and stretched. "I'm glad you have some experience with off-trail hiking, because I'd be completely lost. This is beautiful, but it really is the middle of nowhere."

Emerson didn't say anything.

"You do have wilderness experience, don't you?"

"More or less."

"Well, which is it?" Riley asked. "More or less?"

Emerson pulled a book entitled *The Complete Guide to Wilderness Survival* from his backpack. "It's what you'd call more of a theoretical experience."

"For the love of Mike, Emerson. Do you even know where we are?"

"More or less."

Riley narrowed her eyes at him. "We're completely lost, aren't we?"

Emerson opened the book to the chapter on way finding. "Theoretically, no. It would be a vast exaggeration to say that we're *completely* lost. At worst, we're *partially* lost. And that barely counts because we know where we're going. Sour Creek Dome is the large obstruction directly in front of us."

Vernon and Wayan Bagus crested the hill, rejoining Emerson and Riley.

Vernon dumped his backpack onto the ground. "My

back hurts. I've got blisters on my feet, and Little Buddy won't stop talking about my gun. I could be back at Mysterioso Manor watching reruns of *Baywatch* right now."

"That's the least of your worries," Riley said. "We're lost."

"Lost shmost," Vernon said. "We're going to that big hill in front of us. How can we be lost if we can see where we're going?"

"Precisely," Emerson said. "And I have a book on the subject."

"No man can be lost so long as he follows his Tao," Wayan Bagus said.

"First off," Riley said, "the Tao thing is getting old. Secondly, up until six months ago, when I got sucked into this bizarre vortex, my Tao was being a financial analyst in an office building, saving enough money to pay off my student loans, and going out for an occasional movie date on the weekends."

"Don't sound to me like it compares in any way to hanging out with us," Vernon said.

Emerson offered the *Complete Guide* to Riley. "Would it help if I let you hold on to the book?"

"Thank you," Riley said, "but I don't want to hold the dumb book. I'm going to go sit over there under that tree and eat a PowerBar. Nobody mess with me for ten minutes."

Riley sat under the tree, eating her lunch, while

Emerson, Vernon, and Wayan Bagus sat on a rock eating theirs. The midday sun sparkled off a little lake in the valley below, and Riley closed her eyes, listening to the sound of the wind filtering through the leaf canopy above her. It really was beautiful here, she thought, but it was difficult to relax and appreciate the beauty when the horror of the night before was still so clear in her mind.

She had asked for ten minutes, and that's exactly what she gave herself. She had a job to do. It would seem her life depended on it. She was going to hike to Sour Creek Dome and see for herself if something sinister was taking place there.

In exactly ten minutes she left the shade of the tree and strapped on her pack. "Let's keep moving, boys," she said to Emerson, Vernon, and Wayan Bagus. "We're burning daylight."

Vernon pulled himself to his feet and grabbed his backpack. "I guess you're not so worried about getting lost anymore."

"What could possibly go wrong?" Riley said. "After all, we have a book."

It was late afternoon when they reached the lake on the valley floor. It was deep blue and pristine. And a lot bigger than it looked from the ridgeline.

"We only have an hour or two before sunset," Emerson

said. "I think we should camp here. According to my guidebook it's best to get settled while there's enough light to see your surroundings."

Riley didn't need a book to figure that one out. She'd done her share of hunting and camping when she was a kid. Not nearly as rough as this. They'd had a pop-up camper that they'd supplement with a tent. Still, the basics were the same. Figure out where the bathroom was located, and make sure you could get to it without running into too many critters in the dark of night.

"First thing we want to do is set up the tents," Emerson said. "And we should get a fire started to keep the animals away."

"Do you know how to start a fire?" Riley asked.

Emerson held up the book. "Chapter three."

"Okeydokey then," Riley said. "You make the fire, and Vernon and I will get the tents up."

"I got everything pulled out of the backpacks," Vernon said. "We got four sleeping bags and pads, a couple little pots for cooking, and two tents."

"Are you sure there are only two tents?" Riley asked. "There are four people."

Emerson looked up from his reading. "Four tents would have made the packs too heavy. I decided it was more efficient for two people to share a tent."

"I volunteer to bunk with you," Vernon said to Riley. "You won't have no trouble keeping warm neither. I'm a hot sleeper. And I sleep in the nude, but I promise not to entice you with my nakedness."

"I appreciate the offer, but no."

"I suppose you think you would be too tempted to . . . you know," Vernon said.

"Yeah, that's it," Riley said. "Best not to put it to a test."

Wayan Bagus gave a small apologetic head bow. "It would not be appropriate for us to share a tent," he said to Riley.

"I understand," Riley said. She turned her attention to Emerson. "It seems my choice of a tent mate is limited. Do you sleep in the nude?"

Emerson hesitated. "Would you like me to?" he finally asked.

"No!"

"Anything else?"

"I don't want to wake up and find Post-it notes stuck to me."

"He does that to me too," Vernon said. "He leaves me notes that say there's a zebra in the house or we're all out of orange marmalade. When I wake up, first thing I do is check my forehead for a sticky note."

By the time Riley and Vernon had the tents set up, Emerson had a decent-sized fire started and enough dry wood gathered to keep it going until morning.

Riley sat down next to Emerson. "What are you reading about now?"

"Bear safety. We need to be especially careful through the night."

"Do you think we're in danger?" Riley asked.

"Not just from bears. There are other predators out here too. The fire should keep them away. It's important we take shifts to keep it burning until dawn."

Riley took the book from Emerson. It was open to a section on what to do in a bear encounter. "It says identify yourself by talking calmly to the bear, and stand your ground."

"Running is one of the worst things you can do," Emerson said. "Grizzlies can move at thirty miles per hour, uphill or downhill."

"And if talking calmly doesn't work?"

"If a grizzly attacks you, play dead. Get onto your stomach with your hands around the back of your neck. Spread your legs so the bear can't roll you over too easily."

"Why on the stomach?" Riley asked.

"Harder for the bear to rip out your intestines."

Vernon sat down next to them and blew out a raspberry. "I reckon it's not the bears we need to worry about. These here woods are well-known to be infested with Bigfoots. And let me tell you something. Getting on your stomach and spreading your legs is the last thing you want to do around a Bigfoot."

"I'm almost afraid to ask," Riley said.

Vernon nodded his head solemnly and looked a little choked up. "Yep. I was nearly raped by a Bigfoot."

"You should tell Riley the story," Emerson said. "After all, it just might save her life."

"I reckon that could be true," Vernon said, staring into the fire as if that would conjure up the memory. "When I was just turned twenty, I was out camping with my uncles and their buddies. It was a dark night. No moon at all. Couldn't see nary a thing that was more than six inches in front of your face. Just like tonight."

"The sun has barely set," Riley said. "And it's a full moon tonight."

"Even worse," Vernon said. "Bigfoots are especially 'active' during a full moon. Anyways, we'd all retired to bed after a late night of camaraderie, and by that I mean heavy drinking. I was sound asleep when the Bigfoot crashed into my tent and tried to have his way with me. I fought him off, and he kind of staggered away into the night." Vernon gave a shiver. "I tell you I'm under no illusions what would have happened if I'd just spread my legs and played dead."

"Thanks, Vernon," Emerson said. "I think we're all safer armed with the knowledge of how to properly fend off a Bigfoot attack."

Riley rolled her eyes. "Personally, I think we're all safe unless any of Vernon's drunk uncles show up."

Vernon ignored Riley. "Yellowstone has the biggest, meanest, rapiest Bigfoots in the world. And, I know what you're thinking. You're thinking you've got a fifty-fifty chance that it will be a Bigfoot of the female persuasion, but let me tell you they're the worst of all. They'd sooner rape you than look at you."

Riley stood up. "On that note, I'm going down to the lake to wash up before dinner."

There was no trail to follow, but the slope of the land was gentle. The vegetation was mostly scrub grass and ground cover. She reached the lake and walked a short distance along the shoreline. The sun had disappeared, but the sky was glowing with shades of orange and purple. She dipped her hands into water that was crystal clear and still warm from the afternoon sun. She looked back toward their campsite. It wasn't visible from the lake, but the location was marked by a stand of birch trees. She could hear the faint sounds of Emerson, Vernon, and Wayan talking around the fire.

Her intention had been to rinse her hands and splash some water on her face, but she realized she was totally alone and could actually wade in and get clean. She could wash the sweat and grime and fear away. Modesty wasn't an issue for her. She'd done her share of skinny-dipping in Texas.

She stripped and cautiously stepped into the water.

Once she adapted to the chill it felt great on her skin. She swam out, floated around a little, and swam back. The moon was low on the horizon. The stand of birches was clearly visible, and Riley could see a small ambient glow from the campfire.

She stepped out of the water and stood for a long moment, air-drying. When she moved toward the rocky outcropping where she'd placed her clothes, something rustled through the tall grasses just in front of her, and Emerson emerged, almost bumping into her.

"Crap on a cracker!" Riley said. "What are you doing here?"

"It was getting dark, and we started to worry, so I came looking for you."

"Well, you found me."

"Evidently so," Emerson said, staring at her breasts. "You look . . . cold."

"Stop looking! And turn around so I can get dressed."

Emerson turned around.

"I saw that," Riley said. "You're smiling, aren't you?"

"Maybe a little."

"Well, stop!"

"You should be happy I'm not Bigfoot come to have his way with you."

Riley would have preferred Bigfoot. It would be less embarrassing. She didn't care if Bigfoot got to see her naked. She didn't have a professional relationship with

Bigfoot, and Bigfoot was *always* naked. She tugged her jeans on and thought there was nothing worse than being the only one who was naked. Okay, maybe getting thrown into a pit with a couple dead, bloated buffalo was worse. Still, this was uncomfortable.

SIXTEEN

⊸⊷⊷⊶

D INNER CONSISTED OF FREEZE-DRIED BEEF
stew, Thai curry, and M&M's.

"The fire is nice," Riley said, "but I could see the glow from the lake. It might not be smart to let it burn all night."

"There are other precautions we can take to ward off the animals," Emerson said. "The book suggests that we mark our territory by relieving ourselves around the perimeter of our campsite."

"Count me out," Riley said. "I'd rather be eaten by a grizzly."

"The book also says that you should seal up your food as airtight as possible and hang it from a tree a good distance from your tent," Emerson said.

"You take care of hanging the food," Vernon said, "and I'll take care of peeing the perimeter."

"It sounds like we have a plan," Riley said. "We should douse the fire."

"I will douse the fire," Wayan Bagus said. "It will be my contribution. I will douse the fire with sand."

Wayan Bagus went to gather sand and Vernon wandered off to mark his territory.

Emerson had all the food bagged for hanging. "I should be back in ten minutes," he said to Riley. "If you have a sudden urge to take off all your clothes, just give me a shout-out."

"And what would you do?"

"I suppose I would have a dilemma. On the one hand I would want to come back to look. On the other hand I would want to be sensitive to your puritanical sense of modesty."

"Excuse me? Puritanical?"

"Obviously you have a problem with nudity."

"It's not a 'problem.'"

"I'm merely stating what I've observed," Emerson said. "You seem bothered by nudity."

"And you aren't?"

"Not at all. I'm very secure about my body."

"Well great. If you're so secure, you should take your clothes off."

"What?"

"You heard me," Riley said. "And the more I think about it, the more I think it's a great idea. I don't like that you've seen me naked, and I haven't seen you."

"That contradicts what you said earlier when I asked if you wanted me to come to bed naked."

"It's not at all contradictory. I don't want you rolling around naked next to me. I simply want to get a good look."

"That would be awkward," Emerson said.

"Not at all," Riley said. "I wouldn't feel at all awkward. It would be . . . enlightening."

"Okay, so if I let you get a good look, would it lead to something?"

"Would you want it to?"

"I believe I would," Emerson said.

"You're not sure?"

"There might be things to consider."

"Such as?"

"Precautions."

"You didn't pack any?" Riley asked.

"They weren't on the essentials list in the guidebook."

Vernon ambled out of the brush. "I'm empty," he said. "I got halfway around and ran dry. If I just had a couple beers I could finish the job."

"Confucius wrote that it does not matter how slowly you go so long as you do not stop," Wayan Bagus said.

"Yessir, Little Buddy," Vernon said. "That sure is more sage advice. That's always been my mode of operandi."

155

Wayan Bagus finished smothering the fire and retired to his tent for evening meditation. Emerson trudged off with his bag of food and a coil of rope.

Riley stood close to her tent and crossed her arms to ward off the chill.

"I'm worried," she said to Vernon. "We're in bear country, and the crazy Rough Riders are probably after us. How did we get into this mess?"

"It's not so bad," Vernon said. "We're with a holy man and my genius cousin. And I got my lucky gun. I figure we just go with the flow. Besides, my *unagi* is real quiet so we don't have anything to worry about for now."

A low, guttural growl came from the woods.

"That sounded like a bear," Riley said.

"I reckon," Vernon said.

Wayan Bagus came out of his tent. "What was that?"

They heard another growl. Louder this time. More of a roar than a growl.

"Yow," Vernon said. "That might have been a lion."

"There aren't any lions in Yellowstone," Riley said.

"There might be mountain lions," Vernon said.

"Emerson!" Riley shouted into the woods. "Are you okay?"

Vernon shone a flashlight in the direction of the roaring. "I don't see him. What should we do? We can't just go wandering around in the dark."

They all stared into the woods. "Well, we can't just leave him out there either," Riley said.

"I'm right behind you," Emerson said. "*Wu wei*. This is the perfect example of a situation in which the logical course of action is to do nothing and let the universe solve the problem."

Riley whipped around. "Holy cats, Emerson, you almost gave me a heart attack. What the heck is wrong with you? Haven't you done enough sneaking up on people for one day?"

Another roar shattered the quiet.

"It turns out that it is not, in fact, possible to sit down and reason with bears. At least not with this particular bear."

"No kidding," Riley said.

Emerson nodded. "Surprisingly, it had very little interest in discussing things in a free marketplace of ideas."

"Are you sure it wasn't a Bigfoot?" Vernon asked. "They're notoriously intolerant."

"All living things share a fundamental nature and are equally able to achieve enlightenment," Wayan Bagus said.

"Not Bigfoots."

Wayan Bagus nodded politely. "That is only true because there is no such thing as a Bigfoot."

Vernon gasped. "Whoa. Time out. It's been a long, stressful day, but let's not talk crazy."

"It was definitely a very big, very hungry bear," Emerson said. "The good news is that, in the end, the bear agreed not to eat me. The bad news is that I agreed to give it most of our food in exchange."

Riley hugged Emerson. "It was a good trade. We're just happy you're okay."

"All's well that ends well," Vernon said. "I knew it would. Like I said, I wasn't getting any *unagi* warnings."

"We should take turns standing watch," Emerson said. "We don't want to get taken by surprise by bears or rangers."

"Or a Bigfoot," Vernon said. "Just 'cause we got a doubter among us don't mean Bigfoot is any less real."

At first light, the campsite was disassembled, and everyone prepared to set off for Sour Creek Dome. The bear had eaten 90 percent of the food, but Emerson had managed to salvage enough for a meager lunch and breakfast.

"It should be an easier hike today," Emerson said. "We're sticking to the valley floor until we reach Sour Creek Dome, so it should be fairly flat."

Riley looked at the hill. "It looks out of place. It's just kind of sitting in the middle of the flat expanse."

"It's what geologists call a resurgent dome," Emerson said. "It's formed by the swelling of a volcano's caldera floor. There's a vast supply of underground magma, and it's literally lifting the ground."

"Why here and not somewhere else in the caldera?"

Emerson shifted his backpack. "The magma is a lot closer to the surface at the dome, so that's where the effect is most dramatic. However, more subtle changes are taking place all over the park."

"Like what?" Riley asked.

"For one, Yellowstone Lake, where we started the hike, used to drain to the north. Today, that's been completely reversed by the uplift of the dome, and the lake is now tilting and draining south."

"What do you think we're going to find at the dome?" Riley asked.

Emerson shrugged. "There are a couple possibilities. Whatever it is, it's something worth killing to protect."

"Well, I sure do hope it's a cheeseburger," Vernon said. "No offense, but the freeze-dried mush didn't cut it for me. If I get a chance, I'm going to do a little hunting and see if I can rustle up something that doesn't taste like tree bark." Vernon patted the .45 tucked into his jacket. "I never miss with my lucky gun."

"It is an attachment and bad for your karma," Wayan Bagus said.

Vernon was last in line, lumbering along behind the monk. "No offense, but starving to death is worse for my karma."

"I do not take offense," Wayan Bagus said. "I am just a simple monk. The sun shines on the just and unjust alike. If the sun does not judge, then who am I to do so?"

Vernon looked suspiciously at Wayan Bagus. "Why are you all of a sudden so magnanimous when it comes to my Second Amendment rights?"

"Upon consideration I realized it would be unwise to part with a lucky gun."

Vernon grinned. "I'm powerful glad to hear it. We need all the luck we can get."

"Thank you," Wayan Bagus said. "That is why I threw away the bullets. Bullets are very unlucky."

Vernon stopped walking. "You didn't."

"I did," Wayan Bagus said.

"What good is a gun without bullets?"

"It's even better without the bullets. Now it is lucky for both us and for anyone at whom it happens to be pointed."

Vernon shook his head and muttered to himself that vegetarians know nothing about anything, and that Wayan Bagus wouldn't be so short if he'd eat a cow once in a while.

By noon, they had circumnavigated the lake and the marshy grasslands had given way to a thick forest of conifers. "I can't see a thing through the trees," Riley said to Emerson. "How do we know if we're still heading in the right direction?"

"As long as we continue to walk uphill, we're making progress. Hopefully once we reach a higher elevation, the forest will get a little less dense."

"How are we doing with the food?" Riley asked.

"There's not much left. If we budget it, we have enough for lunch and dinner. After that, we'll have to forage."

"Do you know how to forage?" Riley asked.

"Yes."

"Let me rephrase that. Have you ever actually foraged?"

"No, but I've watched just about every episode of *Naked and Afraid*, so I'm pretty much an expert at this point."

Riley cut her eyes to Emerson. "The people who go on that show mostly just sit around and starve until they go crazy, get sick, or threaten to kill each other."

"That's true, but you have to remember they're disadvantaged in that they are forced to survive naked. Most of us are committed to wearing clothes on this trek," Emerson said.

Riley looked at Emerson. "Keep it up. Your time is going to come. Live in fear."

"I believe I'm being challenged," Emerson said.

"It's going to happen when you least expect it," Riley said. "Total nudity. And we won't need protection because I'll be completely clothed."

"We'll see," Emerson said. "I have excellent *unagi* when it comes to nudity."

They walked in silence for the next two hours, listening to animals rustling in the underbrush, watching for signs that bears might be ahead. Finally the forest opened up into a vast meadow. The lower portions of Sour Creek Dome loomed on the other side, maybe three miles away.

Wayan Bagus pointed into the distance. "What's that?"

"I don't see anything," Vernon said.

Emerson looked through his binoculars. "It's a fence, but it's probably a mile away."

"Is that another one of your *siddhi* powers?" Riley asked

Wayan Bagus. "Being able to see and hear at extreme distances?"

Wayan Bagus shrugged. "I hear and I know. I see and I remember. I do and I understand."

Vernon kicked a stone off the path. "My phone stopped working, which means my ratings are gonna drop like a rock on Fantasy NASCAR. We have no food. I'm hauling around a three-pound hunk of useless metal that serves no purpose other than being lucky, and I have absolutely no idea what Little Buddy is talking about half the time. Good grief. Holy crap. Somebody give me a Snickers."

"We ate all the Snickers," Emerson said, "but I have a couple PowerBars left. Do you want peanut butter or raspberry swirl?"

Vernon took the peanut butter, and the march resumed. A half hour later Emerson pulled up, and everyone stopped behind him. There was a twelve-foot-tall razor wire fence separating them from Sour Creek Dome.

"Looks like somebody has gone to a lot of trouble to keep people out of this area," Emerson said.

"I don't know about that," Vernon said. "That fence looks like something out of *Jurassic Park*. I'm more concerned about what they're trying to keep *in* than what they're trying to keep out."

"You think there's a *Tyrannosaurus rex* in there?" Riley asked.

"Man-eating genetically engineered dinosaurs, Bigfoots,

crazy park rangers," Vernon said. "Who knows? I don't know which one is worse."

Riley looked to the right and then to the left. The fence stretched in both directions with no end in sight. "How do we get across?"

"I reckon up and over," Vernon said, reaching out and grabbing on to the chain-link. There was a loud snapping sound, an arc of electricity jumped from the fence to Vernon, and Vernon went flying in reverse, landing on his back ten feet away.

Riley rushed over to Vernon. "Are you okay?"

Vernon looked up at Riley. His eyes were lazily rolling around from one side to the other, and his boots were smoking.

"Pamela Anderson?" Vernon asked. "Why aren't you wearing your red bathing suit? Did I almost drown?"

Emerson and Wayan Bagus helped Vernon to his feet. Vernon's hair was singed, and most of his eyebrows were burned off.

"Snap, crackle, pop," Vernon said. "Hey, Pam, give me a kiss. Oh yeah, and don't touch the fence. I think it's electrocuted."

"This is bad," Wayan Bagus said. "I should have removed the gun as well. I fear its luck has moved on."

Emerson looked Vernon over. "I think he's okay. He's a little dazed from the shock, and he has some minor burns on his hands."

"Burns shmurns," Vernon said. "I'm good as new. Right, Pam? And by the way, don't touch the fence."

Riley looked at Emerson. "Which one of us is Pam?"

"I don't think it matters," Emerson said. "And obviously we're not going over the fence. We'll have to go around. Sooner or later we're bound to come to a gate."

Several hours later they straggled to the top of a knoll. They'd been walking parallel to the fence line, pushing through tall grass that alternated with low scrubby brush. Emerson was the first to get to the top of the small hill, and he stared out across a swath of pasture.

"That must be the gate," he said to Riley, pointing at a little guardhouse about a quarter mile away down the fence line. He raised his binoculars to his eyes. "There's a crude trail leading to it through a couple hundred feet of open grassland before it disappears into the woods."

"Well, you found your gate," Vernon said. "Now what?"

SEVENTEEN

———⟨∞⟩———

R ILEY WATCHED A JEEP WRANGLER THROUGH
Emerson's binoculars as it emerged from the woods
and meandered down the barely there trail. It stopped at
the little guardhouse before passing through the gate and
disappearing into a thicket of trees.

"This feels surreal," Riley said, crouching down behind
the hill, out of sight from the guards. "We've been watching
this fence in the middle of nowhere for hours. How long
are we going to spy on the gatehouse?"

Emerson was lying down in the grass, using his
backpack as a pillow. "Until we can figure out a way to
get past the sentries."

Riley looked through the binoculars again. Two guards

wearing khaki uniforms and campaign hats manned the station. One had an automatic rifle slung over his shoulder. "There's no way to get past those guys without being seen and/or getting shot. We should find another way."

Emerson shook his head. "We walked the fence line for half a day. This is the only entry point."

"It's going to be dark in an hour," Vernon said. "We can't make a fire without being seen, and without a fire we haven't got a lot of protection against the bears and wolves on account of I'm dehydrated after getting electrified."

Wayan Bagus was sitting under a tree. "They're wearing the same uniforms as the men who forced me off my island. If they're anything like those men, they won't be good hosts."

Emerson sat up. "I have a plan. Ten years ago, a crack commando unit was sent to prison by a military court for a crime they didn't commit. These men promptly escaped from a maximum-security stockade to the Los Angeles underground. Today, still wanted by the government, they survive as soldiers of fortune. We need to contact those guys ASAP."

Riley grinned. "Seriously. Your plan is to hire the A-Team?"

"I have another idea, but it's kind of crazy."

"Crazier than asking a bunch of geriatric actors from a TV show that was canceled thirty years ago to break into a government installation?"

"How do you feel about tattoos?" Emerson asked.

"I'm not letting you anywhere near me with a needle," Riley said.

Emerson pulled a Sharpie from his backpack. "This is more the temporary kind of tattoo. Are you ready to join the Rough Riders?"

"You think a pen-and-ink drawing of two crossed sabers on our wrists will be enough to get us into the compound?"

Emerson uncapped the pen. "No, but I'm hoping it will buy us some time and let us get close enough to overpower the guards."

"Shouldn't you practice first?" Riley asked.

"Excellent idea. It's harder to draw on a human body than on paper, what with all your nooks and crannies."

"Never mind my nooks and crannies," Riley said.

"Understood," Emerson said. "I'll get to your nooks and crannies later. How about if, for now, I practice on the flat of your back?"

Riley rolled up her shirt, giving Emerson access to her lower back.

Five minutes later, Emerson stood up, capped the pen with a dramatic flourish, and surveyed his work. "It's quite good, actually. You may want to consider making it permanent."

Vernon and Wayan Bagus came over to look.

"What do you think?" Riley asked. "Does it look like

two crossed sabers with a number one above them? Do you think it will fool the guards?"

"It is most unlikely this tattoo will fool the guards," Wayan Bagus said.

"Too big?" Riley asked.

Wayan Bagus nodded. "Yes, that's it. It's too big."

"It's nice," Vernon said. "I like it. It's a real conversation starter."

Riley twisted and turned, trying to see her back. "What the heck is this?" she asked. "It doesn't look like the Rough Rider tattoo."

"It's far superior," Emerson said. "It's an octopus smoking a cigar. And I've even signed it. Now that I've mastered more complex forms, I'm certain I can produce an excellent version of the Rough Rider image on your wrist."

"I need a moment," Riley said.

"To enjoy my work?" Emerson asked.

"To stifle the urge to choke you."

"Is it the cigar? It was a last-minute decision."

"It's temporary, right?"

"'Temporary' is a relative term," Emerson said. "It should fade away in no more than two to three weeks."

Riley decided if after two to three weeks she was still alive and not locked away in a dungeon, she'd be so overjoyed that she wouldn't care about an octopus smoking a cigar on her back.

"I suppose you're now going to violate my hand," she said to Emerson.

Emerson nodded. "I'll do my best."

Ten minutes later, Emerson was done with the tattoos.

"I have to admit, it looks pretty realistic," Vernon said. "But what now?"

"Riley and I are going to walk up to the guardhouse like we own the place and tell them we caught two trespassers walking in the woods."

"Vernon and I are going to be the trespassers?" Wayan asked.

"Correct," Emerson said. "There are four of us and only two of them, so if we can fool them into thinking Riley and I are Rough Riders, even for a couple seconds, we should be able to get close enough to distract and overwhelm them."

"Aren't you supposed to be in some kind of uniform?" Vernon asked.

"We're plainclothes Rough Riders," Emerson said.

Riley followed Emerson out of the brush and onto the Jeep path.

"This is never going to work," Riley said.

"You have to believe."

"I do believe. I believe it isn't going to work."

Emerson motioned Wayan Bagus and Vernon to get onto the path and walk in front of them toward the gatehouse.

"Hold your hands up as if you've been arrested," Emerson said. "Look ashamed that you've been caught breaking the law."

"It is difficult for me to look ashamed," Wayan Bagus said, "but I can look humble. I believe it might appear similar."

"They're pointing at us," Vernon said. "They see us."

"Hello," Emerson shouted. "We found these two miscreants trespassing in the restricted area."

"'Miscreants'?" Riley whispered. "Who says 'miscreants'?"

The first guard took the rifle off his shoulder and pointed it in their direction.

"What are they saying?" Riley asked. "Can anyone read lips that far away?"

"They're confused," Wayan Bagus said. "They're saying that there are rangers assigned to reconnaissance in the surrounding woods, but they don't recognize you."

"Are you sure?" Vernon asked. "I can't hear a thing. You're not just making that up, are you?"

Wayan Bagus steepled his fingers. "Altogether, there are eight types of illusions. Magic, a dream, a bubble, a rainbow, lightning, the moon reflected in water, a mirage, and a city of celestial musicians."

Vernon stared at the guards. "Those guys sure aren't celestial musicians, and I noticed you didn't mention assault rifles in that list."

"Only one way to find out for certain," Emerson said. He turned to Riley. "Hold up your wrist so they can see it."

"We're the new recruits," Emerson shouted, pointing to the ink tattoo on his wrist. "Tin Man assigned us to recon."

One of the guards got out a pair of binoculars and looked in their direction. He said something to the second guard, and lowered his gun.

Emerson waved at the guards as he approached. "Don't worry about a thing," he whispered to Riley, Vernon, and Wayan Bagus. "I've read several books on improvisational acting so I know what I'm doing. The most important thing is not to break character. Just follow my lead and wait for me to give the signal before we jump them."

"Let me see your identification," the first guard said.

Emerson waved his hand in front of the guard's face. "I am Park Ranger Kenobi. You don't need to see our identification."

"Protocol is to require identification."

"It's critical that I get these droids to the commander," Emerson said.

"Say what? Are we getting pranked? Billy put you up to this, right?"

"Let me try this again from the top," Emerson said. He shook his hands and rolled his neck. "Red leather. Yellow leather. Red leather. Yellow leather. The tip of the tongue, the teeth, and the lips. The tip of the tongue, the teeth, and the lips. Okay, I'm ready."

"What are you ready for?" the guard asked.

"To give you my identification," Emerson said. He

reached into his pocket and rooted around. "It's in here somewhere." He pulled his hand out and gave the guard the stiff middle finger.

"I reckon that's the signal," Vernon said, jumping on the back of the nearest guard and wrestling him to the ground.

Emerson punched the other guard in the temple, temporarily disorienting him. He flipped him around into a sleeper hold, and in a matter of seconds the guard lost consciousness and slumped to the ground.

Riley stepped in and disarmed both guards.

"We need to get these guys into the guardhouse and secure them before someone comes along," she said.

"I love it when a plan comes together," Emerson said.

Fifteen minutes later the two guards were sitting on the floor, handcuffed to a woodstove in the center of the gatehouse and stripped down to their underwear. Vernon and Wayan Bagus were outside changing into the guards' uniforms. Riley and Emerson were foraging for food.

"You boys don't mind if we borrow your uniforms for a while, do you?" Emerson said. "We'll return them just as soon as we find out what you're hiding behind this fence."

The guards glared at Emerson and struggled against their restraints.

"Screw you," the older guard said. "We're all dead men. Tin Man's going to kill you, and then he's going to kill us."

"Then it might be time for you to reconsider where

your loyalties lie, since your survival is predicated on ours," Emerson said, confiscating a box of granola bars.

Vernon and Wayan Bagus walked back into the gatehouse. "I'm telling you right now, nobody better laugh," Vernon said.

Vernon's khaki pants were three inches too short and tight in all the wrong places. The khaki button-down shirt fit him even worse. Wayan Bagus had the opposite problem. He was absolutely swimming in his clothes, and was holding up his pants with one hand.

"And I thought I looked ridiculous with an octopus on my back," Riley said.

Vernon cut his eyes to Wayan Bagus. "I told you we looked like a couple of grade A morons. But no, you think they fit great. Look at me. I can barely walk, and I can't tell where my doodles end and my dongle begins."

Wayan Bagus hoisted his pants. "You must look on the positive side. Vanity can create a very cruel space for you and, by extension, your doodles, if you don't know how to manage it."

"Lord Buddha?" Riley asked.

Wayan Bagus shook his head. "Lady Gaga. I've recently become one of her Little Monsters."

Vernon rolled his eyes. "Lady Gaga never wore anything as stupid looking as this, and she wore a dress made of meat to the MTV Video Music Awards." He turned to Emerson. "What now?"

"The plan is that you and Wayan will stay at the gatehouse. Riley and I will go inside the fence and investigate."

"When will you be back?" Vernon asked.

Emerson gestured toward the two guards. "We need to be back before sunrise, when the day shift comes to relieve these two. I don't expect there will be too many visitors through the night, but if there are, just ask anybody who comes to the gate for their identification and wave them through."

There was the faint noise of an engine in the dark woods accompanied by a faraway glow of headlights. "Looks like we're getting at least one visitor," Riley said.

Emerson gagged the two guards and handed Vernon his campaign hat. "Just let them through. Riley and I will hide behind the gatehouse until they've passed."

An armored Humvee followed by a heavy-duty military transport truck rumbled slowly out of the woods and approached the gate. "Well, that's something you don't see every day," Emerson whispered to Riley from their hiding place.

Riley leaned into Emerson. "What's an armored military transport doing in the middle of Yellowstone?"

"It's a transport. It's either making a delivery or a withdrawal."

"Of what?"

"You don't send an armored militarized truck to deliver a pizza," Emerson said. "I want to get on that truck."

"How the heck do you intend to do that?"

"*Wu wei.*"

"For once, I agree. There's not a lot of downside to doing nothing in this situation."

Vernon and Wayan Bagus walked outside to greet the Humvee. Vernon was carrying the assault rifle. Wayan Bagus was carrying a clipboard in one hand and holding onto his pants with the other.

"Namaste," Wayan Bagus said to the driver. "May we please see your identification?"

The driver leaned out the window and handed Vernon his ID. "Why do you look like you're waiting for a flood?"

"Wardrobe malfunction," Vernon said. "Anyone else in there?"

The driver handed over two more ID cards. Vernon looked at all the cards and read them aloud for Emerson's benefit.

"Miles Bemmer, Timothy Mann, Bartholomew Young," Vernon said, slightly louder than necessary.

"Tin Man and the director," Riley whispered to Emerson. "What the heck's going on?"

"Proceed," Vernon said, returning the IDs to the driver.

The Humvee drove a short distance, stopped, and idled, and the transport moved up to the gatehouse.

"Namaste," Wayan Bagus said to the transport driver. "May we see your identification?"

"What's with the 'Namaste'?" the driver said, handing over his ID. "Are you on loan from some other army?"

"Many apologies," Wayan Bagus said. "You are correct to be confused. It is my understanding that it is customary to offer a salute in these situations." He snapped to attention, raised his right hand sharply to the brim of his campaign hat, and his trousers fell down around his ankles.

"Cripes," the driver said. "What kind of underwear are you wearing? It looks like a diaper. Is that what central supply is handing out now?"

Wayan Bagus looked down at himself. "I humbly accept whatever gifts the universe bestows on me. I found this in my laundry basket."

"Looks like a towel," Vernon said. "Little Buddy, when we get back to civilization we gotta take you shopping and get you some Calvins."

The transport driver snatched his ID back, rolled up his window, drove through the gate, and both vehicles disappeared into the night. No one in the truck noticed the two hitchhikers who had snuck up behind and grabbed on to the rear handholds.

EIGHTEEN

─────⚬⚬⚬─────

R ILEY AND EMERSON HELD ON TIGHT AS THE
truck rolled and bumped along the rough terrain,
navigating around thickets of woods interspersed with
bubbling hot springs and mud pots. The smell of sulfur
filled the air, getting stronger with every passing minute.

"Do you hear that?" Riley asked. "It sounds like
pounding."

Moments later, the truck passed into a clear-cut section
of the woods with a military-looking compound in the
center dominated by a large Quonset-style warehouse.
The hut was surrounded by what appeared to be at least
fifty immense oil-drilling rigs and an assortment of heavy
machinery. Pipelines ran from each of the drills to the

Quonset hut, like some giant wagon wheel. Several soldiers dressed in the Rough Rider uniforms and carrying assault rifles patrolled the area, keeping watch over a variety of laborers in khaki jumpsuits working the drills.

Emerson and Riley jumped off the back of the truck at the perimeter of the clearing and dashed behind an unmanned drill.

Riley blinked and sniffed the air. The smell of sulfuric acid was so strong now that it stung her eyes.

"What the heck is this place?" she asked. "It looks like they're drilling for oil, but I've never seen any rigs that big, and I'm from Texas."

Emerson examined the drill. "I'd wager no one has ever seen a drill like this. It's not even made from steel. If I had to guess based on the color and luster, I'd say it was constructed from something in the platinum family of metals."

Riley ran her hand over the rig. "That would cost a small fortune. Why would anybody do that?"

"This could easily weigh fifty tons," Emerson said. "Last I checked the spot price of platinum was twelve hundred dollars per ounce. That would make this one alone a two-billion-dollar piece of machinery."

Riley raised her eyebrows. "But there must be fifty or so here in the compound."

"That would be a total of one hundred billion dollars if my math is correct," Emerson said. "Of course, there are cheaper metals, like rhodium, that resemble platinum and cost somewhat less. Still, there's no way around it. Someone spent an obscene amount of money to set up this facility."

Riley shook her head. "It just doesn't make any sense. Why would they use platinum instead of steel?"

"Platinum has two properties that steel does not. It is extremely hard, and it has a melting temperature of about three thousand degrees."

"Neither of which is important if you're drilling for oil."

"Exactly," Emerson said. "They aren't drilling for oil."

"Then what?"

"We're standing over the shallowest part of the underground lava lake. Magma has a temperature of around two thousand five hundred degrees. The only thing that makes sense is that they're mining the magma, and they needed to build a machine that could withstand the heat without melting."

Riley thought back to their conversation with Marion White at George Mason University.

"Why mine the magma?" Riley asked. "The professor said the magma contains osmium, but it's only worth four hundred dollars per ounce. Other than that it's just worthless silica and sulfuric acid gasses."

Emerson nodded. "Yes. It wouldn't make any sense, at least from an economic point of view, to build a one-hundred-billion-dollar facility to mine osmium. There's something else going on."

"Could they be possibly trying to drain the lava lake?"

Riley asked. "Maybe they're trying to relieve some of the pressure to prevent an explosion."

"I doubt it. Where, then, are they dumping all the lava they're removing? And, frankly, I would think it could just as easily have the opposite effect and destabilize the area, sort of like the effects from hydraulic fracking."

The Humvee parked in front of the Quonset warehouse, and the soldiers patrolling the compound rushed over to the truck.

Riley watched the door to the hut open. A tall man in a white lab coat walked out and went to the truck.

"Isn't that Eugene Spiro, the chief scientist for the National Park Service, who we met back at the Department of the Interior?" Riley asked.

"It is. Looks like the gang's all here."

The soldiers opened the rear door to the truck and carefully removed a large metal container that looked like an inner tube connected to a battery-operated power source. The chief scientist pointed toward the warehouse and followed them inside, along with Tin Man and the director. A couple minutes later they all exited and walked into a large construction trailer that obviously served as a makeshift office.

"Looks like a meeting for the American Society of Ruthless Psychopaths," Riley said.

Emerson smiled. "I tend to agree. How do you feel about doing a little snooping?"

"I'm against it."

"Are you totally against it?"

"Yes."

"When you say 'totally' do you mean one hundred percent? As in, it's not even open to discussion?"

"I guess I'm willing to talk about it," Riley said.

Emerson crept through the compound toward the rear of the warehouse.

"Great," he said, motioning to Riley to follow him. "Let's talk about it while we do some snooping."

They snuck around to the rear of the warehouse. There was a small window about six feet off the ground, and Emerson knelt down on his hands and knees in front of it. "Why don't you take a look?"

Riley stood on Emerson's back and peered through the little window. "What am I supposed to be looking for?" she asked.

"Just describe to me what you see."

"It's a high-tech lab of some sort. There's a giant vat in the middle of the room connected to a lot of machinery I don't recognize, except for a bigger version of the metal donut that was in the back of the transport."

"Interesting. Is there anybody there?"

Riley climbed down off Emerson. "No. It looks like everyone's left."

"Interesting."

"I know what you're thinking, and you can just forget

about that," Riley said. "There's absolutely no way I'm walking into the lion's den. Tin Man could be back any minute."

"Now, when you say 'absolutely no way,' does that mean absolutely one hundred percent or just 99.9 percent?"

"This is crazy," Riley said. "It's practically suicidal."

Emerson studied the rear door. "If I can't guess the six-digit combination to this door we're not getting in regardless of whether it's crazy or not."

"Six digits. That's a million different possibilities. It will take us all night, assuming we don't get caught."

Emerson punched a number into the keypad, and the red light on the door stayed lit. He thought a moment and tried again. There was an audible click, and the light turned green.

"I don't believe it," Riley said.

Emerson shrugged. "Sixty-seven percent of the time people choose a birthday or anniversary for the combination when it's exactly six digits. In this case, it had to be a birthday that everyone in this compound could remember. One that's important to all of them. The first one I chose was 102758, Teddy Roosevelt's birthday. The second was 082516, the birthday of the National Park Service."

"I think I would have preferred that you failed to guess the combination."

Emerson opened the door and waited for Riley to enter. "I got lucky. I'm feeling extra discerning today."

Riley and Emerson crept around the dimly lit warehouse, trying to get their bearings. Everything was pristinely clean, including the glass-tiled floor. A variety of white workstations, complete with everything you'd find in chemistry class, occupied one corner of the room. In another corner, robotic arms in a state of constant activity were connected to large pieces of freestanding machinery, each one enclosed behind three inches of what seemed to be bulletproof glass. The large metal donut sat in the center of it all.

Riley walked over to Emerson. He was staring at a big red button on the wall. "Emerson, you're not thinking about pushing that button, are you?"

Emerson continued to stare at the button. "I was giving it some serious consideration."

Riley grabbed him by the arm. "Remember when you once told me it was your life's ambition to avoid terrible ideas?"

"Of course."

"Well, I'm telling you that anytime there's a big red button and you don't know what it does, it's a really awful decision to push it."

"The problem is that is exactly what the button wants you to think. I think we should push it."

"No."

Emerson looked over toward the front door. "Is someone coming back?"

Riley turned to look, and the white milky glass tiles

183

she was standing upon turned clear, revealing a swirling swimming pool–sized pit of boiling red magma beneath her feet.

"Holy crap," Riley said. "What the heck?"

Emerson stared at the magma. "Well, that's something you don't see every day. The floor must be made of electric glass."

Riley cut her eyes to Emerson. "You pushed the red button when I wasn't looking, didn't you?"

"I suppose you wouldn't believe me if I said no," Emerson said.

"Try me."

Emerson looked at Riley. "No."

Riley shook her head. "I don't believe you."

"What was I supposed to do?" Emerson said. "It's a big red button."

Riley threw her arms up in the air. "For the love of Mike, Emerson. Why can't you just be the sort of guy who leaves his shoes all over the house or can never find his car keys? I just don't think I'm the sort of woman who can ever be with a guy who goes around just willy-nilly pushing red buttons."

"I propose a compromise," Emerson said. "I'll continue to push big red buttons, just not in a willy-nilly fashion." He looked at her for a long moment. "About the button pushing and stuff. Are you considering a relationship with me?"

"Um, maybe. I mean, I am your amanuensis. Are you considering a relationship with *me*?"

"It's crossed my mind," Emerson said.

"Is it because you saw me naked?"

"Not entirely, but I think about it a lot."

"In a good way?"

"Sort of in a Vernon way," Emerson said.

"Vernon is a horndog."

"I might also be one."

Riley had no idea where to go with this. She supposed she was happy Emerson was attracted to her, but she didn't know about him being a horndog. "Horndog" didn't exactly describe the man of her dreams.

"We should get on with it," Riley said.

Emerson nodded. "My exact thought."

He walked the perimeter of the pit. It was almost as big as the warehouse itself.

"It's a platinum swimming pool filled with lava," Emerson said. "There's even an intake pipe where the lava gets pumped in, presumably from the drills outside, and an outtake. I'm guessing it eventually gets returned to flow underground."

Riley thought that made sense. There wasn't any evidence in the area of lava being dumped aboveground.

"Why aren't the glass tiles melting?" she asked.

Emerson got down on his knees and examined the floor. "It's not glass. It's some kind of a transparent ceramic. It's an excellent insulator, so it protects us from the heat, and obviously it won't melt unless temperatures reach well above five thousand degrees."

"Is transparent ceramic a real thing?" Riley asked.

"It's a technology used in products ranging from clear orthodontic braces to armored car windows. I've never heard of anybody using it for a swimming pool cover. Of course, I've never heard of a swimming pool filled with lava either."

One of the larger machines on the other side of the room lit up, and a steady stream of magma filled its transparent ceramic enclosure. The robotic arms inside went into operation, pushing the lava through a filter and separating it into different portions. The smaller portion was transferred to another enclosure, where robotic arms again went to work. The larger portion was flushed underground where it gurgled as it moved through the plumbing, eventually flowing outside and away from the warehouse.

Riley watched the robotic arms busy at work. "They're looking for something in the lava, aren't they?"

Emerson nodded. "Definitely. Something much more valuable than money. Something worth killing over. Something that the government's been protecting and keeping secret for more than a century."

They heard the sound of voices outside the warehouse, and the front entrance clicked open. Emerson pushed the red button, and the magma swimming pool disappeared behind the milky white floor. He grabbed Riley by the wrist and yanked her to a dark corner of the warehouse where a large tarp covered an unused piece of heavy machinery.

Riley and Emerson hid under the tarp and listened as the door opened and the voices filled the room.

Riley peered out from under the tarp. Tin Man, Eugene Spiro, and Bart Young were standing next to the large metal donut in the center of the room.

Bart Young pointed at the smaller version of the donut. "Move everything into the portable Penning trap."

Spiro attached the smaller trap to the larger one using a coupling. "You're taking all of it? Where?"

"We have a parallel program in Hawaii," the director said. "We can't find Knight, and I'm not risking leaving any loose ends in light of how close we are to finishing. After today, it's none of your concern."

Spiro went to one of the workstations and sat down in front of one of the computers. He typed in some instructions, and the smaller Penning trap powered up. "It will take a couple minutes for the transfer to be complete," he said to the director. "How are you going to get it safely to Hawaii? You know how a Penning trap works, don't you? It uses a magnetic field to store and isolate charged matter."

"Your point being?" the director said.

"The point being that if you get a little unlucky and there's a power interruption, then there's no more magnetic field."

"And?" Tin Man asked.

"No more magnetic field means that what's inside isn't isolated from the matter outside this canister," Spiro said. "And, if that happens we're all in a world of pain."

"Again, no longer your concern," the director said.

"I've spent ten years of my life developing this program," Spiro said. "I don't want to see it fail."

"This is not your program," the director said. "You are an employee. And you should be very careful, because I'm not impressed with your performance. Ten years have passed, and you've only managed to collect a couple ounces."

"That's enough to obliterate a continent. How much more do you need?"

The director shrugged. "More."

"Collection is difficult. It takes time," Spiro said.

"You are no longer credible," the director said. "It was your call to leave Knight alone. If I had listened to Tin Man in the first place, I wouldn't be thinking about destroying a two-trillion-dollar facility and you wouldn't be out of a job."

Spiro looked relieved that he was only fired. The penalty could have been much worse.

"Why would this have to be destroyed?" Spiro asked.

"Knight has money, and he knows powerful people," the director said. "He also has a blog that's read by thousands. If he learns enough and goes public with it, we'll have all sorts of idiots crawling all over this facility. We won't be able to kill them fast enough. Everyone from conspiracy theorists to Sunday hikers to political watchdogs will be here. Our plans will be savaged, and our technology will be discovered and stolen."

Spiro shook his head. "It will take a year to dismantle."

"On the contrary, one well-placed tactical nuclear device detonated in the underground lava lake beneath the dome should do the trick. The entire area will be buried under fifty feet of magma in no more than a day."

Spiro went pale. "It would destabilize the entire super-volcano. The entire park, not just the dome, could be buried under fifty feet of magma. If that happened, it could kill millions."

Tin Man smiled. "I knew there was a silver lining. I almost hope we don't find Knight and Moon."

The director turned to Tin Man. "Always the optimist. From here on out, you're in charge of Yellowstone. If you don't find Knight and Moon in a week, or if there's even a whisper about Sour Creek Dome on his blog, detonate the nuke."

The little Penning trap beeped and the green light on its side changed from blinking to solid.

"The transfer is done," Spiro said. "I'll get someone to help us move it to the transport."

Tin Man watched Spiro leave the warehouse. "You're not taking him with us?"

"He's leaving with us, but he won't be walking off the plane in Hawaii. You know how I hate loose ends."

NINETEEN

⸺⸺∞⸺⸺

E MERSON AND RILEY WATCHED FROM THEIR
hiding place until the guards left with the portable
Penning trap and the room was empty.

"Wow," Riley said. "What do you think they've got in
that thing?"

Emerson opened the warehouse's back door a crack
and peeked out. There was still a guard hanging around.
"I don't know. The concept of a Penning trap has been
around since 1923."

"You don't know enough to leave red buttons alone,
but you know what year the Penning trap was invented."

"Hans Dehmelt won the Nobel Prize in Physics for its
invention in 1989. It made a major impact in my life."

"You wanted to be a physicist?"

"No, I wanted to be Captain Kirk. The Penning trap is basically a vacuum environment capable of containing charged antimatter in a magnetic prison. Antimatter is what makes warp speed possible, without which the starship *Enterprise* could never have explored strange new worlds."

"Could they be harvesting antimatter?"

Emerson shook his head. "The universe is composed of nearly fifty percent antimatter. If you wanted to get your hands on some you wouldn't have to tap into the earth's core. Besides, a Penning trap that size wouldn't hold enough to destroy this compound, let alone a continent."

"What else can a Penning trap hold?"

"Plasmas."

"Let's pretend I don't know anything about physics or *Star Trek*."

"There are four types of ordinary matter—solids, liquids, gasses, and plasmas. Plasmas are the only type of matter that doesn't naturally exist on the earth under normal surface conditions. They're basically created from neutral gasses, like hydrogen, by ionizing them and giving them an electrical charge. Lightning, neon signs, television screens, and the aurora borealis are all examples."

"So are plasmas rare? Could that be what they're collecting?" Riley asked.

Emerson peeked out the door again. The guard was gone.

"Plasmas are the most common type of ordinary matter

in existence," Emerson said. "The sun and stars are all basically superheated balls of plasma. Plasmas are kind of the building blocks of the universe."

Riley and Emerson walked out into the cold night air and skirted around the perimeter of the compound. There was a lot of activity, but all the attention was focused on the transport and Humvee idling in front of the warehouse.

"This is it," Emerson said. "We're not going to find a better time than this to make our escape."

They sprinted to the surrounding woods, and Riley breathed a sigh of relief when they were hidden from sight. "How far do you think it is back the gatehouse?"

"Not far. Maybe a mile or two. It's going to be slow going in the dark, though. I saw a lot of thermal features on the way in. I don't want to accidentally fall into any pools of boiling water."

They trudged along the Jeep trail in silence for several minutes.

"You know, Emerson, something you said back in the compound reminds me of something Professor White told us back at George Mason University."

"What's that?"

"That plasmas formed the building blocks of the universe," Riley said. "Didn't the professor say that mantle plumes contained trace amounts of cosmic leftovers—the same materials that formed the stars before the earth was created? She said they were a clue to the forces of creation."

Emerson stopped and stared at Riley. "I'm promoting

you to senior amanuensis, effective immediately, for having invaluable insight and a brilliant memory."

"Thank you," Riley said.

"And because you look good naked," Emerson added.

"Would I still get the promotion if I *didn't* look good naked?"

"Yes, but you might not get the additional benefits."

Now that Riley knew Emerson was possibly a horndog, she had some idea of the benefits. She felt a rush of heat curl through her stomach and head south.

"Good to know," Riley said. "Do you know what's in the Penning trap?"

"No, not exactly, but I have a theory. I think it's some cosmic remnant from the swirling nebula of stellar gasses that formed our solar system four and half billion years ago. Some very rare, very dangerous primordial element that can only be found at the earth's core, and every once in a rare while a little bit of it bubbles to the surface, courtesy of a mantle plume volcano."

A diesel engine rumbled from the direction of the compound.

"It's the transport," Emerson said. "They're heading out."

Emerson and Riley ran for cover, flattening themselves under a clump of scrub brush. Lights flashed onto the road and the Humvee appeared, followed by the transport. Tin Man was standing in the back cargo bed of the Humvee methodically shining a spotlight into the woods, first to one side then the other.

"They're looking for us," Riley whispered to Emerson. "We must have been spotted leaving the compound."

"They're looking for something," Emerson said. "Whether it is us or not is unclear at this time."

Tin Man played the light across their bush. Riley held her breath, and the light moved on. The Humvee and transport slowly drove another hundred feet down the road before Tin Man said something into a walkie-talkie and the convoy abruptly stopped. Tin Man hopped off the Humvee, opened the rear passenger door, and dragged Spiro out of the vehicle and onto the road.

Spiro was babbling, and when he passed in front of the transport headlights Riley could see that he was shaking. He stumbled and fell to his knees, but Tin Man yanked him to his feet and shoved him toward the woods. Spiro resisted, and Tin Man hit him hard on the side of his face. Spiro sobbed once and went silent. They disappeared into the woods, and Emerson moved out from under cover.

"Stay here," he said to Riley.

Riley grabbed Emerson by his shirtsleeve. "Telling me to 'stay here' implies that you're not."

"They're going to kill him," Emerson said. "I have to try to do something."

The sound of a brief struggle carried out of the woods.

There was a *SPLOOSH,* and then bloodcurdling screaming. Tin Man reappeared, got back into the Humvee, and the convoy disappeared down the road.

Emerson and Riley ran down the Jeep trail, toward the screaming. By the time they turned into the woods, the screams had turned into whimpers. The smell of rotten eggs hung heavy in the air. Directly in front of them, lit by moonlight, was a large, nasty-looking, steaming, bubbling mud pot.

"Spiro," Emerson shouted. "Where are you?"

A mud-covered hand lifted in response. It was Spiro, lying half in and half out of the boiling, sulfuric mud hole. He was covered with the scorching brown sludge, making him almost indistinguishable from the surrounding dirt.

Emerson knelt beside him. "Hang on. We're going to get you out."

Spiro looked up and blinked. His skin was sloughing off his face, and his blood was mingling with the mud. "Emerson Knight and Riley Moon? Why are you here?"

"I told my friend I would find his island," Emerson said. "I have to know what happened."

"Mauna Kea," Spiro said.

"What's at Mauna Kea?" Riley asked. "What will we find there?"

Spiro closed his eyes and blew out his final breath of air. "Armageddon."

. . .

It was two in the morning by the time Emerson and Riley got back to the gatehouse. The two guards were still half naked and handcuffed to the woodstove. Vernon and Wayan Bagus still looked ridiculous in their ill-fitting uniforms and were playing cards.

Vernon looked up. "Boy, am I glad to see you. Little Buddy cheats something fierce."

"I win only through my superior skills," Wayan Bagus said. "Vernon cannot concentrate."

They walked outside so they could talk without the guards hearing.

"Did the Humvee and military transport come through here a couple hours ago?" Emerson asked.

Vernon nodded. "Yup. Didn't even stop to say howdy-do. Little Buddy and I just stayed in the hut. What'd you two find out? Did you bring me back a cheeseburger?"

"For starters, we're wanted fugitives," Riley said. "That's the good news. The bad news is that the insane director of the National Park Service is tapping into the earth's core to gather materials for making some sort of super-weapon."

"I'll just blow this whole thing wide open on the blog," Vernon said. "It'll get sorted out lickety-split once it's all over the Internet."

"I guess I forgot to mention the hostages," Riley said.

"There is a hostage?" Wayan Bagus asked.

"Try a million. Tin Man's going to blow up Yellowstone if we say even a word to anybody about it."

"I don't see where that's a problem," Vernon said. "We

evacuate all the people, and all's left to blow up are the stupid Bigfoots and stink-hole mud pots. I say good riddance."

"The park is a national treasure," Riley said.

"Treasure shmeasure," Vernon said.

Everyone was silent for a beat, thinking about it.

"Off the table," Riley said. "We are not going to blow up Yellowstone."

"Of course not," Emerson said.

"Very, very bad karma," Wayan Bagus said. "The thought gives me a severe pain behind my eye."

"First things first," Emerson said. "We need to get out of the park."

He walked back inside the gatehouse and knelt down to talk with the guards.

"What do you say we make a bargain?" Emerson asked them.

Four hours of being chained to a woodstove in their underwear had knocked a lot of the fight from the two guards.

"What kind of a bargain?" a guard asked.

"The best kind," Emerson said. "One that is mutually beneficial to both sides. We'll let you go and give you back your clothes."

Wayan Bagus tapped Emerson on the shoulder. "I'm a little attached to the hat."

"Except for the hat," Emerson said.

They looked interested.

"Okay. What do we have to do?"

"You drive us out of the park to the Bozeman airport and forget you ever saw us."

"Why would we agree to that?" the first guard asked.

"What do you think Tin Man would do to you if he knew you let us waltz into a top-secret government installation and steal national secrets?"

The guards exchanged glances.

"Good point," one said. "Will you be needing an SUV or a sedan for your ride to the airport?"

Riley settled into the plush leather seat of the Gulfstream G550 for the seven-hour flight to Kona, Hawaii. "Didn't you have to file a flight plan with the FAA that includes all our names? Aren't you worried the police will be on the tarmac in Hawaii waiting for us when we land?"

Emerson handed Vernon a breadbasket and a tray of meats and cheeses from the cabin's refrigerator.

"This isn't my personal plane," Emerson said. "This is a private charter. I called the owner of the company, and he agreed to help us travel incognito. It took some time for him to get the plane to Bozeman, but it was worth the wait."

"Are you talking about Warren Buffett?" Riley asked.

Emerson selected a piece of cheese from the tray. "Do you know Warren?"

"No," Riley said. "Do you?"

"Of course," Emerson said. "He's a super nice guy. Goes to bed at night and gets up in the morning just like everyone else. Of course, then he hops into his solid gold helicopter and goes to work in a zeppelin made entirely from hundred-dollar bills."

Vernon nodded. "Well, personally, I don't much care for him what with his, quote unquote, 'relaxed island style' and that song 'Margaritaville' playing nonstop in every restaurant in Florida."

Riley rolled her eyes. "That would be Jimmy Buffett. Warren Buffett's the businessman."

Vernon paused. "Huh. No kidding? Does he have a relaxed island style?"

"Not that I know of," Emerson said.

"Okay. Great. Then I don't have a problem with him," Vernon said, and he made himself a sandwich.

Riley closed her eyes just for a moment, and when she opened them again, they were flying over the Pacific Ocean. Vernon and Wayan Bagus were sleeping. Emerson was on his laptop, browsing the Internet.

"So, how are you planning on finding Tin Man and Bart Young once we're in Hawaii?" Riley asked Emerson.

Emerson looked up from his laptop. "The director said he had a parallel program to Yellowstone in Hawaii. It has to be at one of the national parks—either Volcanoes National Park on the Big Island or Haleakala National Park on Maui."

"And you think it's on the Big Island?"

"Spiro's last words were 'Mauna Kea.' It's one of five volcanoes that formed the Big Island. The others are Mauna Loa, Kilauea, Hualalai, and Kohala."

"What's special about Mauna Kea?" Riley asked.

"It's the biggest mountain in Hawaii at more than thirteen thousand feet above sea level. Measured from the ocean floor, it's more than thirty-three thousand feet high. That's bigger than Mount Everest. It's so massive that it depresses the ocean floor beneath the island by six kilometers. One day, eons from now, Hawaii will likely collapse under its own weight."

"Is there a government installation on Mauna Kea?"

"Several," Emerson said. "There's a complex of huge telescopes and observatories on the summit originally built by the U.S. Air Force, although today they're run by an international consortium. The lower elevations of the mountain are home to the hundred-thousand-acre Pohakuloa Training Area, the largest military training ground in the Pacific."

"And that's where you think Tin Man and the director are headed?"

Emerson nodded. "Pohakuloa is extremely remote. Access is restricted by the army. It also has a small military airstrip called Bradshaw Army Airfield. It would be a perfect place to hide an R&D facility."

"I assume you have a plan for what to do if and when we find them," Riley said.

Emerson checked the flight computer. "One hour until we land in Kona."

"You don't have a plan, do you?"

"Of course," Emerson said. "Break into the army base. Steal the super-weapon. Save the world from destruction. Kiss the girl, and live happily ever after. As far as the details go, I thought we would just *wu wei* wing it."

"Would you like to elaborate on the 'kiss the girl' part?"

"It's traditional to get a kiss when you save the world," Emerson said.

Riley smiled. "Tell you what. You save the world, and I'll give you a kiss that will knock your socks off."

"I get a blister if I don't wear socks," Emerson said.

Riley reclined her seat and closed her eyes. She was too tired to roll them. "*Wu wei* wake me up when we land."

TWENTY

───✦───

RILEY STEPPED OFF THE PLANE ONTO THE private runway at Kona International Airport. She'd pictured lush tropical rain forests set against a backdrop of white sandy beaches and blue ocean. The ocean was a brilliant, shimmering blue, but that's where her mental image ended. The paved runway was set in the middle of a huge lava desert that looked a lot like a massive torn-up parking lot. The beach was composed mostly of jagged black rocks. In the distance, a dull haze of volcanic gasses hung over the mountains.

"It looks kind of desolate," Riley said. "I didn't expect to see so much lava."

"This is the dry side of the island. Kona gets very

little rain every year. The only green you'll see is what the resorts irrigate. The other side of the island is beyond wet. Around 150 inches of rain per year and nothing but waterfalls and rain forests."

"You know a lot about Hawaii," Riley said. "Have you spent a lot of time here?"

"My father owned a three-hundred-acre ranch in North Kohala. Vernon and I spent a month there every summer when we were kids. Since I now own the ranch, and we can't risk staying at a hotel without being recognized, I thought we'd stay on my property."

Vernon stepped off the plane with Wayan Bagus and stretched. He looked at Emerson. "Did you say we're going to the ranch?"

Riley thought she heard some hesitation in Vernon's voice. "What's wrong with the ranch?" she asked.

"Nothing," Vernon said. "You're going to love it. It's real pretty. It's only that some of the people in the community are a mite eccentric. By the way, you like cows, don't you?"

"Let me get this straight," Riley said. "Where we're heading, you and Emerson are the normal ones?"

Wayan Bagus took a deep breath and smiled. "I am happy to be back in the Pacific. It has been my experience that the only normal people are those you don't know very well. In any event, I am quite fond of cows. The ranch sounds very nice."

A car was waiting for them on the tarmac. The keys were in the car, and four flower leis were on the dash.

It was an hour's drive to the sleepy little town of Hawi in North Kohala. Riley headed out of the airport, turning left onto Route 19, the belt road that hugged the coastline and encircled the island. Twenty minutes of lava fields later, they passed the Four Seasons Resort Hualalai, a man-made green oasis of golf courses, luxury homes, and bungalow-style thousand-dollar-per-night hotel rooms.

Vernon groaned as they passed. "I don't suppose the ranch has a hot tub, all-day room service, and somebody to bring you ice cream sundaes while you sit by the pool?"

"I don't suppose so, unless there have been some upgrades since we were there last. It does, however, have a tidal pool and a fruit orchard that's open twenty-four hours a day," Emerson said. "Riley will probably be particularly interested in the tidal pool. She's a swimming enthusiast."

Riley cut her eyes to Emerson. "Your time will come."

"Are we almost there?" Wayan Bagus asked. "I would like to have some fruit and swim in the tidal pool and see the cows."

"Not far now," Emerson said.

Riley continued north on Route 19, passing a number of other four- and five-star resorts. As she drove, the lava fields were slowly replaced with scrubby brown grass, arid patches of dirt, and the occasional tree. She turned onto Akoni Pule Highway and passed through Kawaihae Harbor into North Kohala. As she rounded the northern tip of the island, the scrubby brown grass became progressively greener and more lush. Tall guinea grasses swayed in the trade winds.

"This is absolutely beautiful," Riley said as she drove through the little town of Hawi, with its art galleries, restaurants, and little shops.

Emerson pointed at an unmarked dirt road to their left. "It's about half a mile down this road."

Riley bumped down the road, avoiding potholes as best she could. After a couple minutes, the woods and brush opened up into open pastureland. A herd of Black Angus cows looked up in a lazy greeting as their car passed under a sign reading MYSTERIOSO RANCH.

"Oh man," Vernon said, "I hope we don't run into Alani."

"Alani was Vernon's first girlfriend," Emerson said to Riley. "She still lives in Hawi and works as an astronomer at the Keck Observatory. She and Vernon had a small difference of opinion, and Vernon hasn't been back here since."

"She ran me over with an ATV," Vernon said. "She's got anger issues."

"Is she one of the eccentrics?" Riley asked.

"She's *the* eccentric," Vernon said.

Emerson looked at Vernon. "In fairness to her, that was preceded by the Unspeakable Incident."

Vernon leaned over the front seat and clapped his hand over Emerson's mouth. "Hello. It's called 'the Unspeakable Incident' for a reason. Anyway, I'm sure she's forgotten all about it by now. It's been years, right?"

Wayan Bagus rolled down his window to get a better look at the cows. "It is written by the Sage that never by hatred is hatred conquered, but by readiness to love. That is the eternal law."

"I reckon the Sage might feel differently if he had a girlfriend who ran him over with an ATV," Vernon said.

Riley parked the car in front of a small one-story Bali-style house. It sat at the edge of a one-hundred-foot sea cliff with the island of Maui in the distance, separated by the thirty-mile-wide Alenuihaha Channel.

Everyone got out of the car and stood in awe at the sight and sound of the ten-foot swells crashing into the cliffs below.

"It's almost sunset," Emerson said to Vernon. "Why don't you and Wayan Bagus walk into town and buy us some food for dinner. I'll show Riley around the ranch."

Riley watched Vernon and Wayan Bagus disappear down the driveway.

"Is this the only house on the property?" she asked Emerson.

"The ranch manager has a house here, and there's a

larger house that my father preferred. This was built as a guesthouse, but I find the scale more comfortable than the main house. Vernon and Wayan Bagus won't be gone long, but we can do a little exploring. Would you like to walk the perimeter of the property or would you rather see the tidal pool?"

"The tidal pool."

"Good choice," Emerson said. "The tidal pool has always been my favorite spot."

They walked along the cliff for a quarter of a mile in silence before coming to a deep gulch. Seabirds flew overhead, trying to find their roosts before dark, and the occasional humpback whale breached just offshore.

"There's a trail to the bottom," Emerson said. "It's a little rough, but it's worth the effort. It's also the reason for the cowboy boots. That and the cows."

Riley followed Emerson down the muddy, slippery trail, and the pastures gave way to a lush rain forest that smelled of mango trees and freshly cut grass. Behind her, a hundred-foot waterfall plunged down a green cliff into a stream hidden by the thick jungle. In front of her, the jungle opened up onto a rocky beach with a large pool, fed half by the stream coming from the direction of the waterfall and half by the warmer ocean waves.

"We used to swim here every day," Emerson said.

Riley put her hand into the pool. It was a perfect temperature.

"Makes you want to jump in, doesn't it?" Emerson said.

"Are you going to jump in?"

"No," Emerson said. "Unfortunately there's no time. We want to head back before we lose the light. The gulch gets super dark at night because of the double canopy of vegetation."

Thank goodness, Riley thought. Plotting to catch Emerson in the altogether was one thing. Coed naked swimming was something entirely different. She wasn't ready for coed naked swimming. Her head was in other places. She had to save the world and make sure she didn't end up like Spiro.

"How are we going to find the National Park Service research facility without getting killed?" Riley asked.

"No problem. Mauna Kea is very different from Yellowstone," Emerson said. "Once you reach the higher elevations near the training area and the observatory, it's basically an arid, treeless moonscape."

"Is that good or bad?"

Emerson and Riley started back up the path out of the gulch.

"A little of both," Emerson said. "The good is that there's no place to hide an R&D facility, so it should be easier to find. The bad is that there's no place for us to hide either. I have a plan, but it requires a certain amount of diplomacy."

Riley looked at Emerson. Emerson was a lot of things, one of which was definitely not a diplomat.

"We're doomed," Riley said.

"My thoughts exactly," Emerson said. "That's why I wanted to talk with you first, without the others."

"This is going to be good," Riley said. "Let's hear it."

"We need an inside man. Someone who can get us close to the Pohakuloa Training Area without arousing suspicion."

"You have somebody in mind."

Emerson nodded. "Alani."

"Vernon's Alani? ATV Alani? Vernon's going to freak out."

"As long as we keep her away from motor vehicles, Vernon should be fine . . . more or less. She's an astronomer at the Keck Observatory. She can get us access to the Onizuka Center for International Astronomy."

"What's the Onizuka Center?" Riley asked.

"It's basically a hotel for the astronomers. There are usually around seventy people there at any one time, so we should be able to blend in to the background. As the crow flies, it sits about four miles up the mountain from Pohakuloa and about seven miles from the dozen or so telescopes at the summit."

They left the gulch and crossed the meadow that led to the guesthouse. Cows were making cow sounds in the nearby paddock, and the sound of the surf was soft and rhythmic.

It was all calming and wonderful if you could just keep your mind off the scary psycho people who wanted to kill everyone, Riley thought. And then there was the Vernon and Alani thing.

"When are you going to tell Vernon about Alani?" Riley asked Emerson.

"As soon as possible. It's going to be an awkward conversation, so I came up with plan B."

"What's plan B?" Riley asked.

"Send Vernon on an errand, invite Alani over to the house, and find someone tactful to babysit them after the reunion."

"Would this errand happen to involve Vernon getting our dinner tonight? And would the babysitter happen to be me?"

"Yes and yes."

Emerson opened the front door to the guesthouse and held it open for Riley.

"Boy, I wouldn't want to be in your shoes," he said. "I don't know how you get yourself into messes like this."

Riley shook her head. "I ask myself the same thing every day. When can I expect to be in the middle of this new mess?"

"Now."

TWENTY-ONE

⸺❧⸺

THE INTERIOR OF THE GUESTHOUSE WAS A
scaled-down Hawaiian version of Mysterioso Manor.
Four thousand square feet of over-the-top Bali-style
furniture and assorted island-themed bric-a-brac. An
eight-foot-tall tiki of a grimacing Ku, the Hawaiian god
of war, greeted them in the foyer.

A pretty young woman of mixed Hawaiian and Asian
ancestry was sitting in the living room reading a book. She
jumped off the couch, rushed over to them, and punched
Emerson in the shoulder.

"Emerson Knight, I haven't seen you in years!"

"It's been too long," Emerson said.

Alani nodded. "Agreed. I have to say I was shocked to

get your text asking me to meet with you." She turned to Riley. "You must be Riley Moon. Emerson said he was traveling with you. Aloha."

"Aloha," Riley said.

Alani cut her eyes back to Emerson. "You're in trouble again, aren't you?"

"I suppose it's a matter of perspective," Emerson said. "I prefer to think of it as an adventure. We're helping a friend find a stolen island, and we need help."

Alani shook her head. "That's what I thought. Trouble." She paused for a moment and her expression changed. "Wait just a friggin' second. You said 'we' need help. Who's the 'we'? Are you referring to Riley?"

The front door banged open and Vernon walked in, followed by Wayan Bagus.

"Food's here," Vernon said. "I got takeout from the Bamboo Restaurant."

Spotting Alani, he stopped in his tracks, his mouth dropped open, and the food bag slipped through his fingers and crashed onto the floor.

"Surprise!" Emerson said.

"*You!*" Alani said, glaring at Vernon, fists clenched. "*You!*"

"I asked Alani to stop by," Emerson said to Vernon. "I bet you're surprised, right?"

Vernon had a red scald rising out of his shirt collar, staining his cheeks. "I couldn't be any more surprised than if I woke up in the hospital with tire tracks on my back."

Wayan Bagus stepped forward.

"This is Wayan Bagus," Emerson said to Alani. "He's the friend we're helping."

Wayan Bagus tugged at Vernon's shirt. "Isn't this nice, Vernon? The universe has provided you with an opportunity to heal the roots of the past."

Vernon shushed the little monk. "Ixnay on the talk about the astpay," he whispered to Wayan Bagus.

Alani rolled her eyes. "Good grief. What did you tell him?"

Vernon held up his hands. "Nothing. Absolutely nothing."

"You didn't tell him about the Unspeakable Incident, did you? Because that wouldn't end well."

Riley looked at Vernon and Alani. "Okay, I have to know. What happened?"

Wayan Bagus bowed politely. "Vernon accidentally superglued himself to Alani."

Vernon gasped and put his hand over his heart. "That was a *confession*. What happened to the sanctity of the confessional?"

"I know nothing of a confessional. I know only truth," Wayan Bagus said.

"Vernon, you incredible nincompoop," Alani said. "You're not even Catholic, and he's a Buddhist monk, not a priest."

"It was dark. I thought it was lube," Vernon said. "It was an accident. Yeesh, it only took the paramedics twelve hours to get us separated. What's the big deal?"

"The big deal is I live in a town with a population of one thousand. It made the local newspaper. Everybody called me 'Doggie-Style Alani' for a year."

"Well, you ran me over with an ATV," Vernon said. "That wasn't exactly a pleasant experience."

"That was *also* an *accident*," Alani said.

"That wasn't no accident. You ran over me *twice!*" Vernon said. "You're a whackadoodle."

"I am *not* a whackadoodle. How dare *you* call *me* a whackadoodle!"

"This isn't going well," Riley said.

Wayan Bagus picked up the food bag from the floor. "I will take Vernon into the kitchen and allow him to eat his dessert first."

Vernon made a crazy motion with his finger going around in circles, pointed it at Alani, and followed Wayan Bagus out of the room.

"Vernon really didn't know it was glue," Emerson said. "He's always felt horrible about it."

"I know," Alani said. "It's just that seeing him so suddenly brought it all back."

"We really need your help," Emerson said to Alani. "I wouldn't ask if it wasn't important. Lives are at stake, including ours."

"You don't even have to ask. I'm in. You guys are like family to me, even the jackass in the next room who's missing most of his eyebrows. I don't even want to ask. Besides, I haven't had a good adventure since you stopped coming to Kohala. What do you need?"

"A room at the Onizuka with a view down the mountain, and a telescope capable of spying on the runway at Bradshaw Army Airfield."

"Do you think we beat Tin Man and the director to Hawaii?" Riley asked Emerson.

Emerson nodded. "I checked the FAA website. There haven't been any inbound flights landing at Bradshaw in the past forty-eight hours. Of course, they might not have filed a flight plan."

"The entire base has been buried in the inversion layer under thick cloud cover for the past three days," Alani said. "Visibility is zero and, as far as I know, there haven't been any inbound or outbound flights. This is an entirely different weather system from Kona."

"Perfect. All we have to do is wait for the bad guys to arrive and use our telescope to track them to their secret lair, all from the safety of our first-class accommodations at the Onizuka."

"It's a moldy, cramped room with four bunk beds and the combined stench of a thousand dirty, tired scientists," Alani said.

"Then we'll do it from the safety of our barely-third-class accommodations," Emerson said. "The plan is still sound, even if it doesn't smell the best."

Riley raised her hand. "Except for one small detail. What do you intend to do after you find out where they've taken the Penning trap?"

"'Penning trap'?" Alani asked.

"I'll explain it all later," Emerson said. "It's complicated and barely believable."

"About the plan," Riley said.

Emerson rocked back on his heels. "It's a bit fluid at the moment."

Riley narrowed her eyes. "Fluid?"

"Trust me. What could possibly go wrong?"

One hour later, Alani had organized a three-day stay for all of them at Onizuka, and Riley had checked the weather report for Pohakuloa. The cloud cover was expected to dissipate by the next morning and the airfield would be open for business. Vernon and Wayan Bagus were eating in another room. Emerson had disappeared.

Riley looked up from her iPad. "Where's Emerson?" she asked Alani.

"He went into the master bedroom to pack supplies and meditate. He said he needed some private time to come up with an idea that didn't involve Macaulay Culkin."

Riley shook her head. "He's not normal."

Alani smiled. "You like him, don't you? I thought I sensed a spark between the two of you."

"He's the most irritating person I've ever met."

"And you like him."

"He is constantly getting me into trouble. Did I mention he got me fired from my last job?"

"And you like him."

Riley sighed. "Yes. Maybe. I don't know. He has his moments. It's just that some of those moments make me want to punch him in the face. What about you? Did you and Emerson ever have a thing?"

"No. We were always just friends. I had a thing for Vernon. He has his moments too."

Riley checked her watch. "We should be moving on. I'm going to see if I can help Emerson pack."

She left the living room and walked down the short hall to the master bedroom. The door was ajar and she could hear Emerson pacing. She pushed the door open, stepped into the room, and came face-to-face with Vernon in the buff.

"Crap on a cracker," she said, clapping her hands over her eyes. "What are you doing in here?"

"I was using Em's shower. It's better than the one in the guest room."

Riley peeked at him from between two fingers. "Okay, I guess I get that, but why are you still naked, standing in the middle of the room, flapping your arms?"

"I like to air-dry. It's real refreshing and it keeps my skin all silky smooth. I got a butt like a baby. I guess you already noticed that."

"I didn't notice anything!"

Riley spun around and fled the room.

Alani and Wayan Bagus were in the living room when Riley rushed in.

"Are you okay?" Alani asked Riley. "Your face is flushed."

"I just saw Vernon naked."

Vernon followed Riley into the room. He was still damp and he was wearing a towel. "Yep, she saw my doodles and my dongle in all their glory," he said.

Alani gave a bark of laughter. "Your dongle isn't that glorious. I've seen it, along with half the women on this island. You've got a teeny wienie."

Not that Riley had seen hundreds of dongles but from what she'd just seen of Vernon he looked pretty darn good from head to toe, dongle included.

Emerson walked into the room. "What's going on?"

"Riley saw Vernon naked," Wayan Bagus said. "Furthermore, Alani thinks Vernon has a teeny wienie."

"It was an accident," Riley said. "I thought Emerson was in the bedroom."

"I've heard about this on HBO," Vernon said. "It's a fetish called CFNM, or Clothed Female Nude Male. Apparently some women just like to look at as many wieners as they can. You're probably next, Little Buddy."

Wayan Bagus shook his head and looked disapprovingly at Riley. "Not good. Not good at all."

"Criminy," Riley said, "I don't want to see *everyone's* wiener! I only wanted to see *Emerson*."

Emerson glanced down at himself. "And who could blame her."

TWENTY-TWO

B Y FIVE A.M., RILEY, EMERSON, VERNON, WAYAN Bagus, and Alani were loaded into the ranch SUV and passing through the cowboy town of Waimea on their way to the Mauna Kea summit.

"The turnoff to Saddle Road is just ahead," Alani said. "It's about twenty-five miles from there to the Pohakuloa Training Area and another ten miles from there to the Mauna Kea Access Road and the Onizuka Center."

Riley wound her way up the mountain road in the darkness and felt her ears pop. "How high are we going?" she asked Alani.

"Waimea is at twenty-six hundred feet elevation. Pohakuloa is about nine thousand feet. The summit is almost at fourteen thousand feet. It's usually below freezing there through the night and, in winter, it's not uncommon to have snow."

By five-thirty A.M., the thick cloud cover was right above them.

"It's called an inversion layer," Emerson said. "The temperature difference keeps a dense cloud over Mauna Kea at this elevation most of the time."

Riley drove into the cloud. Even with the high beams, it was almost impossible to see more than a foot or two in front of the car.

"This is kind of spooky," she said as the car passed a sign reading POHAKULOA TRAINING AREA. Riley slowed and looked off to the side of the road. The visibility was so bad she couldn't see a single building, let alone the army airfield.

"There's no way a plane could land in this soup," Riley said. "Especially if you're carrying cargo that could explode if you jostled it the wrong way."

"That's what I'm counting on," Emerson said. "There's an eight-hour window tomorrow when the sky will be clear. I'm betting our friends try to land with the Penning trap during that window."

Five minutes later, the car popped through the clouds, and the impenetrable white ceiling turned into an impenetrable white floor. Riley looked up into the predawn sky. "Wow. I've never seen so many stars."

Alani smiled. "Mauna Kea is the world's largest observatory for optical, infrared, and submillimeter astronomy for a reason. The atmospheric conditions at the summit are near perfect."

A couple minutes later, Riley turned on to the Summit Access Road and climbed steadily until reaching the Onizuka Center, where the paved road ended.

"There's a very steep five-mile-long gravel road to the summit from here," Alani said. "It requires a four-wheel drive."

The sun was just beginning to peek above the horizon, and they all got out of the car. The air was noticeably thinner, and even walking up the small hill to the center was a workout. Only Wayan Bagus and Emerson seemed unaffected.

Vernon put his hands on his knees. "It's kind of hard to breathe proper up in this here high country," Vernon said.

"We all need to be alert for signs of altitude sickness," Emerson said. "We haven't had time to acclimate. Mauna Kea is probably the only place in the world where you can go from sea level to fourteen thousand feet in less than two hours."

Alani led them to their dormitory. "The air is even thinner at the summit. Most of the observatories make the scientists spend a night or two at the center before using the telescopes."

"Why?" Riley asked.

"There's forty percent less oxygen up at the top than at sea level, and it can seriously mess with everything from your vision to your mental condition."

"Interesting," Vernon said. "Suppose a person worked where she was chronically deprived of oxygen. Would that cause a perfectly normal person to go all loopy and run over her boyfriend with a motor vehicle?"

Alani cut her eyes to Vernon. "You're a chronic jackass."

Vernon watched Alani walk inside the dormitory. "Okay, so I might be a chronic jackass, but that's no reason not to like me. Some people even think I'm a *fun* jackass."

Wayan Bagus put his hand on Vernon's shoulder. "It is written by the Sage that you, yourself, as much as anybody in the entire universe, deserve your love and affection."

"Thanks, Little Buddy," Vernon said. "Right back at you."

Alani returned with a key and handed it to Emerson. "You're all set. I have to get to work at the observatory. Call me on my cell if you need anything."

Alani had given them an accurate description of the dormitory room. It was a small, serviceable room with two sets of bunk beds and a distant view of the Bradshaw Army Airfield. A telescope had been placed on a tripod next to the window.

Wayan Bagus looked around the room and out the

window. The sun was up and the clouds had disappeared, revealing a breathtaking view of South Kohala all the way to the Pacific Ocean.

"This is very nice," Wayan Bagus said. "I've never been on a stakeout. I'm having such a good time saving the world that I almost don't care if we find my stolen island."

"We'll find it," Emerson said, peering through the telescope and adjusting it to focus on the runway.

"Now what?" Riley asked.

"We wait," Emerson said.

Over the next several hours, a steady stream of airplanes landed on the airstrip, but none were carrying cargo or any passengers wearing park ranger uniforms.

Vernon groaned and tilted his head back. "Here's something they don't tell you about stakeouts. They're really, really boring."

"It's about to get really, really exciting," Emerson said, turning the telescope over to Riley.

Riley focused on a medium-size jet taxiing down the runway. It had two crossed sabers and a number one above them painted on the side of the plane.

"For a secret society, they're not very good at keeping themselves under the radar," Riley said.

"Pure arrogance," Emerson said. "They've been an untouchable secret quasi-military unit for the past hundred years and don't think anybody can take them out."

"What chance do we have then?" Vernon asked.

Emerson watched the plane pull up to the terminal and power down. "If we can expose the secret they're protecting, they'll no longer be useful and will become more of a liability than an asset."

"They're crazy," Riley said. "If we expose them, they'll destroy Yellowstone and who knows what else. You heard Spiro. He said we'd find Armageddon waiting for us in Hawaii. I don't know what that means, but it sounds really bad."

Emerson focused the telescope on the plane's door. "Then we'll just have to steal the super-weapon they're creating here on Hawaii, find a way to neutralize Tin Man, and then expose the secret to the world."

"Yeah, that sounds like a walk in the park. We can do that, no problemo," Riley said. "And then we can end world hunger by growing tomatoes on the moon."

The plane's door opened, and Emerson watched as the pilots walked down the stairs and waited for the passengers to disembark.

"They're coming out now," Emerson said. "It's Tin Man and Bart Young. An SUV is driving onto the tarmac to meet them. And now two Rough Riders wearing khaki uniforms and campaign hats are unloading something from the cargo storage into the SUV."

"Is it the Penning trap?" Riley asked.

"It's a crate, but it's the right size to contain the Penning trap."

Emerson watched as Tin Man and Bart Young climbed into the SUV with the two soldiers. They drove through the airfield's gate and onto Saddle Road. After a quarter mile, the SUV turned left onto a rough Jeep trail and headed into the barren wasteland.

"Where are they going?" Riley asked. "The army base is in the other direction. There's nothing where they're heading but lava desert."

Emerson watched them drive for a couple more minutes in silence. "Well, that's interesting."

"You found their base?"

Emerson looked up from the telescope and turned to face Riley. "Not exactly. It turns out there is someplace to hide. They've disappeared."

Riley looked through the telescope. There was still a cloud of dust where the SUV had passed, but no SUV. She scanned the surrounding area. Nothing but miles and miles of desert without a structure in sight.

"That's impossible," she said.

"It's improbable," Emerson said. "Clearly it's possible, because it happened."

"Maybe that SUV is with Little Buddy's island," Vernon said. "Like they both got sucked into one of them black holes and got spit out someplace else."

Emerson returned to the telescope. "What do you think happened to the SUV?" he asked Riley.

Riley allowed herself a grimace. "I've got nothing."

"So what are we going to do now?" Vernon asked. "Do we go out to look for the black hole?"

Emerson lay down on one of the bunk beds. "Nothing. We do nothing. The universe will provide the answer."

"We can't sit around in this hotel room forever *wu wei* waiting on the universe," Riley said. "We're sort of in a time crunch. Tin Man plans to destroy Sour Creek Dome in less than a week if we don't either get ourselves killed or stop him first."

Emerson closed his eyes. "We don't have to sit around forever. Just until three P.M."

"Why three P.M.?"

Emerson smiled. "The clouds may drop down titles and estates, and wealth may seek us but wisdom must be sought."

Riley rolled her eyes. "*Wu wei* whatever."

Riley woke from a sound sleep at two-thirty P.M. to the sound of her cellphone alarm. She hadn't intended to take a nap, but she'd been up since four in the morning and was exhausted. Vernon was kneeling next to a snoring Wayan Bagus with a can of shaving cream he'd appropriated from the dormitory bathroom in one hand and a feather in the other. Emerson was looking out the window and down the mountain.

Vernon held his index finger up to his lips, grinned at

Riley, and pointed at Wayan Bagus's hand. It was filled with a giant glob of shaving cream.

"Little Buddy, wakey-wakey," he whispered, tickling the monk's cheek with the feather.

Wayan Bagus snorted and turned his face from side to side. "Spiders, spiders," he mumbled.

"Get those spiders," Vernon whispered.

Without ever opening his eyes, Wayan Bagus lifted his shaving-cream-filled hand and smacked Vernon in the back of the head.

"Son of a bitch," Vernon said. He wiped the shaving cream off his head and went to the bathroom to clean up.

Riley crossed the small room and stood behind Emerson. "What are you looking at?"

Emerson pointed down the mountain toward Pohakuloa. The clouds had returned, and white tendrils of fog were creeping around the airfield and buildings at the army base.

"I'm looking at the fog," Emerson said. "I'm waiting for the universe to solve our problems. Another half hour and the entire area will be completely socked in. We could be right on top of Tin Man and he wouldn't see us."

Riley watched the clouds as they continued to roll in. "We also won't be able to see *him*. How did you know the universe would send you fog at precisely three P.M.?"

Emerson held up his iPad. "The universe works in mysterious ways. In this case, the universe sent me a

Weather Channel app. Besides, the clouds always come back in the afternoon."

Thirty minutes later, Emerson, Riley, Vernon, and Wayan Bagus were standing outside the Onizuka Center. Thick clouds covered the lower elevations of the mountain, and the temperature was noticeably cooler.

Vernon shifted from foot to foot. "What the heck are we doing out here?"

"Waiting for our transportation," Emerson said.

"Is it being provided by the universe?" Riley asked.

"In a manner of speaking," Emerson said.

Alani pulled up to the front of the center in a six-person Polaris ATV. "Ready to go?" she asked.

"I'm ready to go *nowhere* with you behind the wheel of this thing," Vernon said. "I'd rather walk."

"Good idea," Alani said. "You go wandering around in the zero-visibility fog. I'll follow you in the ATV. I'm sure you'll be perfectly safe. I'm an excellent driver. Only had one accident."

"Emerson, did you hear that? Devil Woman threatened me," Vernon said. "She's probably planning on driving us all over a cliff."

"There aren't any cliffs here," Alani said. "You're safe . . . for now."

"Okay then," Vernon said, getting into the back seat next to Wayan Bagus, "but I'm keeping my eye on you."

Alani drove into the cloud cover down the access road to Saddle Road and toward Pohakuloa.

"I wouldn't think it was possible, but it's even more dense than it was this morning," Riley said.

Emerson pointed to an unimproved Jeep trail, barely visible through the fog, off to the right side of the road. "Turn there."

Alani turned onto the gravelly path and followed the tire tracks as best she could.

"We need to stay on the trail," she said. "We're officially trespassing on the army training area, and there's unexploded ordnance left over from past military exercises all over the place. As long as we stay on the trail we're safe."

"Well, I don't feel safe," Vernon said. "I feel like I'm a character in some horror movie. You know, the kind of dumbass who's being chased by a serial killer and decides to hide in a graveyard or an abandoned warehouse or some seriously scary fog."

"I am certain that this is perfectly normal fog," Emerson said. "Except for the unexploded artillery and top-secret government research facility guarded by a sociopathic axe murderer. But other than that, it's a perfectly normal fog."

"It would be easier to stay on the trail if someone walked in front of me," Alani said.

Emerson got out of the ATV and picked his way over the disturbed gravel with the ATV bumping along behind him, making slow progress. After ten minutes of walking he held his hand up as a signal that they should stop.

"We should park the Polaris and go on foot from here

on," Emerson said. "We're getting close to where the SUV disappeared, and I don't want to risk them hearing the sound of a motor approaching."

Riley looked around. She couldn't see more than a couple feet in front of her face.

"This cloud cover is completely disorienting," she said. "If someone accidentally wanders off the trail they'll never find their way back."

"I have that all worked out," Emerson said. He reached into his daypack and fished around. "When I was packing our gear at the ranch, I had the foresight to pack whistles for each of us. Wayan will stay with the ATV while the rest of us snoop around. If we get separated or can't find the Polaris in the fog, all we have to do is blow our whistle."

Emerson pulled from his pack five long metal tubes with pistons on one end and mouthpieces on the other.

"Here you go," he said, handing everyone a whistle.

Riley's eyebrows went halfway up her forehead. "For real? It's a slide whistle. What are we supposed to do with these?"

"They're multifunctional," Emerson said. "Blow once if you're lost. Twice if you're in danger. You can also use it to add some drama to the otherwise ordinarily mundane actions of sitting down, getting up, or turning the page of a book. The possibilities are endless."

Alani cut the engine on the ATV and tried her whistle. *Weeeoop!*

Everyone smiled.

"It's a slipping on a banana peel whistle," Vernon said. "I always wanted one of these." *Weeeoop! Weeeoop!*

"No more whistling," Emerson said. "We don't want the bad guys to hear us." He handed his iPad over to Wayan Bagus. "I downloaded *Rocky III* for you. Vernon said you needed to know about manly hugging. We should be back in no more than three hours. I don't want to be stuck here overnight."

TWENTY-THREE

RILEY TOOK POINT FOLLOWING THE TRAIL IN the fog. Emerson, Vernon, and Alani walked close behind her.

"We've been walking forever," Vernon said. "This is like the road to nowhere."

"Unfortunately that's a totally accurate description," Riley said. "We've come to the end of the tracks. There's no more road. And there's also no more anything, including the missing Jeep."

Everyone looked around. Riley was right. No more road. No more tracks. No Jeep.

"If it wasn't for my cool new whistle I'd say this trip was a big waste," Vernon said. "It's cold, it's spooky, and I can't see where I'm going. I near broke my foot a minute ago on that stupid pipe sticking out of the ground."

"I didn't see a pipe," Riley said. "Where was it?"

Vernon retraced his steps and pointed down at the ground. "It's just some old waypoint left over by a surveyor."

Emerson got down on his hands and knees to examine the pipe. "It's not a surveying monument."

"How do you know?" Alani asked.

"Because heat doesn't come out of a survey pipe. This is an exhaust."

Riley put her ear to the pipe. "It sounds like there's a generator down there."

"That would explain the need for an exhaust pipe," Emerson said. He turned to Alani. "Are there any caves in the area?"

"In this area? None that I know about. There's a big one on the eastern side of the mountain. It's called the Paauhau Civil Defense Cave, but it's really more of a lava tube."

"What's a lava tube?" Riley asked.

"It's a conduit formed by lava flowing beneath the surface of already cooled and hardened magma," Alani said. "Once the volcano is no longer active and the lava's no longer flowing, what's left is a cavelike channel with solid rock walls."

"Do you think there could be a lava tube under us?" Riley asked. "One that was big enough to hide an R&D lab?"

235

Alani went still for a couple beats. "I suppose it's possible. Some are up to fifty feet wide and can be very long. The Kazumura Cave in Kilauea, the active volcano in the southern part of the island, is almost forty-one miles long and the longest known lava tube in the world. There's also one on Mauna Loa, the mountain just to the south of this one, that runs all the way from the summit to the Pacific Ocean thirty-one miles away, but there's no record of anything like that on Mauna Kea."

Emerson looked at the pipe sticking out of the ground. "It all makes sense."

"Oh boy," Riley said. "Here we go."

"I'm listening," Alani said.

"A hollowed-out volcano is every super-villain's dream lair. It's all about location, location, location."

Riley looked around. "If you're right, the entrance has to be close."

"Agreed," Emerson said. "We just need a bit of luck to find it."

Everyone froze at the sound of a large, heavy door rolling open.

"It sounds like it's at the bottom of this hill," Riley whispered.

Footsteps scuffed somewhere out in the fog, and a male voice carried up to Riley, Emerson, Alani, and Vernon.

"Every time the motion detectors go off they send us out here," the man said. "I don't know what we're supposed to find in this fog."

"It's probably just the stupid feral goats," a second voice said. "It's always the goats."

"Okay, you found the entrance," Riley whispered. "You got your lucky break. Now let's get out of here before they change their minds and come looking for us."

"That would be ignoring our unique opportunity," Emerson said. "An opportunity like this doesn't come up every day."

"Do you mean an opportunity to get killed? You get those opportunities all the time."

"You're absolutely right," Emerson said to Riley. "When presented with an interesting opportunity, you have a responsibility to the universe to acknowledge it."

Riley stared at Emerson. "I didn't say anything remotely like that."

"Perhaps I paraphrased."

"Perhaps you live in fantasyland."

Emerson looked at Vernon. "How's your *unagi* today?"

Vernon grinned. "I'm just chock-full of it. Then again, who needs *unagi* when you've got a big-ass gun." He pulled his lucky Glock from his jacket. "Even put bullets back in it when Little Buddy wasn't looking."

"You see," Emerson said. "It's a sign. We have luck, an interesting situation, *unagi,* and a big gun. It would actually be grossly negligent of us not to overpower the guards and infiltrate the top-secret hollowed-out volcano."

Riley nodded. "I'm sure I'll regret it, but I'm in."

"Let's do it," Alani said. "Mauna Kea is sacred ground

to Hawaiians, and I don't like what's going on here on my mountain."

"I'm all about the lair," Vernon said.

Emerson, Riley, Vernon, and Alani carefully walked in the direction of the voices. As they got closer, the faint outlines of the men took shape. Two sentries were standing just outside a gaping hole in the hillside. They were smoking, and they'd laid their rifles against a rock wall.

"Howdy," Vernon said, pointing his gun at the guards. Both men jumped.

"What the—" the first guard said.

"Oh crap," the second one said.

"We're from Human Resources," Vernon said, positioning himself between the guards and their guns. "A couple of feral goats called and complained about the secondhand smoke. This is a nonsmoking mountain."

Alani collected the rifles and walked into the dimly lit tunnel that appeared to be about fifty feet in diameter.

"This is definitely a lava tube," she said.

The rolling metal door was large enough for a truck to pass through. It was half closed and covered with jagged pieces of cinder. When the door was completely closed it would be perfectly camouflaged in the lava desert.

"This explains the disappearing SUV," Emerson said. "I wouldn't have noticed the entrance if I'd walked right past it."

"What are we going to do with these two?" Alani said, motioning toward the guards.

"I'm prepared for all events," Emerson said. "I have zip ties in my pack. We'll truss them up, and you and Vernon can stay behind to watch them. Riley and I will do a little snooping. We'll be back in no more than an hour."

Riley took one of the guards' rifles from Alani. She checked the clip for ammo and shouldered the gun.

"What about you?" Alani asked Emerson. "Do you want the other rifle? Do you know how to use it?"

"Sure," Emerson said. "I read about it in a book." He pointed at the barrel. "This is the end where projectiles exit, right?"

"Maybe Riley should be in charge of firearms," Alani said.

"Emerson don't need a gun," Vernon said. "He can do all kinds of lethal stuff. You should see him do the Vulcan nerve pinch."

"There's no such thing," Alani said. "That was made up for *Star Trek*."

"Excuse me, but that is a total load of baloney," Vernon said. "I've seen him do it. We were in this fight at the Pig 'n' Whistle bar one time, and I saw him do the pinch. You probably don't believe in Bigfoot either."

Alani did a gigantic eye roll. "You are so *gullible*," she said to Vernon.

"Yeah and you are so—"

"So what?" Alani asked.

"I don't know. Actually, you're kind of pretty."

"Oh jeez!" Alani said.

"Anybody got a Snickers?" Vernon said. "I really need a Snickers."

Emerson pulled a roll of antacids out of his pack. "This is all I've got," he said.

"Good enough," Vernon said. "Hand them over."

"We're losing time," Riley said. "Let's get this show on the road."

TWENTY-FOUR

───✺───

E MERSON AND RILEY WALKED INTO THE TUBE. Almost immediately they came to a large diesel generator that hummed and buzzed, providing power to the flickering electric lights lining the slick black rock walls.

"I wouldn't have thought it was possible, but this is even spookier than the fog," Riley said.

"I rather like it," Emerson said.

The tunnel opened up into a large man-made cavern with a poured cement floor. The SUV was in the corner of the room, parked next to several Ford F-150 pickups, a bunch of ATVs, some heavy machinery, and a military transport like the one at Sour Creek Dome.

Riley inspected the SUV. "Looks like we found the bad guys' secret hollowed-out volcano parking lot. But where are the bad guys?"

Emerson pointed to the other side of the cavern. "The lava tube continues that way."

Riley crossed the cavern with Emerson and peered into the adjacent tunnel. There was a heavy-looking steel double door blocking their path and muffled voices on the other side. She put her ear to the door.

"It sounds like someone is crying and calling for help," Riley said.

Emerson carefully opened the door and peeked inside. "It's a bunch of jail cells lining one side of the lava tube. There's a woman in one. I don't see any sign of Tin Man or the guards."

"If we're caught, there's nowhere to run. We're trapped in this tunnel," Riley said. "We'll end up in one of those cells."

Emerson pushed the door open wide enough for them to squeeze through and closed it quietly behind them. The woman in the cell was standing at the bars and sobbing hysterically.

"Are you okay?" Riley asked.

The woman scrambled away from them into a corner of the cell.

Riley stepped closer. "I'm Riley and this is Emerson. Maybe we can help you."

The woman cautiously approached the bars. "I'm Margo Tanner. We were hiking in Kilauea and got lost. We ended up spending the night in a cave. The park rangers who found us told us we were trespassing in a restricted area."

"Did you see anything unusual?"

"They were drilling for oil," Margo said. "I didn't even know there was oil under Hawaii."

Emerson and Riley exchanged glances. "We have to get her out of there," Riley said. "I'd shoot the lock, but the gunshot would definitely be heard."

Margo pointed at the wall on the opposite side of the tunnel. "There's an electrical panel over there that locks and unlocks the doors."

Emerson pushed the button marked CELL THREE. There was an audible click, and the door popped open. The woman rushed out and hugged Riley.

Emerson looked around the room at the other cells. They were empty.

"You said '*We* were hiking.' Is there somebody else here too?"

Margo nodded. "His name is Richard. I don't really know him. We met on the hiking trail and were walking together when we got lost." She pointed down the tunnel. "About half an hour ago some scary military-looking guy with a close-shaved head and a three-day-old beard came and dragged him away. I thought I was next when you two came in."

Riley grimaced. "Tin Man."

"You're in a lava tube underneath Mauna Kea," Emerson said to the woman. "There's a bunch of ATVs in the next room. Take one and follow the tube about a half mile to the exit. We have some friends there, and they'll help you get back to the main road."

Margo looked nervously in the direction Tin Man had taken Richard. "What about my friend?"

"We'll try to find him," Riley said. "You just get out of here, and don't tell anybody about what you saw. You can't trust anybody."

Margo ran down the tube, and Riley turned to Emerson. "What do you suppose Tin Man did with the other hiker?"

"He didn't take him to Disneyland," Emerson said. "You stay here. I'm going to go further down the tube and look for him."

"We'll both look for him. I don't want you to have to rely on that pathetic Vulcan nerve pinch if you run into the bad guys."

They walked past the cells and down the tunnel for another hundred yards before it opened up into a large, clean, well-lit room set up similarly to the laboratory in Yellowstone, minus the equipment for processing the magma.

Riley and Emerson paused, plastered themselves against the side of the dark lava tube, and looked inside. A large Penning trap sat in the middle of the room, surrounded by four smaller portable traps. Tin Man and Bart Young were there, as well as a dozen soldiers wearing Rough Rider uniforms. They were all standing around watching a glass cage in the southwest corner.

A small Asian woman, dressed entirely in black, was manning a control booth in front of the cage. She had a slim, athletic build and long black hair, and she was wearing large, round glasses with black frames.

A middle-aged man with a bloody lip and a bruised eye stood in the center of the cage, shackled to the floor, like a zoo animal.

"That must be the hiker," Riley whispered.

Bart Young was fixated on the enclosure. "Berta, are you certain we're safe out here?" he asked the Asian woman.

"Absolutely. I can't say the same for him," Berta said, gesturing toward the man in the glass cage.

"How does it work?" the director asked.

"The enclosure was built based on the same principles behind the Penning trap. There's a magnetic field surrounding it and acting as a barrier between what's on the inside and what's on the outside. Everything outside the case is safe, and the glass is also protected. You will soon see what happens inside the case."

Tin Man was staring at Richard. "And if the magnetic field fails?"

"We'll all be destroyed. Possibly the whole mountain will be destroyed. It's hard to say how far it would progress before reaching a state of equilibrium. That's why we need to conduct more field experiments before we load it into the weapon. I don't want a repeat of the fiasco in Samoa."

"In a way, I'm jealous of him," Tin Man said, motioning toward the man in the cage. "This is a historic moment. No one in the history of the world has ever died this way. It's like being the first person to walk on the moon."

"Yes, yes, yes," Bart Young said. "Enough talking. Let's see the demonstration."

"We need to do something," Riley whispered to Emerson.

"You would need to take out almost everyone in the room," Emerson said. "You're not the only one with a weapon. And the lady in black has the ultimate weapon."

"I'm turning on the magnetic field now," Berta said, pushing a button on the controls in front of her.

There was a low hum from the direction of the cage, and the man inside struggled against his chains.

"Is he in pain?" the director asked.

"No. Just scared," Berta said. "The magnetic field is harmless to him. Its only purpose is to contain the strange matter."

Emerson did an audible intake of air. "They're not using the Penning trap to contain plasma. They're using it to contain strange matter."

"What's strange matter?" Riley whispered.

"Do you remember in Yellowstone I said there were four types of ordinary matter—solids, liquids, gasses, and plasmas?"

"Sure."

"Well, there are other theoretical forms of matter, called exotic matter. Forms that exist in the far reaches of space, but not on earth. At least, nobody thought they existed on earth."

"Like what?"

"All the matter on earth is what physicists call baryonic, which is just a fancy way to say that things are made up of protons and neutrons. The number of protons and neutrons in an atom determine whether something is made of helium or carbon or uranium or some other element in the periodic table. Strange matter is, in very basic terms, stuff that's not made up of protons and neutrons, because all the protons and neutrons have been squished superhumanly hard into a mass of disorganized basic particles called quarks. Under the right conditions, it could be, to put it mildly, dangerous."

Riley lowered the rifle and watched as Berta pressed another button. A robotic arm dropped a small canister into the enclosure. It shattered on the floor next to Richard, revealing a tiny dollop of what looked like a shimmering, rainbow-colored bit of liquid mercury. The cement floor collapsed and was consumed by the shimmering little blob. Everything went quickly after that. The chains were compressed and sucked into the tiny ball, and Richard followed. He screamed in pain and horror and then he was gone. Ten seconds later, the little ball stopped shimmering, turned a gray color, and melted away into a flat mass. All that was left of the little glass room was the enclosure itself protected by the invisible magnetic field.

"What the heck just happened?" Riley asked Emerson.

No response. Emerson was gone. He was standing in the center of the room by the Penning traps. He waved at Riley and held his breath as he unplugged one of the four portable traps from a wall outlet. The machine switched to battery power. Emerson picked it up and walked back over to her, cradling the trap in his arms.

Everyone else in the room was gobsmacked, stupidly staring open-mouthed at the glass enclosure. No one seemed to notice Emerson skulking away with a Penning trap.

"Crap on a cracker," Riley whispered to Emerson. "What . . . did . . . you . . . do?"

"I know. I clouded their minds. Great idea, right?"

"Wrong. You're holding enough strange matter to probably destroy the entire island of Hawaii."

"Or . . . I just got the evidence we need to put the bad guys out of business."

"Okay," Riley said. "Let's very quietly leave with the evidence."

Tin Man was the first to turn away from the glass enclosure and the first to see Emerson and Riley. He snatched a rifle from one of the soldiers and fired off a shot.

The director knocked the gun out of Tin Man's hands. "You fool. They've got one of the traps. If you hit it, we're all dead."

"Run!" Riley said to Emerson. "Run fast."

"Go after them," the director ordered. "Don't let them get away, but be careful of the trap."

Tin Man and a handful of Rough Riders ran toward the tunnel. Riley fired off a round and the soldiers scattered, taking cover behind whatever they could find.

"I'll buy you some time," Riley said to Emerson. "That Penning trap probably weighs at least fifty pounds, and it will slow you down."

Emerson looked at Riley and shook his head. "I'm not leaving you."

Riley took aim at where Tin Man was hiding. "Don't worry. I'll be right behind you. I'm just going to buy you a thirty-second head start. Go."

Emerson ran in the direction of the jail cells, and Riley fired a couple more shots into the laboratory room.

"There's no escape," Bart Young shouted. "You're just delaying the inevitable."

Riley backed into the tunnel, took a final shot, turned, and sprinted through the passageway. She reached the metal double door and heard footsteps behind her. Tin Man and two guards were no more than fifty feet away at the other end of the line of cells.

Tin Man raised his gun and pointed it in Riley's direction. She ran through the metal door, slammed it shut, and heard the bullets ricochet off the door on the other side.

Emerson was waiting for her in the back seat of an ATV. The Penning trap was sitting next to him.

"They're going to be in a lot of trouble with the director," Emerson said. "They aren't supposed to be shooting at the Penning trap."

Riley jammed her rifle through the handles of the double door, barricading Tin Man on the other side. She jumped into the driver's seat, turned the key in the ignition, and raced down the tunnel in the direction of the exit.

"It's only a matter of time before they break through," she said. "Hang on to the Penning trap."

Riley could see the light from the tunnel's entrance in front of her, and she could hear Emerson behind her. He was blowing on the slide whistle, trying to alert Vernon and Alani.

Riley burst out of the tunnel entrance and into the fog, braking hard and coming to a sudden stop in front of Vernon and Alani.

"Get in," Riley said. "We don't have much time."

Vernon and Alani piled into the ATV, Riley floore
the gas pedal, and they took off along the Jeep trail, bac
toward Wayan Bagus.

"What is that thing?" Vernon asked, pointing at th
Penning trap.

"A doomsday machine filled with strange matter," Rile
said.

Vernon eyed the trap. "Is it dangerous?"

Alani rolled her eyes. "What do you think, dumb
dumb? It's a doomsday machine."

"It contains some thick liquidy substance that sucked ;
guy right into itself, like some little black hole," Riley said

Emerson patted the Penning trap. "Not exactly. Th
simplest analogy is that it ate him."

"No kidding? Like the Blob," Vernon said.

"Under the right conditions, strange matter will attract
normal matter and convert it into strange matter. That's
what happened to the man in the cave. The strange matter
came in contact with the floor and converted it into more
strange matter and that came in contact with the man
and converted him into a little superdense ball of strange
matter too."

"So it's a chain reaction," Riley said. "Little by little,
everything gets converted."

Emerson held his hand over the trap to stabilize it as
they bumped along the road. "Yes and no. Like I said,
there are certain conditions that must be met. The first

is that the strange matter has to be more stable than the normal matter."

"And the second?"

"It has to be negatively charged," Emerson said. "That's also why it can be contained safely within a magnetic field."

Riley scanned the road ahead for Wayan Bagus. Still no sign, but she thought she heard faint sounds of Survivor's "Eye of the Tiger" through the fog.

"All the baryonic matter on earth has positively charged atomic nuclei," Emerson said. "For the strange matter to be attracted to the normal matter on earth, it would need an opposite negative charge. Otherwise, the two would repel each other, kind of like two positively charged magnets. Positively charged strange matter would just sit in a glob, not eating anything in its path."

"And if you had a stable supply of negatively charged strange matter?"

"Theoretically, under ideal conditions, it could destroy the earth, gobbling up everything until there was nothing left but a little superdense ball of strange matter."

"Armageddon," Vernon said.

Emerson nodded. "Under ideal conditions, so to speak."

Riley looked at Emerson in the rearview mirror. "You know a lot about strange matter."

Emerson shrugged. "I've been told on occasion I'm a strange man."

"We study strange matter at the Keck Observatory," Alani said. "Astronomers believe that on a cosmic level, exotic matter is much more common than normal matter and was probably created during the early stages of the universe. Around ninety-six percent of the universe is exotic matter. It's just that none of it, before now, was ever discovered on the earth."

Riley saw the outline of Wayan Bagus's ATV ahead through the fog and slowed down.

"That doesn't exactly explain how the National Park Service got their hands on it," Riley said.

"I have a working theory, but it will have to wait," Emerson said. "We're about to get company. I can hear ATVs on the trail behind us."

TWENTY-FIVE

E MERSON QUICKLY TRANSFERRED THE PENNING trap to Wayan Bagus's ATV.

"Here's the plan," Emerson said. "They don't know we have a second ATV, and they're going to assume we'll try to outrun them down the mountain."

Riley looked down the mountain. The undulate terrain looked very steep and treacherous.

"Do you think we can outrun them?" she asked.

"Doubtful," Emerson said. "That's why Alani, Vernon, and Wayan Bagus will take the ATV with the Penning trap up the mountain to the summit and hide out at the Keck Observatory while you and I act as decoys and lead them down the mountain."

"What about the unexploded ordnance?" Riley asked.

"It's one thing if we blow up. It's another if the entire island of Hawaii is destroyed."

Emerson nodded. "The bad guys won't be looking for Alani and Vernon's ATV, so they can drive at a safe speed, sticking to the Jeep trail and main roads."

"And what about us?" Riley asked.

"We'll be off-road, speeding down the mountain in the fog at breakneck speeds, trying to avoid hitting any explosives."

Riley rolled her eyes. "That's a relief. I was afraid we'd be doing something dangerous."

"Be careful," Vernon said. "Pay attention to your *unagi*."

The three of them took off down the Jeep trail and disappeared into the fog. Riley and Emerson buckled in and waited.

"The dogs won't chase the fox unless they are allowed to pick up its trail," Emerson said.

Riley cut her eyes to Emerson. "Have you ever been to a fox hunt? Nine times out of ten it ends up badly for the fox."

Four sets of headlights shone through the cloud cover, and seconds later Riley could make out four ATVs loaded to the gills with Rough Rider soldiers.

"Do you know how to drive one of these things off-road?" Emerson asked.

"I'm the daughter of a small-town Texas sheriff, and I have four brothers," Riley said. "What do you think?"

She gunned the engine and took off down the mountain,

fishtailing through the lava cinders before getting her bearings.

Emerson looked behind them. The four sets of headlights were still in pursuit.

"They took the bait," Emerson said. "The good news is that they're coming after us. The bad news is that they appear to be gaining on us."

Riley checked the speedometer. "We're going forty miles per hour. I'm driving blind in this fog. Any faster, and I'm afraid we'll lose control of the ATV."

"If you don't, Tin Man will catch us."

"I see your point," Riley said. She pressed on the accelerator and the ATV surged forward, bumping over the rough terrain.

The wheels of the ATV lifted off the ground as they launched off a knoll and were airborne for several seconds. They hit the ground hard and Emerson blew a *weeeooop* on his slide whistle.

"For the love of Mike," Riley said, reaching across, ripping the whistle from Emerson's hand, and throwing it out of the ATV.

Emerson watched the whistle bounce on the ground and out of sight. "That's a shame. I was really beginning to get good on that thing. Another year of practice and I think I would have been ready for what we in the slide whistle game refer to as 'The Show.'"

" 'The Show'?"

"You know. Playing the 'bankrupt' sound effect for

Wheel of Fortune. The guy who has that job is just living the dream."

The ATV burst out of the cloud cover, and Riley could see the Pacific Ocean far in the distance. "How far from civilization are we?"

"It's about fifteen miles until we get to the Hawaii Belt Road," Emerson said.

Riley looked down at the speedometer. It read sixty miles per hour. "At this speed, that's fifteen minutes. Maybe we can stay ahead of them that long."

The four pursuing ATVs emerged from the cloud cover, and Emerson turned to look.

"It's Tin Man and about a dozen goons wearing khaki uniforms and campaign hats," Emerson said. "They're maybe a hundred yards behind us."

Riley applied more pressure to the gas pedal, and the ATV leaped forward. They could see green pastures in the distance at the lower elevations, and the cinders lining the ground were starting to give way to scrubby grasses.

"I have my foot all the way to the floor," Riley said. "We can't go any faster."

The pursuing ATVs were keeping pace, but they weren't closing the gap.

"It looks like they're at maximum speed too," Emerson said.

Riley passed a rusty, tarnished metal tube with fins on one end. "Um. What was that?"

Moments later there was the sound of a tremendous

boom, and one of the pursuing ATVs was catapulted at least thirty feet into the air before crashing to the ground and exploding into flames.

"I have good news and bad news," Emerson said. "The good news is that there are only three ATVs and nine Rough Riders chasing us now."

"And the bad news?"

"I think we're passing through an artillery dump. The rusty metal tubes stuck into the ground all around us look to me like unexploded shells."

Riley swerved, narrowly missing one.

"There's one dead ahead," Emerson said.

The ATV was going too fast to steer around it without rolling the vehicle and killing them both.

"Hold on," Riley said, launching the ATV over a hillock and flying over the shell before landing roughly on the other side of it.

"This is nice," Emerson said after they'd passed completely through the dump. "We've been on the island for less than twenty-four hours and already we've seen so many off-the-beaten-path things most tourists don't even know about."

Riley glanced behind her. The pursuing ATVs had made it through and were still a football field's distance away.

"We could have died," Riley said. "That's not nice."

"Do not dwell in the past," Emerson said. "Do not

dream of the future. Concentrate the mind on the present moment."

"Buddha?"

Emerson shook his head. "Fence."

"Who's Fence?"

Emerson pointed at the green pasture ahead. There was a barbed wire fence strung across their path, stretching on for miles in either direction.

There was nowhere to go but through. "Ramming speed," Riley shouted, slamming into the barbed wire at seventy-five miles per hour. The fence strained for a moment and snapped as the ATV plowed through.

"More good news," Emerson said. "We must be off the Pohakuloa Training Grounds and onto private property."

Riley squinted into the distance. "What's that sea of black ahead of us?"

"You don't want to know," Emerson said.

"I really, really do."

"We're on one of the biggest privately owned ranches in the state," Emerson said.

"Crap on a cracker. They're cows. There must be a thousand of them."

"Black Angus," Emerson said. "They're the Cadillac of cows."

"Good to know. Are they dangerous?"

"I wouldn't run into one at seventy miles per hour. They weigh up to two thousand pounds. It would be like smashing into a brick wall. We should be fine as long as you don't excite them."

"Hello. I'm driving an ATV at seventy miles per hour right through their herd. I think they're going to get excited."

Emerson gripped the side door of the ATV. "Yes. That might complicate things," he said as Riley weaved around the first of the cows.

Startled cows snapped to attention as the other three ATVs invaded the herd as well. In a moment, the docile mass of cows was transformed into an angry sea of black, thundering down the mountain, together with the unwelcome ATVs.

"Ten years from now this will be an amusing anecdote," Emerson said. "You don't get to be a part of a stampede every day."

Riley looked around her. All she could see was a swirling vortex of two-thousand-pound cows.

"This is even worse than the artillery dump," she said. "At least the shells didn't move."

Emerson looked around. "Did you know the average cow produces 200,000 glasses of milk in her lifetime? The highest lifetime yield of milk for a single cow, named Smurf, was 478,163 pounds."

"That's really fascinating, but I'm sort of trying to concentrate on not getting us killed right now."

Emerson was silent. He squirmed in his seat a little.

"You're dying to tell me more about cows, aren't you," Riley said.

"A dairy cow makes 125 pounds of saliva every day," Emerson blurted out in one breath. "I have more fun facts about cows, but I suppose we can discuss them later."

One of the pursuing ATVs swerved hard right to avoid a cow, and the driver lost control, the ATV rolling several times and launching himself and the two other passengers through the air.

"One more ATV down. Only two left," Emerson said. He watched the three soldiers scramble to their feet. "Looks like they're okay."

A mass of stampeding cows collided with the three men, knocking them down and trampling them before continuing to run down the mountain.

"Whoops," Emerson said. "They might not be so okay anymore."

Riley worked her way to the front of the herd and sped down the hill. The ATV containing Tin Man and one other were still behind them.

"I see a road," Riley said.

Emerson looked. "I think it's the Old Mamalahoa Highway. There's nothing in the area but uninhabited cattle ranches. Just cross the road and keep going."

A couple minutes later, Riley burst through another barbed wire fence and launched the ATV across the Old Highway. Emerson was right. Just more pasture on the other side, but at least it wasn't as steep as the upper slopes.

"Are they still there?" Riley asked. A bullet whizzed by Riley's head. "I guess that answers my question. I thought they were afraid of hitting the Penning trap."

"Something tells me Tin Man doesn't care too much. He's flat-out crazy."

Riley passed through a grove of trees and exploded across Hawaii Belt Road, barely missing an eighteen-wheeler. Across the road, the landscape was more lush and lightly forested.

"This is good," Emerson said. "We may be able to lose them in the trees. Just keep going and look for an opportunity."

Riley dodged the trees and entered a meadow covered in tall guinea grass.

"I can't see a thing," Riley said.

"Neither can they."

Seconds later, the ATV rocketed out of the guinea grass and Riley slammed on the brakes. The ATV fishtailed and rolled over several times, coming to a stop at the edge of a thousand-foot cliff overlooking a green rain forest in the valley below.

Riley unbuckled herself from the ATV and struggled out and over to Emerson. He had blood on his forehead and was still dazed from the impact. She unbuckled him and dragged him out of the ATV.

"Emerson, are you okay?"

"Cows can walk upstairs but not downstairs because their knees don't bend that way," Emerson said.

Riley smiled. "You're fine."

She looked up and saw Tin Man and six armed Rough Riders standing over her.

"You won't stay that way for long unless I get back what you stole," Tin Man said. "It's not in the ATV, and I'm assuming it's not at the bottom of the cliff, or there'd be no more cliff by now."

Tin Man grabbed Riley and put a gun to her head. "Tell me where it is, or I'll shoot her."

"If I tell you, you'll shoot her. Then you'll kill me too," Emerson said. "And, if you do shoot her, I'll never tell you anything. That's a promise."

Tin Man held tight to Riley but lowered the gun. "What do you suggest?"

"Let her go and keep me as a hostage. She'll get the Penning trap and we can arrange a swap. Me for the trap."

"I have a better idea," Tin Man said. "I keep the redhead and you get the trap and bring it to me. And if you break our agreement, I'll hurt her and then I'll kill her. That's *my* promise."

TWENTY-SIX

———⊗⊗⊗———

R ILEY LOOKED OUT THE WINDOW OF THE SUV
as they drove south along the Hawaii Belt Road
toward Captain Cook. She was sandwiched in the middle
of the back seat between Tin Man and a hulking Rough
Rider. Bart Young was in the front.

"We're not going back to Mauna Kea?" Riley asked.

"No," Bart Young said. "That location is obviously
compromised. Everything of value, including you, is being
moved to our other base of operations in Kilauea."

Riley thought it probably wasn't a good sign that they
hadn't blindfolded her and were taking no precautions to
hide the new location from her.

"Why are you doing this?" she asked the director.

"Are you familiar with the writings of Machiavelli?"

"Wasn't he the sixteenth-century philosopher who thought it is better to be feared than loved?"

"That's part of his writings. Taken as a whole, they were a guidebook for how to rule. He believed that a prince who tries to be good all the time is bound to come to ruin among the great number who are not good."

"And you fancy yourself a prince?"

"Why not? For a century, my predecessors have been protecting a secret that they never truly understood. Yes, they knew it was a destructive force the likes of which the world has never seen. But I alone saw its potential. I alone set about to harvest and refine it into a weapon. With it, I can obliterate whole nations in the blink of an eye. Who would dare to stand in my way?"

"How many innocent people have died because of your quest for power?" Riley asked.

Bart Young shrugged. "Immaterial. A prince who wants to keep his authority must learn how to be ruthless, and to use that knowledge as necessity requires."

"You're no prince," Riley said. "You're just a thug in a thousand-dollar suit."

"Time will tell. Was Napoleon a thug? Was Alexander the Great? Was Genghis Khan?"

"Yeah," Riley said. "Those guys were thugs."

Bart Young shook his head. "You're not seeing the big picture. The winners write the history books. Only two things stand in my way. Emerson Knight and the Penning trap he stole."

"Why?" Riley asked.

"That particular trap contains a little more than a third of my supply of strange matter, and I need it to complete Armageddon."

Riley leaned forward. "'Armageddon'?"

"The weapon my troops will carry into battle."

"You don't have enough from your other collection sites?" Riley asked.

"In microscopic quantities, it isn't stable enough to do any significant damage. The larger the mass of strange matter, the more stable it becomes."

"How much do you need?"

The director turned around in his seat and stared directly at Riley. "If I want to conquer the world, I need enough to instill fear in every man, woman, and child. I need the ability to threaten the planet Earth with annihilation. Unfortunately, without that Penning trap, I barely have enough to destroy North America."

"Right," Riley said. "That would be unfortunate if you couldn't destroy the entire world."

Riley sat in silence as the SUV drove around South Point and continued north on Highway 11 toward the Kilauea Crater. Riley stayed alert as they entered Volcanoes National Park. Vast fields of jagged lava ran from the road down to the ocean, ten miles away. The SUV drove past the turnoff to the visitor center and continued on along Highway 11, out of the park and toward the little town of Volcano.

"I thought we were heading to Kilauea," Riley said.

"We are, and we aren't," Bart Young said, smiling. "It's nice to know there are still some secrets that we've managed to hide from you and Knight. I just might keep you around for a while. Where we're going, nobody will ever find you."

"How the Sam Hill are we going to find her?" Vernon asked.

Emerson was pacing in his living room. He'd phoned Alani minutes after Riley was kidnapped and told her to bring everyone to the ranch. They now had the task of rescuing Riley without sacrificing the Penning trap.

"Tin Man won't try to arrange an exchange until morning. That gives us twelve hours," Emerson said.

Alani leaned forward in her chair. "We have absolutely no idea where they took her. Hawaii might be an island, but it's a really big island."

"Well, we can't give up the Whatsamadoodle either," Vernon said. "I don't like the idea of handing over a doomsday machine to those maniacs."

"We have it stashed away in the storage locker at the Keck Observatory," Alani said. "It's hooked up to power and there are two backup generators, so it should be safe. I told my assistant it was part of an experiment I was conducting and not to touch it but to call if there were any problems."

Emerson got out a map of the Big Island. "Every riddle has an answer. It's somewhere here on this map."

"Mauna Kea?" Alani asked.

Emerson shook his head. "No. I'm certain that by now they've already disassembled the lab, moved everything, and sealed off the entrance to the lava tube."

Wayan Bagus studied the map. "Do not seek answers but seek instead to understand the question."

"There you go talking in riddles again," Vernon said.

Wayan Bagus shrugged. "Would you search for a branch taken by a river? Instead, ask yourself what is the nature of the river. Everything on earth seeks its proper place."

"If I were them my proper place would be somewhere I felt in control," Emerson said. "Somewhere that I felt comfortable." He pointed at the map. "Like Hawaii Volcanoes National Park. It's part of their system."

"Volcanoes National Park is huge," Alani said.

"The woman we rescued from the lava tube on Mauna Kea said she was taken from a cave on Kilauea," Emerson said. "Are there any restricted areas there?"

"There are some restricted areas near the active vents, but they're not big enough to hide a research facility. And they're so dangerous that nobody, not even Tin Man and Bart Young, would go there."

Emerson returned to the map. "There's a little square piece of land on the map that isn't contiguous to the rest of the park. It looks out of place."

"That's Ola'a Forest," Alani said. "It's a crazy dense jungle. Hardly anybody ever goes there."

Emerson tapped on the map. "There's got to be a reason why the NPS annexed this little unrelated property into the park. How big is Ola'a?"

"Nine thousand acres, more or less," Alani said.

Emerson smiled. "It's the perfect place to hide a government compound. I think I know where we can find Riley."

"We can't search eighteen square miles of rain forest in twelve hours in the dark," Vernon said.

"We don't have to," Emerson said. "They used the lava tubes at Mauna Kea to make a hidden base. It stands to reason they did the same at Ola'a."

Alani's eyes widened. "The Kazumura."

Emerson nodded. "Correct, one of the biggest lava tubes in the world. And it starts in Ola'a."

"The Kazumura is forty miles long and runs from the coastline near Puna all the way up to the summit of Kilauea. It takes a minimum of two days to hike," Alani said.

"Well, we can't just go walk right up to the entrance in Ola'a and knock on the door," Vernon said. "If it is being used by the Rough Riders, it's sure to be guarded."

Emerson pulled up a detailed map of the lava tube on

his iPad. "There are more than a hundred known entrances to the Kazumura. We just need to find an entry point close to Ola'a, that isn't Ola'a."

Alani looked at the map. It was divided into five sections. The one adjacent to Ola'a was described as Sexton's Maze.

"What about here?" she said. "It looks like there are a couple entrances in the area."

Emerson clicked on that portion of the Kazumura. The next Web page revealed a complex network of side channels, some of which were dead ends and others of which linked up and eventually connected to the main tube.

Wayan Bagus looked over Emerson's shoulder. "A labyrinth. Very Zen."

"I bet it's a dark, moldy, cramped cave, probably chock-full of Bigfoots. We're going to get lost for sure," Vernon said.

"No man can be lost so long as he knows himself," Wayan Bagus said.

Vernon rolled his eyes.

Alani looked at Vernon. "Don't forget about the Night Marchers."

"'Night Marchers'?"

"They're the ghosts of ancient Hawaiian warriors that come forth from their burial places to roam the countryside at night," Alani said.

Vernon looked a little nervous. "Do they roam in caves?"

Alani nodded. "Absolutely. Caves are what they like best of all."

Vernon looked up in the air. "Oh Lordy. This just keeps getting worse and worse." He narrowed his eyes at Alani. "Are you joshing me? Are they for real?"

"They're no less real than Bigfoot."

"Oh Lordy," Vernon repeated. "Assuming we get through the maze without getting raped by a Bigfoot or a ghost, what's next?"

Emerson pointed to the section above Sexton's marked Ola'a. "We have to navigate through a series of lava falls."

"Lava falls," Vernon said. "Seriously."

"There hasn't been any lava in the Kazumura for five hundred years, so they're more or less just cliffs we'll need to scale. There are at least twelve falls in this section, some as tall as forty-five feet. Hopefully, we'll see something while we're exploring that leads us to where they're keeping Riley."

"It's a good theory," Alani said. "But what if we're wrong and Riley isn't there?"

Emerson shrugged. "We have until morning to try. If we fail, then we still have the option of bargaining with Tin Man."

"It's a three-hour drive just to Volcano," Vernon said. "By the time we get to the Kazumura it'll be past midnight. That's going to put us way behind schedule."

Emerson smiled. "Not to worry. I've already arranged

for a ride and supplies. We should be at the entrance to Sexton's Maze in less than an hour."

Riley jiggled the handcuffs binding her to the heavy metal desk in the corner of the cavern and looked around the room. Tin Man, Bart Young, and the other Rough Riders were nowhere to be seen. Berta was at a workstation across the room, calibrating what looked to be a large, complicated bomb. A couple dozen similar devices were stacked neatly nearby.

"What are you working on?" Riley asked.

Berta continued her work. "It's a delivery system for the strange matter."

"You mean a bomb."

"I suppose you could call it that."

"Then you're Bart Young's bomb maker."

Berta looked up. "I'm a mechanical engineer. Spiro and I spent the past ten years designing the technology to harvest and contain the strange matter."

"Spiro is dead," Riley said.

Berta went back to her work. Riley guessed she had nothing more to say on that subject.

"If you've really discovered strange matter, you deserve a Nobel Prize in Physics," Riley said.

"I didn't discover anything. It was discovered more than a century ago when the U.S. government was exploring the area known today as Yellowstone. Of course, all they knew at the time was that once in a very rare while a little blob of matter, which was like nothing ever seen before, would bubble to the surface of a mud pit or a hot spring and, well, you've seen what it can do under the right conditions."

"It was horrible," Riley said. "What did they think it was?"

"They didn't know. It was impossible to collect and study because it bubbled to the surface so rarely and randomly and always in such small quantities. The reaction would be over in seconds and, as you saw, there was nothing left to study. Later, they discovered more in Hawaii and then in Samoa and so on. The government decided to create the National Park system to protect and study the mysterious substance that had such an enormous destructive potential. They didn't know what it was at the time. They only knew that it was connected to volcanic activity. The real breakthrough was in 1970."

"What happened in 1970?" Riley asked.

"We realized that certain volcanoes were formed over mantle plumes and were drawing magma directly from the earth's core."

"Cosmic leftovers from the big bang," Riley said.

Berta looked surprised. "That's right. The world we know is composed of normal matter, but at the earth's core there are small bits of exotic matter leftover from the early universe."

"Like strange matter."

Berta nodded. "Correct."

"So why hasn't the earth been destroyed long ago?"

"Most of the strange matter we find is no bigger than the size of a light nucleus. They're called strangelets, and they don't seem to have the mass to do any significant damage. Every once in a couple hundred thousand years, a larger mass is extruded, and the results can be devastating."

"Destroy-an-entire-continent devastating?"

Berta shrugged. "You've heard of the lost continent of Atlantis? We also suspect strange matter is the catalyst responsible for the past couple magnitude-eight eruptions at Yellowstone."

"And you've discovered a way to collect strange matter?" Riley asked.

"Strangelet by strangelet. It's been a painstakingly slow process. Even after ten years all we've managed to put together is the size of a tennis ball."

"Is that enough to destroy a continent?"

"It's enough to destroy the earth and turn it into a little dense ball floating through space. The little field experiment you witnessed was mostly plasma. The actual strange matter was less than a single drop, and it would have destroyed all of Mauna Kea if it wasn't contained within a magnetic field."

Riley looked around the room. She needed to find a way to escape before Berta decided to conduct another field experiment on her.

"Why doesn't it destroy the earth's core?" Riley asked.

"We don't know yet. There's a powerful magnetic field at the core. Maybe it's the intense heat or pressure. Maybe something happens to change its charge from positive to negative when it reaches the surface. For whatever reason, it's not until it reaches the surface that it seems to react with normal matter."

"It seems to me that you're a scientist, not a killer."

"Your life means no more to me than a lab rat's. If the director wants me to experiment with human subjects, I have no problem with that. If he wants me to build him a super-weapon, that's just fine with me too."

"Why?" Riley asked. "What's in it for you?"

"Just a little thing called France. It's the bonus I've been promised once Director Young conquers the world."

"A friend of mine recently told me that greed leads to suffering," Riley said.

"I guess I'd rather suffer as a rich empress than be a happy, dead scientist like Spiro," Berta said. "You and your friends picked the wrong fight."

Riley jiggled her chains and glared at Berta. "Funny, I was just about to say the same to you."

TWENTY-SEVEN

———⊗⊗⊗———

THE UNMISTAKABLE *WUP, WUP, WUP* OF A hovering helicopter filtered through the windows of Mysterioso Ranch.

"Ride's here," Emerson said, springing out of his chair, gathering up his backpack, and going to the door.

Vernon, Alani, and Wayan Bagus joined him on the front lanai. A six-seat Airbus Eco-Star helicopter was landing in the pasture behind the house, stirring up the grasses in the process.

Vernon looked at the chopper and groaned. "Tell me you didn't," he said to Emerson. "There must be a thousand helicopter pilots in Hawaii and you chose Mr. Yakomura, Alani's dad, didn't you?"

"It was the only helicopter I could find at short notice, and who would fly us around at night, no questions asked."

Yakomura hopped out of the Eco-Star and walked over to them. He gave Alani a hug, then saw Vernon and shook his head.

"Good evening, Mr. Yakomura," Vernon said. "I reckon it's been a while."

"Dad, you remember Vernon," Alani said.

Yakomura frowned. "How could I forget? Are you still a degenerate?"

Vernon looked around for help. "No, Mr. Yakomura." He reached out to Wayan Bagus. "In fact, this here's my personal spiritual adviser. He's teaching me the ways of the Sage and such."

Mr. Yakomura looked skeptically at Vernon. "Really. What ways would those be?"

"Oh, you know. Showing my elders respect and not objectifying women's racks and things like that. Isn't that so, Little Buddy?"

"No," Wayan Bagus said politely.

"This is my father, Steven Yakomura," Alani said to Wayan Bagus.

Wayan Bagus steepled his fingers and bowed ever so slightly in greeting.

Half an hour later, they were airborne and flying over the interior of the island. The sun had just set and they had a full-on view of Kilauea. Glowing red rivers of lava flowed down the dark mountain and into the sea. Huge plumes of smoke and steam obscured the entry points. Even from a distance it was impressive.

The helicopter banked to the left, and the dark lava fields were replaced with lush rain forests.

"That's Ola'a," Alani said.

Everyone looked down. A thick blanket of trees covered the area completely. Emerson reached into his backpack, pulled out a large telescopic camera, and aimed it at Ola'a Forest.

"What's that?" Alani asked.

"It's a long-range infrared camera I appropriated from the security system of the main house at Mysterioso Ranch. It basically picks up any heat signature and takes a picture using temperature differences the same way a regular camera uses light."

Vernon, Alani, and Wayan Bagus looked at the camera's viewing screen as Emerson scanned the forest through the thick canopy. Except for the occasional pig or goat displayed in a rainbow of yellows, reds, and greens, initially there was nothing but complete darkness.

"The detail is amazing," Alani said. "We have an infrared telescope at Mauna Kea, but I had no idea the image quality for terrestrial cameras was so good."

"It used to be strictly a military technology," Emerson said. "It provides an accurate image up to a distance of two miles."

Emerson aimed the camera at the center of Ola'a. A good-sized red and yellow blob of an unknown heat source filled the screen.

Emerson pointed at the area. "It looks like we may have found Riley."

"I don't know," Alani said. "It's just a blob of heat. It could be anybody down there."

Emerson shook his head. "It's not a campfire. We'd see the light from the air. I think it's an exhaust, just like the one we saw on Mauna Kea. And it's coming from the center of an unspoiled wilderness that just happens to be owned by the National Park Service."

The helicopter circled over Ola'a and the little town of Volcano. The town of Puna was ahead, and beyond that the Pacific Ocean.

"Where do you want to set down?" Yakomura asked.

Emerson looked at his map. "There's an entrance to the Kazumura Cave on the outskirts of Ola'a Forest called Wild Pig Drop Falls." Emerson pointed to a fifty-acre pasture at the outskirts of the forest. "Can you land there? The falls are somewhere at the edge of the field, and there's supposed to be an ATV trail used by the local guides that leads to it."

"Why don't we just land in Ola'a near the heat source?" Vernon asked.

Emerson shook his head. "The jungle is so thick, there's no place to land. And even if we did find some clearing,

Ola'a is not a lava desert like the summit of Mauna Kea. It would be nearly impossible to find an exhaust pipe in the dense vegetation. Most importantly, if by some miracle we did find the compound, it's certain to be heavily guarded. If we have any chance of rescuing Riley, we need to take Tin Man completely by surprise. Our best chance is to sneak up on them through the lava tubes."

"I have a fix on the ATV trail," Yakomura said. "There's just enough moonlight to see the tire ruts."

The helicopter landed and everyone piled out. Emerson spread a map of Ola'a Forest on the ground and circled the area in red pen where he had seen the heat signature. He overlaid a map of the Kazumura Cave on top. "Here's where we need to head once we find the entrance to the Kazumura."

Alani looked at the map of Ola'a and frowned. "Assuming the heat source is where they're keeping Riley, the bad guys' base of operations isn't near any of the mapped portions of the Kazumura."

Emerson nodded. "That's true. It's not near any of the mapped portions. However, the Kazumura is actually a vast network of independent lava tubes that became connected into a maze of tunnels over a hundred years of active lava flows and water erosion."

"So you think Tin Man has Riley in some unmapped side channel?" Vernon asked.

"I'm hoping so. The main tunnel is too well-known

and used regularly by tour companies and spelunkers." Emerson pointed at the red circle. "There has to be a secret underground route to this area. If there was an aboveground road in, everyone would see them coming and going."

"If it's a huge maze of unmapped tunnels, how the Sam Hill will we know we're heading in the right direction and not into a den of Bigfoots?" Vernon asked.

Emerson smiled. "There are hundreds of mapped entrances, mainly through naturally occurring holes called skylights in the ceiling of the tunnels. There are bound to be hundreds of other unmapped entrances. We won't have cell reception when we're underground, but when we reach a skylight we'll pop out of the hole and get a GPS reading on our location."

"Let me get this straight," Vernon said. "We're going to be popping in and out of hundreds of holes."

Both Wayan Bagus and Mr. Yakomura slapped him on the back of the head.

Vernon jumped away from the two men. "You guys have dirty minds. How do you know that's what I was thinking? And in fact I was only thinking it for a minute, and then I was thinking something entirely different. I don't get how popping out of the holes is gonna help us. Won't we still be under jungle canopy? Doesn't the canopy screw up, excuse my French, the GPS?"

"Mr. Yakomura will be our eyes from the air," Emerson

said, handing him the infrared camera. "He'll fix on our ground location, and he'll give us direction on which way we need to go in order to reach where we saw the heat source."

Alani nodded. "Kind of like a high-stakes game of Warmer and Colder."

Emerson nodded. "The highest."

Emerson stuffed the maps into his backpack and led the way down the trail toward the falls.

Five minutes later, Vernon, Alani, Wayan Bagus, and Emerson were staring into a dark hole at the outskirts of the Ola'a rain forest.

"Why do they call it Wild Pig Drop Falls?" Vernon asked.

Emerson shone his flashlight down into the hole, draped in jungle vines. The beam illuminated the skeleton of a massive wild boar submerged in a plunge pool at the bottom, forty-five feet below.

Alani looked down at the bones. "I guess that answers the question."

Emerson took a rope from his pack, tied one end to a tree, and attached a harness to himself with a carabiner.

"We're going to have to rappel down. Does everyone know how this works?" he asked.

"Yes, of course," Alani said.

"You betcha," Vernon said.

"No," Wayan Bagus said.

"Tell you what, Little Buddy, you just wrap your arms around my neck and hold tight, and I'll have us down lickety-split," Vernon said.

Emerson went first, swinging out a little to avoid the pig, splashing down in a foot of water. Vernon pulled the harness back to the top and handed it to Alani, who got into the rig and descended next.

"Look out below," Vernon yelled, as he slid down the rope with Wayan Bagus riding piggyback.

Vernon sloshed out of the shallow pool and set Wayan down on solid ground.

"This here's gonna be creepy," Vernon said, taking in the pitch-black tunnel that led away from the pig bones. "Good thing I'm big and brave and not afraid of the dark."

Emerson handed out headlamps. "This should help. Pay attention to where you're walking and don't lag behind."

They walked ten feet into the tunnel, and Wayan Bagus reached out to touch the smooth, ropey black walls.

"It is like being inside a sculpture," Wayan Bagus said.

"There are two main types of lava flows in Hawaii," Emerson said. "A'a is the jagged, rocky stuff you see all around Kona. This is called pahoehoe, and it tends to form when the eruption is slower and less violent. Most lava tubes in Hawaii are made from smooth pahoehoe lava."

They spent the next half hour scrambling over a series

of lava cascades and smaller falls. It was fairly easy going. The tour guide companies had left an assortment of ropes, ladders, and handholds to make the trip possible for tourists. Finally, they came to a skylight in the ceiling about fifty feet above them with a rope dangling down.

Emerson looked at the rope. "That's convenient," he said.

"I wouldn't call it convenient," Alani said. "You'll have to hand climb four stories to reach the skylight. If you fall, you'll kill yourself."

Emerson shrugged. "When faced with situations such as this one I ask myself WWSMD?"

"WWSMD?" Alani asked.

"What would Spider-Man do?" Emerson grabbed the rope. "I'll be back." He scurried up and disappeared out the hole.

"That's impressive," Alani said. "That takes real strength."

"Strength shmength," Vernon said. "I could do that with Little Buddy on my back."

Alani looked at Vernon with a single raised eyebrow.

"I'd show you," Vernon said, "but it would leave you down here unprotected if I went up there."

"Nice to know you care," Alani said.

"Of course I care," Vernon said. "I've always cared. I'd care even more if you weren't frickin' nuts."

Alani flapped her arms out. "There you go ruining the moment. You always ruined the moment."

Vernon stuffed his fists on his hips. "Did not."

"Yes, you did. Remember that time we went to my cousin's luau wedding and I caught the bouquet?"

"Un-huh."

"Do you remember what you did with the bouquet?"

"Um, no."

"You fed it to one of the feral goats."

"That wasn't good?"

"Catching the bouquet was significant. It meant I was supposed to be the next one married."

"So you're not married because of me?"

Alani narrowed her eyes. "Yes, and for many reasons."

Emerson appeared at the skylight edge. He was back on the rope and descended hand over hand.

"Did you get a fix on our position?" Alani asked when Emerson got his feet on the tunnel floor.

Emerson nodded. "It's a wet, muddy rain forest. I couldn't see anything but ohia trees and massive hapu'u tree ferns. I called your dad, and he says we're about two miles inside the forest, and he gave me new directions."

They walked another half mile down the tunnel and came to a dead end. They were facing a forty-foot cliff with a pool of water at its base. Emerson looked at the map.

"This has got to be Skylight Falls. It's the second highest lava fall in the main tube. The main tunnel continues west from here. Mr. Yakomura says we need to find a side channel going north fairly soon or we'll be getting *colder*."

A series of ladder rungs had been embedded into the three-story cliff. Emerson sloshed through water two feet deep and pulled himself up onto the ladder.

"Be careful, they're slippery," Emerson said, climbing the rungs and waiting at the top for Vernon, Alani, and Wayan Bagus.

At the top, the tunnel became wide and low, barely tall enough for Emerson to stand upright. They walked another quarter of a mile before it opened into a cavern with another cliff and plunge pool at its bottom. This one was thirty feet tall, and no one had left behind a rope or ladder.

Vernon looked up at the cliff. "Well, this is a real pickle," he said.

Emerson started to unpack his rock-climbing gear from his pack. "Not a problem. I'll climb to the top and throw down a rope."

"Wait," Wayan Bagus said. "There is a sound."

Everyone listened. Somebody or something was coming their way, and the sounds were getting louder by the second. There was no place to hide. They were trapped between the cliff and whatever was approaching.

"It sounds big," Alani said.

A family of wild pigs suddenly burst into the cavern and ran past Vernon.

"Holy bejeezus," Vernon said, plastering himself back against the tunnel wall.

The pigs panicked at the sight of the humans. They ran in circles, squealing and grunting, flashing in and out of the headlamp beams, their eyes reflecting the light. And then just as suddenly as they came they disappeared back into the tunnel.

"Stupid pigs," Vernon said. "They near gave me a heart attack."

Alani grinned. "At least they weren't Bigfoot."

"I should never have told you about Bigfoot," Vernon said. "Next you're gonna be telling me it's another thing that ruined a moment."

"It did!" Alani said. "There was the camping trip at Keokea Bay. We were having a romantic moment, and you were sure you heard Bigfoot."

"Hey," Vernon said, "that Bigfoot encounter I had was traumatic. Anyways I'm not currently worried about Bigfoot because everybody knows Bigfoots lack the hand-eye coordination to climb ladders, and the only way they could get to us is by climbing that rickety three-story one back at Skylight Falls."

Emerson looked at Vernon. "An excellent observation."

"It is?" Vernon said. "I was just kind of winging it."

"Bigfoots can't climb ladders," Emerson said. "And last I checked neither can pigs. So where did they come from and where did they go?"

Everyone nodded. They'd missed an offshoot tunnel. They retraced their steps back toward Skylight Falls. They went slowly, carefully examining each fold and crevice. A small pig darted across their path and disappeared.

"There," Emerson said, shining his light at the tunnel wall.

There was a small hole in the north side. It was just wide enough for a large pig to squeeze through.

Emerson got down on his stomach and peered into the opening. "I think it's big enough for us to crawl through, but I can't see the end."

"If it gets much narrower, we'll be stuck," Vernon said. "Just like Winnie-the-Pooh in Rabbit's hole."

"I am small," Wayan Bagus said. "I will go first." He wriggled into the hole. A minute later he called back to Emerson. "I am in another tunnel, and it seems to head in the direction we wanted to travel."

Vernon stuck his head into the hole. "Can we fit?"

"It should not be a problem," Wayan Bagus said from the other side. "As long as you make yourself as small as possible."

Vernon looked himself over and sucked in his gut. "You didn't use your special powers to go where thought takes you, did you?" Vernon asked. "'Cause that's not really an option for the rest of us."

"The mind is everything. What you think you become," the disembodied voice of Wayan Bagus echoed through the hole.

Emerson got into the hole and wriggled through,

pushing his backpack in front of him. He was followed by Vernon and Alani. After about fifty feet, they emerged in a lava tube on the other side. It was slightly smaller than the first tube, and only Wayan Bagus could stand completely upright.

"This is good," Emerson said. "I don't know if it will connect to Tin Man's compound, but at least we're heading in the right direction according to Mr. Yakomura."

TWENTY-EIGHT

—◦◦◦—

A FTER ABOUT AN HOUR OF WALKING, THE
sounds of coqui frogs filled the otherwise eerie
silence of the tunnel. Emerson looked up to see a skylight
just ahead and about eight feet above them. He got a boost
from Vernon and hoisted himself out of the hole in the
ceiling.

"Nothing but more trees and ferns," he called back into
the hole. "I'm going to check with the helicopter."

Alani looked at her watch. "I'm not feeling good about
this," she said to Vernon and Wayan Bagus. "It's taking
us too long. It's three A.M. Riley is at the mercy of these
psychopaths. We have no idea if she's even alive. And if
she is alive, heaven knows what they could be doing to
her."

"I know what you mean," Vernon said. "My *unagi* is acting up. I'm feeling all tingly. That's either a sign of a naked woman nearby or some kind of danger. And I don't see no naked women. Although now that I think about it the tingling is pretty strong, so it could be some naked woman is in danger. I sure hope it isn't Riley."

"Silence is a great source of strength," Wayan Bagus said to Vernon.

Emerson dropped back into the tunnel. "We're close," he said. "We're walking in the right direction. Mr. Yakomura can't circle overhead much longer without refueling so we're on our own for a while."

"I don't like that," Vernon said. "That feels real insecure being that my *unagi* is giving me a stomach cramp. There's something bad happening up ahead. I know it for sure."

"What's with this *unagi* thing?" Alani asked Emerson. "Didn't I see that on an episode of *Friends*?"

"Wait a minute," Vernon said to Emerson. "You told me I had *unagi*. I mean, I got it, right? It's not like the time Tom Hanks brought you the sculpture, is it? I never bought into that one."

"As you believe, so will you be," Emerson said, once again leading the way into the black tunnel.

"So what's wrong with me if it's not *unagi*?" Vernon said.

"Maybe you need a bathroom," Alani suggested.

"It's not the same thing," Vernon said. "I'm all in a

knot. It's like in *Star Wars* when you hear the Darth Vader music and your heart gets real tight, like it's squished into a little nugget."

"My heart feels like that too," Alani said. "I'm worried about Riley."

Emerson stopped and held up his hand. "This is interesting," he said. "We've come to a brick wall."

Everyone sidled up next to Emerson and stared at the wall.

"Here's something you don't see all the time," Alani said. "Not many brick walls in lava tubes."

"I reckon we're at a dead end," Vernon said. "I guess the only choice is to go back to that skylight we passed a mile or so back and search aboveground."

"It's precisely because somebody has taken the trouble to erect a brick wall that it's imperative we find a way through," Emerson said.

Vernon waved his hands at the sealed tunnel. "It's a brick wall. How the Sam Hill are we going to do that? You got explosives in your pack?"

"No explosives," Emerson said. "I have a Swiss Army knife and a spoon."

"There goes my *unagi* again," Vernon said. "Now I got a cramp in my ass. I'm telling you something is wrong."

"I hear a noise," Wayan Bagus said. "It sounds like a machine."

Everyone stood still, holding their breath, listening.

BANG! An object crashed into the other side of the brick wall, and everyone instinctively jumped back. The wall vibrated slightly, and some brick dust sifted down.

"I told you something bad was happening," Vernon said. "They're coming to get us."

BANG! Another thunderous crash and a forklift exploded through the wall, sending bricks flying, raising a tremendous dust cloud. The forklift stopped short once it had demolished the wall, and Riley leaned forward in the driver's seat, mouth open, eyes wide.

"Crap on a cracker," Riley said. "I had no idea you guys were out here. I almost ran you over!"

"Holy cow," Vernon said. "Holy guacamole."

Riley swung down from the forklift. A handcuff dangled from her right wrist. "It's not safe to stay here."

"What's with the bracelet?" Alani asked.

"Berta made the mistake of unshackling me for a bathroom break," Riley said. "She might know how to build a bomb, but she sure can't take a punch."

"Who's Berta?"

"She's the woman who's tied to the lab bench."

Everyone peeked through the hole in the wall and stared at Berta, tied up and sitting on the floor. Several tables and chairs were knocked over, and there had clearly been some sort of a struggle.

Alani looked around the room. "What is this place?"

"It's a weapons lab," Riley said. She pointed at the bombs in the corner of the room. "They're making a weapon capable of detonating and releasing a payload of the strange matter. They've got the Penning trap on the table by the bombs."

"Where are Tin Man and Bart Young?" Emerson asked.

"I don't know. They left me here with Berta. I'm sure they're close. I barricaded the door to the lab but it won't stop them for long. We should get out of here ASAP. I'm sure they heard me breaking through the wall."

Emerson looked at the steel door on the other side of the room. It had a small reinforced-glass window at its top and a professional stainless steel refrigerator tipped over in front of the bottom.

Emerson kneeled next to Berta. "Does the Penning trap hold all of the strange matter?"

Berta stared at him in stony silence.

Emerson rose and walked over to the bombs. He studied them for a moment and set the timer on one of them to ten minutes.

"I assume that even without the strange matter loaded, these can still do some damage," Emerson said.

"You don't know what you're doing. You'll kill us all," Berta said.

"Not all of us," Emerson said. "Only those remaining

in this lab. The rest of us will die only if we leave some strange matter behind."

"You mean to steal the strange matter," Berta said, eyes wide in disbelief and fear.

"Yes," Emerson said. "All of it."

"You might want to reconsider your priorities," Riley said to Berta. "It might be better to be a poor live scientist than a rich dead empress."

"I'll ask you one more time," Emerson said to Berta. "Does the Penning trap on the table hold all of the strange matter?"

"Yes," Berta said. "Except for what you already have in the other trap. Just don't leave me here."

Emerson unplugged the trap, Vernon grabbed it, and Riley got Berta to her feet. Someone was banging on the lab door, trying to get in. Riley and Berta looked at the door. The enraged face of Tin Man filled the little window.

"He looks pretty angry," Riley said.

"He's insane," Berta said. "If he catches us he'll chop us into pieces, fingers and toes first, and then ears and breasts. I've seen him do it."

Riley felt a wave of revulsion roll through her, and she pushed it away. No time for emotion, she told herself.

"Let's get out of here," she shouted above the banging.

Emerson lugged the Penning trap back into the tunnel and got into the passenger side of the forklift.

"What are you doing?" Riley asked.

"Making our getaway."

Riley climbed into the driver's side. "In a forklift that drives less than ten miles per hour?"

"The only way back to the main line of the Kazumura from here is through a crawl space. The Penning trap won't fit."

"And a forklift will?"

"There's a skylight about a mile into the tunnel. We can use the forklift to lift the trap to the surface and make our escape."

Vernon, Wayan Bagus, Alani, and Berta piled onto the blades of the forklift, and Riley turned the ignition. It reluctantly started up and rumbled slowly through the bricks, down the tunnel. By the time they reached the skylight, they could hear footsteps and voices echoing in the tunnel behind them.

"We have about a six-minute head start," Emerson said. "Let's get topside with the Penning trap."

Riley raised Vernon, Alani, Wayan Bagus, and Berta close enough to the hole in the ceiling that they could scramble out and then lowered the blades so Emerson could get on, holding the Penning trap. Once the trap was safely aboveground Emerson slipped back into the lava tube.

A deafening explosion reverberated through the tunnel, followed by the sound of a cave-in coming from the direction of the lab.

"I guess the bombs work," Emerson said.

Riley looked in the direction of the lab. "Do you think we got Tin Man?"

"Probably not," Emerson said. "I imagine he's leading the horde running after us."

The sounds of footsteps and angry voices were getting closer.

"What have you got in your pack?" Riley asked. "Matches, flares?"

"Yes and yes."

"Give me the Swiss Army knife you always carry."

Riley took the knife from Emerson and flipped the large blade out into the locked position. She dropped to the tunnel floor and cut the fuel line on the forklift, allowing the diesel fuel to pour out.

"Brilliant," Emerson said. "And impressively diabolical."

Emerson and Riley scaled the forklift and joined the others topside in the pitch-black jungle. Emerson fished around in his backpack and pulled out a signal flare. He lit it and handed it to Riley.

"Do you want to do the honors?" he asked.

"It's not like the universe provides you with the opportunity to blow up a forklift every day," Riley said. "I suppose it would be negligent of me not to drop this flare."

Emerson smiled. "My thoughts exactly."

Riley tossed the flare into the hole, and everyone jumped back. Seconds later the lift exploded, and a fireball rose out of the skylight.

"Guess we don't have to worry about the crew in the tunnel," Alani said. "Between the debris from the explosion and the destroyed forklift, I imagine they're trapped for a while."

Emerson and Vernon tugged Berta over to a large ohia tree and tied her up so that she was hugging the tree.

"We'll send the authorities to pick you up once we get the Penning trap to safety," Emerson said.

"You said you'd take me with you!" Berta screamed. "You can't leave me alone in this jungle."

Emerson stuck a Post-it note to her back. It said "I'm an evil murderer. Please leave me tied to this tree until police arrive."

"We did take you with us. And now we're leaving you here," Emerson said. "You'll be perfectly safe. There aren't any predators out here, assuming Tin Man doesn't find you."

"You don't think he's imprisoned below?" Riley asked.

Emerson shrugged. "No way to know for sure."

The sound of ATVs and human voices carried from far off in the jungle.

"They're organizing a search party," Alani said. "They know we're here and that we have the Penning trap. I'm sure reinforcements are on the way."

"Bart Young is desperate," Emerson said. "He'll throw anything he can at us now. Soon this entire forest will be crawling with Rough Riders."

Alani called her dad on her cellphone. "Is there a clearing where you can pick us up?" she asked. She nodded and turned to Emerson. "He's refueled and is back in the air. He's flying over Ola'a now. I'm going to give him our GPS coordinates so he can aim the infrared camera at our location, and you can link up to it on your iPad."

Emerson powered up the iPad and loaded the app for the security camera.

"I hope that's not us," Vernon said, pointing at six human figures clustered together at the center of the image.

"Unfortunately, yes," Emerson said.

All around them other human figures in shades of red and yellow crept around the jungle while several ATVs patrolled the perimeter.

"There must be thirty soldiers," Riley whispered. "They're sweeping the area."

"My dad says there's a small clearing he can land in two miles east of our location," Alani said. "If we can make it there, he can pick us up and fly us out of here."

"How will we get past the patrols?" Wayan Bagus asked.

"It won't be easy, but with the infrared camera, we have a chance. We just have to be extra sneaky," Emerson said.

Riley grinned. "I'll take those odds. You have superior skills when it comes to sneaky."

TWENTY-NINE

⊶⊷

R ILEY, EMERSON, WAYAN BAGUS, VERNON, AND Alani lay facedown in the muddy rain forest, waiting for the patrol to pass. They'd come close to being discovered several times in the past half hour and had spent more time hiding in the dense vegetation than they had making forward progress toward the clearing.

After the soldiers were gone, Emerson stood up and looked at the iPad. "They're slowly tightening their search grid, basically herding us into a smaller and smaller pen. And that's the good news. The bad news is that I'm sure they hear our helicopter making passes and have called in one or two of their own."

Vernon stood. "Part of the problem is we're lugging

around this here Penny trap. I'm plumb worn out," he said, resting the trap on the ground.

Alani looked at her cellphone. "We have another problem. Dad just texted. He can only fly around for another hour, then he'll have to go refuel."

"That's not good," Riley said. "If he's not up in the air taking infrared video for us, we'll lose any small advantage we might have. Plus, it's going to be sunrise soon and they'll find us for certain."

"Right," Emerson said. "This isn't working. Time for plan B. We need to go on the offense."

"Offense? There are thirty of them, and they have assault rifles," Riley said.

"We need to get one of the ATVs," Emerson said. "That means we need a distraction."

"I know what we need," Vernon said. "We need Bigfoot. Bigfoot could distract the hell out of them."

Everyone stared at Vernon.

"What?" Vernon said. "Did I say something stupid again?"

"No," Emerson said. "You said something helpful."

"So we're all thinking the same thing?" Riley said.

Alani nodded. "It's genius. Total typecasting."

"He is very big enough," Wayan Bagus said.

"Take all your clothes off," Emerson said to Vernon. "We're going to make you into Bigfoot. Then we'll hide in the brush and wait for an ATV. You can jump out in

301

front of it, and they'll be so startled they won't notice us ambushing them from behind."

"But why do I have to be naked?" Vernon asked.

"When was the last time you ever saw a Bigfoot wearing a Brooks Brothers suit?" Emerson said. "Your nakedness adds to the illusion. Besides, the idea is to gobsmack them into a state of utter stupefaction."

Vernon looked doubtful. "And my being naked helps to stupefy them?"

Emerson nodded. "It's essential."

"Well, okay. I sort of like the idea that I could stupefy people with my nakedness. Regardless of what *some* people say, I am impressive in my altogether."

Five minutes later Vernon emerged from behind some bushes. He was naked and plastered with mud. Ferns and twigs were stuck to him, his hair was spiked up every which way, and he had something that looked like a bird's nest covering his privates. At least Riley hoped it was a bird's nest.

"So what do you think?" Vernon asked.

"I have no words," Alani said.

Vernon turned around so everyone could get the full impact. "I'm scary, right?"

Everyone nodded. Truth is when you caught sight of him in a headlamp beam he was downright frightening in a ridiculous, lunatic kind of way.

"I'm sexy too," Vernon said. "I'm a sexy Bigfoot."

"That might be stretching it," Alani said.

"Here's the plan," Emerson said. "We wait in the shadows by this ATV path. When I spot them on the iPad, Bigfoot will jump out in front of the ATV and distract them while the rest of us rush the ATV from the sides and overpower them."

"I hope they come along soon," Vernon said. "I'm starting to get cold with nothing but mud on me, and it's giving me shrinkage. It's hard to look ferocious when you got shrinkage."

"We have an ATV approaching," Emerson said. "Everyone take cover."

Moments later, an ATV carrying two Rough Riders slowly rumbled down the path. The one in the passenger seat had a spotlight he was shining from side to side into the brush.

"I hope they aren't in a mind to shoot a Bigfoot," Vernon said.

"Showtime," Emerson said, shoving Vernon out of the thick vegetation.

Vernon jumped into the middle of the road and ran awkwardly toward the ATV, stopping abruptly in front of it and waving his arms.

"*Abugga, bugga, bugga!*" Vernon said.

The ATV stopped, and the passenger shone his light directly at Vernon. "What the heck is that?"

Vernon performed some impromptu ungainly capoeira somersaults and kicks for his audience.

The driver grimaced. "It looks like it's doing some sort

of bizarre mating dance. I can see its twig and berries," he said, pulling out his cellphone and taking a video. "I always thought Bigfoot would have bigger, you know."

Vernon stopped dancing and raised his arms, shaking his fists and growling.

"You angered it," the passenger said. "Say something nice about its junk."

Alani rushed out of the shadows and whacked the driver in the head with a chunk of lava rock while Emerson, Riley, and Wayan Bagus pulled the passenger from the ATV and disarmed him.

"Nobody insults Bigfoot's junk but me," Alani said, demonstrating her calf-roping prowess and tying the driver up.

Riley jumped into the driver's seat of the ATV, and Emerson grabbed the Penning trap and climbed into the seat next to her, holding the trap in his lap. Alani collected the Rough Riders' rifles.

"Phase two of the plan," Emerson said. "We haul ass and make a run for the clearing."

Wayan Bagus and Alani hopped into the back with a still naked, still muddy Vernon sandwiched in between them. Riley gunned the engine and took off in the direction of the clearing.

"I texted Dad," Alani said. "He's hovering over the landing spot."

A patrol of four Rough Riders was dead ahead. They

raised their guns, and Riley pressed her foot to the accelerator. They managed to fire off a couple shots before Riley plowed through them, knocking them over like bowling pins.

"Is everyone okay?" Riley asked.

Wayan Bagus held his hand over his shoulder. "I am bleeding, but I am unhurt."

Vernon examined Wayan's shoulder. "It just nicked him. He'll need some stitches, but it's not too bad."

Riley exploded out of the woods and into the meadow and looked up at the helicopter. Its lights were off but she could hear the *wup, wup, wup* of the blades.

Alani was on the phone with her father. "It's us! You can land now."

The Eco-Star touched down just as a second ATV drove out of the woods behind Riley.

"We've got company," Vernon said.

Riley reached the Eco-Star a minute later. Its blades were noisily chopping through the air, and Mr. Yakomura had his hand on the control stick, ready to lift off as soon as everyone was on board.

Emerson climbed into the back, settled the Penning trap next to him, and Alani, Riley, Vernon, and Wayan Bagus jumped in and buckled up. Headlights from Rough Rider ATVs flashed into the clearing from four directions. Shots were fired at the Eco-Star, and Alani and Riley leaned out the open helicopter door and returned fire.

"Here we go," Mr. Yakomura said. "Hang on."

Two bullets pinged against the fuselage. The helicopter quickly rose out of the field. It took one more hit as it sped away.

Vernon was squashed between Mr. Yakomura and Alani, trying to cover himself as best he could. Mr. Yakomura, for his part, was trying hard not to look at Vernon.

"Well, sir, I guess this is a little awkward," Vernon finally said to Mr. Yakomura. "You're probably wondering why I'm naked and covered in mud. There's a perfectly good explanation, which I'll tell you as soon as I can wrap my head around it. By the way, would this be a good time for me to ask for permission to date your daughter?"

"Yes," Mr. Yakomura said. "No. You can't date my daughter, and I'm going to have a restraining order written against you."

"Again?" Vernon asked.

"It's okay," Alani said to her dad. "Vernon was a hero. He risked his life pretending to be Bigfoot so we could all get to the helicopter."

"Hot damn," Vernon said. "I always wanted to be a hero."

"Where are we going?" Mr. Yakomura asked.

"The first stop is the Keck Observatory to collect the Penning trap hidden there. Once we turn it, and the one we have with us, over to the proper authorities, it should be enough evidence to put Bart Young and Tin Man away for the rest of their natural lives . . . if they're not already dead."

It was six-thirty A.M. when the Eco-Star touched down on the small landing pad at the Onizuka Center. The helicopter had been damaged in the firefight. Not so much that it couldn't fly, but enough that it was decided it couldn't safely fly any farther.

Riley, Emerson, Alani, and Wayan Bagus were almost as muddy as Vernon. They showered, changed into clean clothes, scarfed down a fast breakfast, and kept moving. Riley was afraid if she stopped and closed her eyes she wouldn't open them again for days.

THIRTY

ALANI COMMANDEERED A GOVERNMENT CAR SO they could drive Wayan Bagus to the hospital in Waimea.

"The first-aid kit here at Onizuka doesn't include instructions on how to suture a gunshot wound," Alani said to Riley.

"What about your dad?" Riley asked. "Is he going with you?"

"He's elected to stay with his helicopter and wait for the flatbed."

Riley filled a to-go cup with coffee and watched Alani drive off. Emerson had both Penning traps secured in the back seat of the ranch SUV. It had only been two days since they'd left the car at Onizuka, but it felt like a year.

"Are you ready?" he asked Riley.

Riley gave him a thumbs-up and got behind the wheel. They drove in silence down Saddle Road. It was almost eight A.M., and the sun was shining. They passed through Waimea and started down the Kohala Mountain Road toward Hawi and Mysterioso Ranch.

"This is a nightmare," Riley said. "I can't believe we have enough strange matter in this car to destroy the world."

Emerson nodded. "I called the governor of Hawaii. My family has known him for a long time, and he's a good man. He's sending the Hawaii National Guard to Mysterioso Ranch to meet us and take possession of the Penning traps."

"And after that?"

"The federal government will take over and find a way to neutralize it. Rocket it into space perhaps. I had a short conversation with someone at the highest level. As it turns out, the Department of the Interior is supremely grateful. They were in the dark about Bart Young and his plan for world domination. The direction the labs took, the militarization of the Rough Riders, the collection of the strange matter, and the whole evil plan, including the hiring of nutcases like Tin Man . . . it was all Bart Young."

"It's shocking how one man almost brought about the destruction of the world."

"It was one man leading," Emerson said, "but he had complicit followers. And there were others who turned a blind eye."

Riley drove down the mountain into Hawi and made the turnoff to the ranch. She passed the cows, parked the car in front of the guesthouse, and she and Emerson got out of the car.

"Looks like we beat the National Guard here," Riley said.

Emerson looked at his watch. "They should be showing up any minute. Let's get the traps inside the house."

He carefully slid the first trap off the seat and carried it to the front door. He stopped when he saw Bart Young and Tin Man waiting for him in his living room. Tin Man had a hatchet in each hand. The Park Service version of a ninja warrior.

Under other circumstances Riley might think this was a ridiculous display of machismo. Problem was she'd seen Tin Man's hatchet work firsthand, and now the sight of the short axes evoked visceral fear.

Riley and Emerson backed off the porch, and Tin Man and Bart Young followed them out of the house.

"The entire ranch is surrounded by my soldiers," Bart Young said. "There's really no place to run. Just give me the Penning traps and we'll be on our way."

Emerson shook his head. "I'm holding all the cards. I've

got the strange matter, so I'm thinking I call the shots. I have my own army on its way, and it's bigger and more powerful than your army. If you leave now you might escape. Run as fast as you can and get out of the country. Maybe open a bakery in Argentina."

"Here's the flaw," Bart Young said. "You're basically a good person. You don't especially want to kill us, and you don't want to turn the earth into a tiny ball of death that will get spit out of the solar system."

"I'm not that good," Emerson said. "I have my moments."

"Yeah, and I have *a lot* of moments," Riley said. "I would actually *like* to kill you."

Okay, so this had an element of bravado to it, but there was also some truth there. Not that she really wanted to kill anyone, but these men were monsters.

"I understand you're a businessman," Bart Young said to Emerson. "Perhaps we can make a deal. I can use someone like you and Ms. Moon in my regime. How does it sound if I give you France?"

"I thought you promised France to Berta," Riley said.

"She won't be needing France anymore," Bart Young said.

Tin Man smiled. "We found her tied to an ohia tree in Ola'a Forest. She resigned her commission."

"Well?" Bart Young asked Emerson.

"I'm thinking," Emerson said. "Before I decide, I'd like to know what happened to my friend's island."

"Destroyed," Bart Young said. "I saw it all from the

air. It collapsed into a little ball of strange matter and disappeared into the sea."

"It was inspiring," Tin Man said.

"But why?" Riley said.

"It wasn't by design," Bart Young said, "although it did convince me we needed to conduct some field experiments to test the strange matter's destructive potential. Samoa, and particularly the deserted island your friend was living on, sits over a mantle plume. We'd had a secret collection facility there for years. We found the little monk on one of our security sweeps of the island and evicted him. If I'd known then that he'd make so much trouble I would have just had him killed."

"But how was the island destroyed?" Riley asked.

"There was an earthquake almost immediately after the monk left. We accidentally lost the magnetic field, and some of the strange matter was released. I managed to escape with Tin Man."

Emerson had raised eyebrows. "And everyone else working there?"

Bart Young shrugged. "Casualties of war. If you want to make an omelette, you have to be prepared to break a few eggs."

"Enough talking," Tin Man said. "They're just stalling until their army arrives . . . if there even is an army. This is obviously an impasse, so maybe I should just put a hatchet in the Penning trap he's holding and get on with it."

"You're an idiot," Bart Young said to Tin Man. "You're a psychopathic imbecile. Let me handle this."

Tin Man swung his hatchet and in one fluid movement he sliced Bart Young's head from his neck. The head fell to the ground and lay there with its eyes still open. The rest of the body went over like rigor had already set in. *Crash.*

"I'm not an imbecile," Tin Man said. "Nobody calls me names like that and lives."

"He was a bit of a bully," Emerson said, holding tight to the Penning trap, "but decapitation seems extreme."

"*He* was the imbecile," Tin Man said. "He had small goals, motivated by greed. I have no interest in anything as profane and temporal as power and wealth."

"What then?" Emerson asked.

"Armageddon. The end of the world. Rulers and conquerors come and go with the passage of time. Some are remembered. Most are forgotten. There is only one way to truly be eternal and omnipotent. Destroy that which God created, and you become as a god yourself."

This isn't good, Riley thought. He wasn't just evil. He was insane. And evil and insanity was a bad combination.

"I'll give you a choice," Tin Man said. "I'll allow you to die as a gift to the strange matter. Or I can bury my hatchet in you."

"I can't let you do either of those things," Emerson said, carefully inching away from Tin Man.

"You can't escape me," Tin Man said. "I have an army. They're watching. They'll advance if I give the signal. You have no way out. My army controls your access to the road, and to the west there's nothing but ocean."

Emerson was moving in the direction of the ocean. He was backing up across the meadow behind the house, keeping his eyes on Tin Man.

Riley was following, walking parallel to Tin Man.

"Thinking of suicide?" Tin Man asked. "Maybe leaping off the cliff with the trap? That would be interesting. I could watch it swallow the ocean and the cliff and work its way up to me inch by inch. And then there would be the glory of the ultimate death and rebirth."

"There might not be rebirth," Emerson said. "It's one of those things that's open to debate. And from what I've seen, the death part isn't good."

"The pain will be exquisite," Tin Man said. "And it's inevitable. I have you trapped."

Emerson stopped and stood his ground. He and Tin Man were of similar height and build. Emerson was the younger of the two. Neither man showed any fear.

"I can't give you the trap," Emerson said.

Tin Man smiled. "Then I suppose I have to kill you."

Emerson set the trap on the ground and moved between the trap and Tin Man.

"Take the trap back to the car," Emerson said to Riley. "I'll join you when I'm done here."

Riley rushed in and grabbed the trap. She wasn't a cream puff. She went to the gym and worked with free weights, but the Penning trap was heavy and awkwardly shaped. She hugged it to herself and backed away until she was at a safe distance.

Tin Man crooked his finger at Riley. "Bring it here."

"No," Riley said.

Where the heck are the National Guard troops? she thought. Why weren't they here? Why were they taking so long?

"I'm losing patience," Tin Man said. "I have a mission. A destiny."

He threw a hatchet at Riley, she jumped away just in time, and the hatchet sailed past her.

She wasn't sure if he'd tried to sink the hatchet into her or the Penning trap. Not that it mattered. The result would have been equally deadly. Her heart flipped around a little, and she felt a shot of adrenaline get pumped into her system. It burned in her chest and took her breath away.

Tin Man ran at Riley and the trap, and Emerson tackled him, sending the hatchet flying into space. He struck Emerson several times with quick jabs to his head. Emerson's head snapped back, and a trickle of blood rolled down his lip. They locked on to each other, rolling on the ground, doing a lot of punching and attempted eye gouging before ending up near the land's end. Tin Man disengaged from Emerson and kicked him toward the cliff and the crashing waves a hundred feet below.

"Falling to your death isn't the fate I imagined for you, but it will have to do," Tin Man said, continuing to kick Emerson.

There were no thoughts in Riley's head. Just instinct and adrenaline. She scooped the hatchet off the ground, charged Tin Man, and with as much strength as she could muster rammed the hatchet into his back.

Tin Man suddenly paused, hands in the air, shock registering on his face. "No," he said. "This isn't right. This isn't the way it's supposed to end." He reached around, pulled the hatchet out of his back, and turned to face Riley. "You could have had a spectacular death, but now you're just going to die."

Tin Man raised the hatchet above his head and lunged at Riley.

Emerson pulled himself up, grabbed Tin Man's arm from behind, and yanked him off his feet with enough force that Tin Man sailed off, hatchet and all.

Tin Man flew over the cliff like a giant Frisbee, plunging a hundred feet onto the rocks below. Emerson and Riley peered over the edge as a wave rolled in and washed the mangled body out to sea.

"Oops," Emerson said. "I didn't mean to do that."

"He had bad karma," Riley said.

Emerson nodded agreement and looked back at the

Penning traps. Multiple military trucks, police cars, and an assortment of emergency vehicles were streaming down the driveway.

"They're our guys, right?" Riley asked.

"Right," Emerson said. "They're our guys. The bad guys are the ones walking out of the woods with their hands up."

"We should get back to the guest house and secure the Penning traps," Riley said. "The police will want to talk with us."

Emerson looked at the cliff and then back at Riley. "You saved my life."

She grinned. "And you saved the world."

"*We* saved the world," Emerson said. "Now there's only one thing left to accomplish." He put his hands on her waist and drew her closer. "You need to knock my socks off."

"Not until I see you naked," Riley said.

"Deal," Emerson said. "I was planning on getting naked anyway."

ABOUT THE AUTHOR

JANET EVANOVICH is the #1 *New York Times* bestselling author of the Stephanie Plum series, the Knight and Moon series, the Fox and O'Hare series, the Lizzy and Diesel series, the Alexandra Barnaby novels and *Troublemaker* graphic novel, and *How I Write: Secrets of a Bestselling Author.*

Evanovich.com
Facebook.com/JanetEvanovich
@JanetEvanovich
Instagram.com/janetevanovich
Pintererest.com/JanetEvanovich
plus.google.com/+JanetEvanovichOfficial

ABOUT THE TYPE

This book was set in Minion, a 1990 Adobe Originals typeface by Robert Slimbach (b. 1956). Minion is inspired by classical, old-style typefaces of the late Renaissance, a period of elegant, beautiful, and highly readable type designs. Created primarily for text setting, Minion combines the aesthetic and functional qualities that make text type highly readable with the versatility of digital technology.

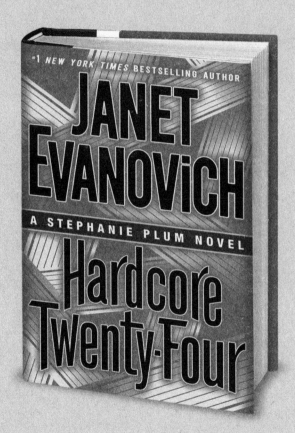

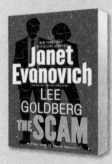
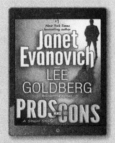
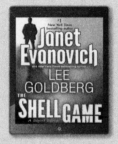
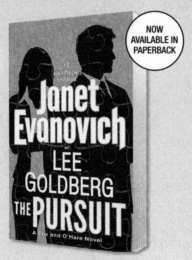